Dedication

To all those who have royally screwed up, it's never too late to right your wrongs. Everyone deserves a second chance, you just have to earn it. And for those who have been hurt, no one is perfect not even you. Don't live life holding grudges. It's too short.

Prologue

ASHLEY

"**EVERYTHING WILL BE** just fine, Sweets," Quinn says, squeezing my hand.

"I know," I agree, giving her a small smile because it's all I can manage at the moment. The butterflies in my belly feel more like dragons. I can't remember the last time I was this anxious or nervous.

A knock on the door grabs our attention, and the bubbly blonde technician from earlier wheels in a huge cart holding what looks like an old-style computer, like the machine in Dr. Marcus' office, only bigger. There's a keyboard with a big rolling ball in the middle. There's also a slot in the side that holds a bunch of wands.

"This is the machine we'll be using," she says, showcasing the ultrasound machine like Vanna White. "And I'll be the one doing your scan today." She smiles brightly. She must really love her job. "This is what is commonly referred to as your first trimester scan. It will take about half an hour, and when I'm all done, I'll send over my findings to your doctor. He'll go over everything at your next appointment."

Her bright pink scrubs with dancing kittens make it impossible not to smile back at her, so I do, while nodding to acknowledge my comprehension of what she just said.

"Okay, I'm going to hit the lights. I just need you to roll down your pants and push your shirt up a little bit," she tells me as she stands from her little wheeled stool.

I do as she asks, and when she sits back down, she squirts some jelly on my stomach. The coldness causes me to jump.

"Sorry, I should have warned you," she says apologetically.

"It's okay."

She presses a bunch of buttons on the keyboard and shows me the monitor, asking if everything has been spelled correctly before grabbing one of the wands from the holder. "I'm sorry. I can't believe I didn't ask earlier. Are we waiting for the father to join us?"

"No," I reply in a nasty tone that she really doesn't deserve. "There is no father."

Her smile fades. "Okay, let's get started then."

Chapter One

TANNER

"**YOU'RE RUNNING LIKE** you just robbed a bank and cops are chasing you, son."

"Something like that, Coach," I huff out, breathless.

He doesn't leave, so I know some kind of lecture is coming. I slow down the speed of my treadmill. I've been maintaining a decent speed over the last hour, so I'm kind of annoyed with his interruption.

"You've been pushing yourself pretty hard lately. Be careful, would you? It'd cripple this team to lose you over something stupid like overtraining," Coach says in the stern voice he always uses when he's trying to get a point across. He uses it a lot with the rookies when they need to be knocked down a peg or two. I always get a kick out of watching him hand them their asses during training camp.

"It's either training or drinking, Coach. Which do you think would be more beneficial?" I ask sarcastically, focusing on adjusting to the new pace.

He leans over the side of the treadmill to look at the display, shakes his head, and then returns his attention to me. "Well, Tanner, you're at sixteen miles already, and it looks to me like you have no intention of stopping anytime soon, so I'm starting to think drinking may have less of an effect on your body."

"You telling me to drink my problems away instead?" I ask, stunned the suggestion has even left his mouth.

"What I'm trying to tell you is that I've watched you push yourself ridiculously hard for the last two weeks, and it's going to wind up biting you in the ass sooner or later. You can't run yourself into the ground. The team needs you. You know it's an important time of the season. We can't afford any stupid mistakes. I don't want you to go down because you're pushing yourself too hard. You can't train away whatever it is that's bothering you, Son. If you need to keep yourself busy to avoid whatever it is that has you all wound up, find more than one vice. I'd rather you go out and tie one on once a week if it means that you'll take a day off from running yourself ragged in here. Everything is fine in moderation. Just make sure whatever you do, it's on the right side of legal, please. This team won't stand for any stupid scandals." He doesn't wait for a response from me, just turns and walks away.

Is he for real? He'd rather see me go out and get shitfaced than be in here training? I mean, sure, I've been here a lot lately, but it hasn't been that bad. Like I told Coach, it's either this or drinking myself into oblivion the way I did the first few days after Ashley fucked me over. I spent as much time as I could completely wasted over her betrayal, and it showed in my game that weekend. Thank God the defense picked my sorry ass up because if not for them, that game would have been a complete massacre. I was sacked more in that one game than I've been all season, and I felt each and every one of those hits for two days afterward, but at least we didn't lose. Ashley has ruined a lot of shit for me with her little stunt; I'm not going to let her take football from me too. That'll be the only time she affects my game.

I used to fuck away my frustrations, and it worked for years, but now it's one of the many things that has been ruined for me, thanks to Ashley. I haven't been able to think about sex without freaking out since I left her. I wish I could. Maybe I could if I got drunk enough. Maybe then I'd be able to stop thinking about all the ways a chick could screw me over the minute I put my dick in her. I've even considered the possibility of double bagging it. You'd think that weeks later, I'd be over her. I haven't heard a word from her since, so I don't really know why I can't seem to get her out of my mind. It's really fucking annoying.

Glancing down at the treadmill display, I notice I've run another five miles since getting lost in my thoughts. I really should call it a day. At least all this training has improved my long-distance stamina. I used to only be able to handle around ten to twelve miles but not anymore.

Grabbing my towel, I start wiping away all the sweat that seems to be dripping from everywhere. Coach might have a point about pushing myself too hard because I'm feeling pretty beat down and I'm dying of thirst. A nice, long shower sounds like heaven after a workout like that. My once light gray shirt is completely soaked with sweat, and my basketball shorts are sticking to my legs, causing my boxers to stick to my balls.

I roll my cold bottle of water along the back of my neck as I head toward my locker. The coldness against my overheated skin makes me break out in goosebumps and shiver. I probably look like I'm having a bunch of muscle spasms as my body shakes involuntarily. Thank God no one else is in here now. Stopping at my locker, I chug the rest of my water and grab my shower bag, my thoughts now strictly on getting into the shower to cool off and figuring out how to distract myself for the rest of the day.

After showering and throwing on clean clothes, I go to the projection room and start going over the game film from last week. I'm almost embarrassed to say that's me out there on the field. Unable to watch myself get my ass kicked for very long, I switch over to watching films of Buffalo's defense to prep for this week's game. By the time I'm done, I think I can honestly say I know every play their defense has called this season. Having watched each play over and over, I can now tell which ones are going to be blitzes just from reading the linebacker's face. With their defense down, I start reviewing our new plays one by one until I'm sure I could recite them in my sleep.

How has my life come down to keeping myself distracted from a woman's deception? I'd had everything down to a science, and I'd been content with the way things were. Why did I have to go and fall for her and convince myself I could have something so pure? I should've learned from my mistakes by now, but I guess I'm as hard-headed as they come. I shake off those thoughts and decide that I just need to suck it up and move on. I may never fully understand the 'what's and 'why's and 'how's of this mess, but it's time to man the fuck up and get over it. I'm Tanner Garrison. When did I become such a pussy?

Enough of this shit. Time to pull my head out of my ass. I stare at the new passing scheme another few minutes before deciding it's time to call it a night. It's time to get out of here and clear my head. As I close my playbook, my phone rings. It's Melissa. She's a perfect distraction. The call is like a sign directly from above that I'm ready to move past all this nonsense with Ashley.

"Hey, Melissa," I answer, trying for a cheery tone.

"Well, you sound awfully happy for a change."

"Yup, I've decided it's time to move on and stop feeding into the shit with Ashley," I inform her, but the resolve is missing from my voice.

"Oh yeah? Good. I was wondering how long you were going to mope around about that tramp." There's a snarky bite to her voice that can't be missed. I don't really know why Melissa is so hostile toward Ashley. It's nothing I need to worry about anymore, even if it still rubs me the wrong way.

"You can retract the claws. She's not a part of my life anymore… Well, unless the kid is mine, but I doubt it."

"I have to say, I wasn't all that impressed with her to begin with. I mean, she's very plain. And what kind of girl doesn't like to go shopping?" she asks, sounding incredulous. Melissa's whole life revolves around shopping and looking like a runway model, and she can't understand someone who doesn't enjoy the same things.

"Melissa, you need to be a little more open-minded. Not everyone loves to shop like you. Could you imagine if I didn't like anyone who didn't have the same passion for football as me? My social circle would be very limited." I laugh a little, shutting off the light in the projection room. As I make my way to the door, I'm trying to figure out why— even though I just made myself a promise to move on—I still don't like Melissa trashing Ashley. The fact that I still care grates on my nerves.

"Your social circle is barely a circle as it is, Tag. Anyway, I called because I'm worried about you and this funk you're in, so I wanted to go to dinner. What do you think? Say, like, an hour?" Thankfully, she doesn't seem to have noticed my slight irritation at her comments about Ashley. Or maybe she's just smart enough to pretend she hasn't.

"Sure, why not? Where did you have in mind, and are we meeting there?" I could use a night out of the house and some interaction with people that doesn't happen on a football field.

"How about Dina and Harrison's? You love it there," she suggests. Damn, this woman really does know me well.

Why didn't I stick with the arrangement we'd had when it had been working for years? I haven't been to Dina's since the last time I took Ash to dinner there. But I've had many dinners there with Melissa over the years, so I'm hoping that'll be my saving grace and the restaurant won't be tarnished by memories of Ashley.

"Perfect. Meet me there?" I push thoughts of Ashley back out of my mind. Even with my total disgust for her, she still finds ways to creep into my head every damn chance she gets.

"I'm near your house. How about I just meet you at home and we can go to dinner together?" she offers up. It has been a while since Melissa was over… since before I started seeing Ashley and fucked her on my kitchen counter.

"Sure. Were you at your parents'?" Her mom and dad live about fifteen minutes from me on the outskirts of Paramus—much closer to me than Melissa's place in the city.

"Yeah." She sighs. "So now you know why I can totally use a drink."

"You can tell me all about it at dinner. See you soon," I tell her, heading out of the locker room.

"YOU KNOW YOU always order the same thing whenever we come here," Melissa points out with a smirk.

"I like it. It's hard to find a good steak these days. I didn't realize you'd been cataloging my dinner choices over the years." I give her a smirk of my own as I tip my wine glass toward her.

I look around the restaurant as our waitress delivers our salads and find myself thankful that Dina's is quiet for a Thursday night. I'd needed to get out, but I really hadn't wanted to be in a crowded place where there was the possibility of unwanted attention. The last thing I need is for some overzealous sports fan with a camera phone to see us out and assume something scandalous is going on, and I definitely don't need anyone posting pictures of Melissa and I together. Then people would start asking questions—questions that would lead to talk about me and Ashley, which would lead to people tracking down Ashley and asking her questions. I don't need to give her the opportunity to spew her lies for the public to read. I don't know if she would do that, but it's apparent my judgment isn't always the best when it comes to women. Well, with the exception of the woman sitting across from me who's currently bitching about her parents.

"I mean, how many times are they going to harp on this? It's been four years!" she says with angry exasperation in her voice, her fork stopped midway to her mouth as if her point is too important to wait until after she had a bite. "It's not my fault that I'm his only child and he has no one else to pass his legacy onto—his words, not mine."

"I can see where he's coming from though, Melissa. Think about it from his perspective. He's worked his whole life building that company from the ground up. He wants to pass it on to you, give you something that means the world to him. Is that so bad? I know he's not always so eloquent in his way of trying to persuade you to change your mind, but there are always worse things," I tell her and take a sip of my wine as I give her a *think about it* look.

"Damn you, Tag. No wonder Daddy loves you so much. Maybe you should take over the company then, if you think it's so great. Lord knows that would probably make Daddy happy. You can't play football forever, and you're like the son he always wanted." She pushes her plate aside and rests her forearms on the table, awaiting my response.

"I doubt he'd love that. He wants you to have it. Maybe your future husband will have an interest in it. Then you can have your dad teach him all about it, and he'd still be leaving it to you." It's a good suggestion, if I do say so myself.

A mischievous look overtakes Melissa's features, and she smiles a smile that's nothing but trouble. "Maybe, Tanner. Just maybe." That's all she says on the subject before changing gears. "You have anything else going on with the kids?"

We haven't talked about the work I've been doing with the underprivileged kids lately. I spent Thanksgiving going from boys' home to boys' home for the majority of the day. I was more than happy to spend my day with them. I love giving back and making those kids feel important to someone—especially on a day when we're all supposed to be thankful. Unfortunately, most of those kids have a hard time finding something to be thankful for, so I was glad I could give them something to smile about. Spending time there also kept me away from Ma's for most of the day, which was important because I wasn't ready to tell them all about what had happened with Ashley. I got to my parents so late that I was able to tell Ma that Ashley had gone to her parents' house after spending the day with me, and she didn't question it.

"Not until closer to Christmas," I reply to Melissa's question, breaking out of my thoughts of Thanksgiving revelry. "I'm going to go to some the houses I wasn't able to get to on Thanksgiving with some gifts. Maybe I should do what that player in Houston does and take a few kids to the Toys "R" Us and let them have a one-minute shopping spree. He's the shit for doing that. I don't know how he just picks a few kids though. I wouldn't be able to say no to all the others. I'm thinking about maybe getting something big for each group home, like an Xbox or something else they wouldn't otherwise get." It's a shame that things most kids have and take for granted are such a big deal for those at the boys' homes.

"You really are something special, Tanner. Don't ever forget that. Maybe you should start your own foundation. That way you could reach more kids than just the ones in the nearby communities." She gives me a sincere smile.

"That's a brilliant idea." It really is. I'll have to get Davis on this idea as soon as possible. I can't believe it hasn't ever crossed my mind before. It would be the perfect time too. With all the publicity I've gotten from standing up for that little boy, Jesse, when that asshole from the open practice nearly got him trampled, everyone has been super supportive of my little "missions".

We finish up our dinner and wine with our usual banter before I take care of the check, and we make our way to the car to head back to my house. I spend the ride telling Melissa all about how I plan to have Davis look into the possibility of starting a foundation and find out everything that's involved. Like the true friend that she is, Melissa offers to help me any way possible.

As we head into the house, I tell Melissa to grab a bottle of wine from the wine rack in the dining room while I grab some glasses from the cabinet. We meet back up at the island with said glasses and a bottle of Bordeaux. I open it, pour us each a glass, and set it aside, giving it a few minutes to breathe.

I notice Melissa staring at the kitchen island. Her cheeks have a slight pink tinge to them that wasn't there a minute ago, and her breathing has picked up a little bit. I have a feeling she's remembering the last time we were here and is looking for a repeat of our exploits. She glances from the counter to me and back to the counter again, before pushing off of it and rounding the island in my direction. I know what she's planning, but my brain still takes a minute to process everything that's going on.

Melissa's mouth molds against mine, and she rubs the tiny tip of her tongue back and forth over the seam of my lips, waiting to gain entrance. I open my mouth, giving her what she wants. She has herself pressed tightly up against my side as she rubs her hand up and down the plains of my stomach. I wait for the arousal to kick in. Hell, I'd even take a twitch of my dick, anything to tell me that the lower half of my body is on board with this. I give myself time to adjust. Maybe it's just that this is a new person so my brain is confused—but Melissa *isn't* a new person. When she places her hand on my cock and it doesn't even flinch, I know this isn't going to work right now.

I pull away from her and look down at her pouty lips, noticing they don't look nearly as irresistible as Ashley's do after a make out session. *As irresistible as Ashley's?* Why the fuck am I thinking about Ashley's lips when I have Melissa's ready-and-willing, non-betraying lips right in front of me? No wonder my dick doesn't want to join the party.

"What's the matter?" Melissa asks, looking up at me with confusion and sounding slightly put out.

"Honestly, I don't know." I shake my head, trying to get my thoughts as far away from Ashley as possible.

"Is this about her?" She closes her eyes as she mumbles something under her breath that I don't quite catch.

"No," I say, scrubbing my hands up and down my face, trying to gain some insight into what the hell is going on. "Yes. I don't know. Maybe." I give her honesty because that's what Melissa and I have always had together: honesty.

"I'm sorry." She sounds more remorseful than angry. "You had said that you were ready to move on, and tonight had felt like old times. I miss the old us. I guess I just got the wrong impression." Her eyes are glued to the floor, and her shoulders are slumped. I think she's embarrassed. I don't think I've ever seen Melissa embarrassed before.

"You have nothing to be sorry for, Melissa. I *am* ready to move on, but I guess I'm not ready to go there yet. Let's just focus on making our friendship about more than just sex," I tell her, pulling her to me for a hug and kissing the top of her head.

"It's okay, Tag." She sighs into my chest. "Our friendship has always more than just sex."

I'm slightly alarmed at the way Melissa seems to be hurt, but then again, we're in uncharted territory here. Neither one of us has ever broken off our arrangement for a relationship and then come back to start things up. I wonder if there's some type of etiquette for this thing.

Chapter Two

ASHLEY

THE KNOCK ON my door startles me from my writing zone. I'm working on an article about some of the upcoming holiday events going on in the city. Christmas here is always beautiful. Watching the decorations being erected on almost every block always puts a smile on my face. I never miss the tree lighting either, which happened two nights ago. I always watch, whether it be in-person or on television. My article about all the festivities shouldn't even be considered work. Christmas is by far my favorite time of the year, and I love this month. It may also have something to do with the fact that my birthday is this coming weekend.

Setting my laptop down on the coffee table, I get up to answer the door. I don't know if shocked is the proper word to describe my feelings when I look through the peephole and find Melissa standing on the other side.

What the hell?

"Melissa, what are you doing here?" I ask, opening the door.

"I'd like to have a word with you." The tone of her voice is cold and harsh.

Opening the door fully for her to come in, I let out a sigh. I have a feeling this isn't going to be a friendly visit. By inviting her inside, I'll save face, and the whole floor won't hear my business.

She looks annoyed as she enters, as if she's the Queen of England and I'm inconveniencing her. I follow her gaze as she looks around with distaste, clearly thinking she's better than me and Quinn. I wonder if the *I-just-sucked-on-a-lemon* look is because she's just figured out that Quinn's home décor is as high end as hers—if not more.

"What can I do for you, Melissa?" I ask, moving into the living room.

She doesn't follow. She just stands in the entryway, looking at me as if I'm a speck of dirt on her shoe. "It's more like what can *I* do for *you*, Ashley. I'm going to give you some advice and save you some time and heartache. Tanner will never fall for this. You aren't the first one who's tried it. There's a reason Tanner and I have the relationship we do. I understand him in ways no one else can. Why do you think we've lasted so long? I was fine letting him play with you, knowing it would never go anywhere. As you can see, I was right. You played your cards too soon. Do yourself a favor and just get rid of that thing. I've been by Tanner's side since you dropped this little bomb on him, and I can assure you, he wants nothing to do with you or that little scheme you call a child."

I stand tall, bringing myself up to her level. "Who the hell do you think you are? How dare you come into my home and tell me what to do with my baby?" No way will I let this bitch think I'm beneath her.

"Well considering you planned on using it to trap Tanner, I have every right. You're not going to fuck up my life with that baby. I'm sure it's not his anyway. Do yourself a favor and get rid of it. Try and save some of your dignity. Who do you think he ran to when you pulled this stunt? Me. I'm the only woman he trusts. Just last night, he said what a mistake it was to ever let another woman into his life." She emphasizes the words *last night*, obviously trying to rub it in my face that she was most likely helping him fuck out his frustration. I guess it didn't take him long to go back to his old ways. "It's been me for almost a decade. It will always be me. Now, thanks to you, he sees that even more. You'll never stand a chance now." She sneers.

"You're in love with him, aren't you?" I knew it. I'd known from the beginning that this bitch wasn't who Tanner thought she was. Fake fucking twat.

"I will be the one he chooses in the end, Ashley. We've even been discussing him taking over Daddy's business when he retires. We're planning a future. Together. And I don't want that bastard baby fucking up my vision. I haven't stood by patiently all this time for you to come in with your cliché little plan and mess it all up. Get rid of it. Because Tanner will never accept it, and neither will I. You should really think about all that, Ashley." She turns to head for the door, but I can't let her leave without making sure she understands nothing will stop me from having this baby, including her threats.

I let her have it as I approach her. "As much as I wish he wasn't, Tanner is this baby's father. There's nothing you or I can do about it. Get over it." Fucking bitch.

She stops to face me once more, giving me an '*oh please*' look, which vanishes quickly as I continue toward her. Each step I take causes her to take one backward.

"Oh, and if you were really *with* Tanner last night, you would know I want nothing to do with that asshole. I'm glad you think I'm competition, but you can have him. I'm too good for him." I feel proud of the nasty look she's giving me and decide to share another piece of my mind with her as she backs through the open doorway. "And by the way, desperation doesn't look good on you, sweetheart. Coming to a pregnant woman's home and telling her to abort her baby is pathetic. Please tell Tanner not to send any more messengers over. I won't change my mind. My baby and I are no longer his concern. *We* don't accept *him*, and he'll never be a part of our lives again!" I want to scream that last part in her face, but I refuse to sink to her level. "Get the fuck out of my house, you stupid bitch." I slam the door in her face, wishing I had gotten a picture of her shocked expression before I did.

Who the fuck do these people think they are? I couldn't make this shit up if I tried, and I'm a writer! I won't let her get to me though, because that's what she wants. I don't know if I should believe her claims about Tanner, but my gut's telling me that I should. Of course, he has run right back to her. And why wouldn't he? He thinks the sun shines out of her ass and has no clue what a nasty snake she really is. If he's going to be with her from now on, I'm glad I've made the decision to keep him as far away from my baby as possible. I don't need that bitch anywhere near the baby either. I can only imagine the horrible things she would do and say the minute Tanner turned his back. No, thank you! Those two really deserve each other after all. They both hide their true colors well. Lucky for me, I seem to be able to bring the truth out.

I turn on the stereo and scan until I reach the local radio station that plays Christmas music twenty-four seven. No one can be in a foul mood when Christmas music is playing; it's truly impossible. Then I get back to my writing, picking up where I'd left off in my article and immersing myself in the land of Christmas. I stay there until I finally glance at the clock and realize it's time to shower and get ready for my shift at my new second job. I'm the new waitress at a local sports bar called Legends.

After Tanner ripped out my heart, I went looking for a second job immediately, and I was hired on the spot. For obvious reasons, a sports bar isn't exactly an ideal work environment for me, but they were the only place I found hiring short-term and willing to let me stay on past the holidays. I finished my training last week, and this is going to be my first night on my own. Everyone there has been great so far, and they're aware that I'm pregnant. Marshall, the owner, said I'm a perfect fit for right now since I won't be able to work at a bar for very long. They only need temporary help because of the extra rush from the Jets having a great season. Marshall also said that after a while, I'll be a liability because of the nature of the job, so at least he won't feel bad letting me go in a few months. I'm set to stay through March Madness, and then I'm leaving. He did tell me that, if things work out and I like it there, if he needs help here and there in the future, I'll be his go-to girl.

I'll be working four to five shifts a week for the time being, three of which are during football games—Thursday nights, Sunday afternoons or nights, and Monday nights. I'm doing Fridays too since that's a busy night in Hoboken. The bar is on the opposite side of the city from my condo, but it's only a ten-minute drive with no traffic.

I'm stoked to think that between four shifts, I can hopefully squirrel away a decent chunk of money each week. Bella, the girl who trained me, also told me to take advantage of Thursdays while I can because after football season, they're kind of dead. Apparently not all the cable companies carry the channel that the Thursday night games are on, so anyone who doesn't have the channel and wants to watch them heads out to local bars. That's the only thing that sucks about this job: football. How can I escape Tanner when four times a week, I'm hearing all about him on five different big-screen televisions? He's everywhere.

I hear the door slam just as I turn off the hair dryer, alerting me my darling best friend, Quinn, is home.

"Ash?" she yells from the entryway.

"In my bathroom."

"What's up, slut?" she asks when she reaches the doorway between my bedroom and the bathroom.

"Such a lovely greeting, my dear." I smile at her.

"Blow me, bitch. How was your day?" She plops herself down on the closed toilet and grabs her copy of *Cosmo* off my counter.

"Fine, until that bitch Melissa showed up to inform me that it'll be best for everyone if I kill my baby," I tell her, rolling my eyes as I wrap a section of hair around my curling wand.

"Shut the fuck up. No, she didn't!" Quinn actually looks shocked.

"Yup." I unwind my hair from the wand and turn toward Quinn, giving her my full attention. "She also informed me that she and Tanner were together last night, discussing their future, and my baby doesn't fit into it. Oh! And she also admitted she's totally in love with him and swears they'll wind up together now that I've 'played my cards too soon,'" I explain, making air quotes.

"Fake fucking twat," she says.

I can't help but crack up, laughing so hard, my eyes tear up.

Quinn gives me a weird look, as though she doesn't understand my reaction. "Not that I don't love seeing you laugh like this, but care to share what's so funny?"

"I called her the same thing—a fake fucking twat," I say while I settle myself down from my laughing fit.

"No, you didn't!" She gasps.

"Well, not to her face, but I did in my mind. When I figured out she was basically telling me what I knew all along, my first thought was 'fake fucking twat.'" I pick my curling wand back up so I can finish my hair for work.

"Well, she is. She's got some balls, though. Might even give mine a run for their money," she says, going back to flipping through the magazine.

I stop, curling wand midair and give Quinn's reflection a pissy look in the mirror. "Who cares about how big her balls are?" I snap before proceeding to replay every detail of the conversation back to her.

"Good for you, bitch. It's about time you started hardening that spine of yours. You're going to need to make it bulletproof soon," she says with a sad look in her eyes. We both know she's right though. The road ahead isn't going to be easy, and I know people are going to be criticizing me left and right, the same way they do to every other single mom out there.

I smile at Quinn to let her know that it's okay. I'm prepared for it.

"So, tonight's your first shift by yourself, huh?" she asks with her nose still in her damn magazine. That thing is like Quinn's Bible.

"Yup. And Bella said you can make a killing on a busy Friday night, so I'm really hoping it's packed tonight."

"Me too. You better use that ass of yours to make a few extra dollars before it gets all fat on you." She chuckles.

"Fuck you, bitch. My ass will not get fat." I turn around so I can check out my ass in the mirror, giving her with a nasty look in the process. "You're just jealous that my ass now looks better than yours."

"Yeah, sure. That's what all preggos say before they get as big as a house. You're lucky the bar has a lax dress code. You're not going to fit into those jeans much longer." She laughs again, sounding way too much like a hyena. Glad she finds herself so funny.

"Go fuck yourself, Quinn. I'm going to look amazing and that's a really mean thing to say to your hormonal, emotionally vulnerable best friend. You're lucky I'm controlling my urge to slap that stupid smirk off your face. I know you're just trying to get a rise out of me so beat it. I need to finish getting ready for work, slutbag." I growl at her.

She leaves the bathroom, laughing to herself but not before slapping my ass with her stupid magazine. Some best friend she is.

I PLOP ONTO my bed, exhausted. Tonight has been grueling but oh so worth it. I didn't sit down once from the minute my shift started at seven until the bar closed at two—seven straight hours of non-stop running. The three hundred and twenty dollars in my pocket make it more than worth it. Bella hadn't been kidding when she'd said that you can kill it on Fridays. I'm sure it wouldn't have been so bad if I hadn't already been tired simply from being pregnant, but I won't complain—not out loud anyway.

I know I should probably take a shower before I fall asleep, but I can't force myself to get up and do it. Then I remember how many drunk men have grabbed my ass or some other part of my body tonight, how many times I had to dip my hands into that nasty 'sanitizing' bucket to wipe down tables, how many bar glasses I helped rinse and put in the dishwasher, and how much beer was spilled on me throughout the night. Remembering all of that has me running to the shower to scrub off the grime. Feeling decontaminated, my eyes close the moment my head hits the pillow.

It feels as though I've just fallen asleep when Quinn barges in and starts bouncing on the bed and poking me in the side over and over. "Wake up, bitch! It's your birthday, and you're going to sleep the whole day away,"

"I just went to bed. Leave me alone," I grumble back, swatting her hand away.

"No, you didn't. It's almost one in the afternoon. Get your soon-to-be-fat ass out of bed now!" She bounces harder now, and I'm jostled completely out of my much-needed sleep.

"Shut the hell up and stop that fucking jumping! It's too early for your shit. It's my birthday, and I want to sleep, so fuck off," I yell from under the pillow I've pulled over my head to muffle the sound of her raised voice.

"Ashley, come on. Get up. I have the whole day planned out before dinner," she whines, finally sitting still. I look up to see her batting her sad puppy dog eyes at me.

"Fine." I admit defeat and drag my tired ass out of bed. "There had better be breakfast waiting for me, or so help me God, I'll kill you."

"You're even more of a bitch in the morning now that your precious coffee has been banned." She laughs as she flees from the room. She really is a total fucking brat sometimes.

Quinn hadn't been kidding when she'd said that she had the day planned out. We start out at the spa where we have facials, massages, mani's and pedi's. Then we go shopping for an outfit to wear to dinner. Quinn claims the shopping trip is because most of my regular wardrobe is starting to get snug and I won't spend any extra money right now on clothes I would be comfortable in. She swears she wants to treat me to a few new outfits, including one I can wear out to dinner. I reluctantly agree as long as we keep it simple and stick to stretchy pants and some cotton tops—nothing fancy. I get choked up quite a few times during the day by how thoughtful she really can be. She doesn't even push to go somewhere else when I suggest we go to the outlet mall in Elizabeth, even though I know she hates any sort of outlet.

After shopping, we head back to the condo to hang out for a little while before dinner. We plan to end the night out at a new posh restaurant, Paradox, which Quinn has been dying to try. She'd asked earlier in the week if I minded her inviting Alex to celebrate with us, which of course I didn't. I have no problems with Alex. It's not his fault his best friend is a complete douchebag. I do make Quinn promise me that they won't leave me sitting all alone while they sneak off for a quickie in some closet or something. She laughs at me and thanks me for the suggestion. Bitch. At least one of us is getting laid.

Dinner goes surprisingly well. The food is great, but I don't think the restaurant is anything special. Actually, the design of it kind of creeps me out. Everything is done in silver, black, and white, like some weird futuristic design.

There's a little tension between Alex and me before he breaks the ice. "I need you to know that I don't agree with what Tanner's doing," he says. "I've told him as much. I don't know what the hell's wrong with him. I mean, I know he can be a dick but never with you. This shit really has me thrown for a loop."

"It's okay, Alex. Don't worry about it. I'm sure I'm better off in the long run. But he's your best friend. I understand your need to stand by him." I don't want Alex to feel torn. My situation with Tanner shouldn't have any bearing on Alex's non-relationship with Quinn or even his potential friendship with me—if that's what he's looking for.

"It's hard to stand by him right now. I don't agree with him. But thank you for understanding my shitty position. Don't believe a word he's said to you. You really are a special girl, Ash. Too good for his sorry ass." He smiles, raising his glass for a toast. I raise my virgin daiquiri, and with the clinking of the glasses, any signs of awkwardness dissipate.

"Now that's a perfect toast. Guess you're good with more than just your cock and hands." Quinn smirks at him with fire in her eyes.

"Now you know how good I am with my mouth, *Sugar*," he jibes right back, throwing the stupid pet name she loves to use so much back at her.

"Guys, seriously, I just got the nausea under control. Do you need to make me want to puke again?" I say, causing all three of us to laugh uncontrollably.

It's a perfect birthday dinner. We talk about my new job, the baby, and all the awesome things Quinn has done for me today. It's refreshing to see the interaction between Quinn and Alex—the secret glances they think they're sneaking, the hand-holding, the innuendos. You can totally see something deep is brewing there, but I don't dare tell them that. It kind of makes me miss being a half of a whole.

"You'll let me know if you need anything? I'll do anything I can to help you out," Alex says sincerely before we all part ways.

"I will. That means a lot to me. Thank you," I tell him before pulling him into a hug that startles him, and we both laugh.

"Sorry, I'm overly emotional these days. Thanks for the beautiful flowers too," I say, holding up the bouquet of lilies he's brought me. Then I step back to allow him and Quinn a moment.

Quinn's kept me going nonstop today, and I'm exhausted by the time we get home. Forgoing a shower, I change into my sweats and climb into bed, where Quinn and I lie together, talking about my doctor's appointment at the end of this week.

"Do you think that they'll be able to tell you the sex of the baby?" Quinn asks while snuggling down under the covers trying to get warm. It's so blistering cold outside that being out there for more than a second freezes you into a Popsicle.

"I doubt it. I'll only be fourteen weeks and a few days. From what I've read, most doctors don't like to tell you until at least sixteen weeks." I've spent most of my spare time researching pregnancy and everything that relates to it. It's crazy how much stuff I didn't know about when it comes to being pregnant.

"Maybe we'll get lucky," she says, burrowing into my side.

"Maybe," I say before snuggling her back and closing my eyes, thinking about nothing but tiny little babies.

FRIDAY MORNING ROLLS around a lot quicker than I thought that it would. I've been so excited about my doctor's visit I'd been expecting the week would drag. My shifts at Legends and the stack of articles I need to write have helped keep my mind otherwise occupied.

Quinn and I are still trying to defrost from the freezing temperature outside when my name is called to head back to the exam room. Lacey, the same nurse as last time, informs me today I just need to give a urine sample. I don't have to change into the gown this time. I just have to come back to the room after doing my business.

After peeing, I leave the sample on the counter, just like last time, and sit on the exam table to wait for Dr. Marcus.

"I think I'm more nervous this time than I was last time," I tell Quinn, picking at the ends of my hair, looking for split ends. I do that a lot when I'm anxious.

"You had a lot going on in your mind last time, and nothing was really real yet. Now it's real, and you have real fears. I'm sure it's normal," Quinn says, giving me a sincere smile. I'm so glad she was able to come with me today. I'm sure everyone must think we're a lesbian couple since Quinn is always the one holding my hand through these visits.

Dr. Marcus knocks on the door, alerting us to his presence, and strolls in with a smile on his face. "Good morning, Ms. Mitchell. How are you today?" He offers me a hand with his greeting.

"I'm doing well, thank you," I tell him, shaking his hand.

"Good to hear. How's the vomiting? Did the Zofran we prescribed last appointment help?" he asks, glancing over my chart.

"Yes, the extreme morning sickness let up about two weeks ago." I'm so thankful that I'm not puking my brains out anymore.

"Good. Good. It usually does work itself out by the second trimester. So, today I want to do a quick scan just to double check how everything's progressing. Before you get all worked up, no, I don't think that there's anything wrong, but I always like to double-check." Man, he's good. But I guess that after dealing with pregnant women every day, he must be able to sense a freak out coming a mile away.

"I just need you to roll or push down your pants to your pubic line and pull your shirt up to your bra line," he says, pushing some buttons on the ultrasound machine he's just wheeled over to the table from the corner of the room. He squirts some cold jelly around my belly button before pushing the wand down on my tummy and moving it around as he turns his attention to the monitor.

He hits a button on the keyboard, and suddenly, a loud whooshing sound reverberates throughout the room.

"That's the baby's heartbeat, right?" I ask even though I'm pretty sure it is. I just want to make sure. I heard it for a few seconds during the last ultrasound, and it's almost impossible to confuse that beautiful sound with anything else. Everything except that amazing whooshing just fades out. It makes the fact that there really is a little person growing inside me more of a reality. The baby becomes a little more real every time I hear it.

"Yes, and it sounds great. Everything else looks great too. I don't see anything abnormal," he says, still moving the wand around as he checks things out. I can't tear my eyes away from the screen. It's hard to believe that little peanut is inside me—although she's not really a peanut anymore. I can definitely make out the shape of a baby now.

"So, do you think you might be interested in finding out the sex of the baby, Ashley?" Dr. Marcus asks.

I see Quinn bouncing in her chair and shaking her head up and down.

"Yes, but I thought it was still early to tell," I reply.

"You're at about fourteen and a half weeks. We don't normally look for the sex at this point, but I'm already here, and I can tell for sure what the sex is. So if you want to know, I'd be more than happy to share." He smiles down at me.

"Yes, I would love to know," I answer, my voice full of excitement.

He points to an area of the screen that looks as though it could be the baby's butt. "This view is what we sometimes refer to as the potty shot, and that right there tells us that you're having a bouncing baby boy."

I gasp, and my eyes fill with tears as I stare at the image that is my son.

Chapter Three

TANNER

A **FEW DAYS** after having dinner with Melissa, I called Davis, my agent, about my foundation idea. He must have jumped on it right away because it only took him a little over a week to get back to me with good news. While trying to start my own foundation to benefit underprivileged children could take months and even years to get off the ground, Davis has found something that he thinks is even better for me. The Tony Mathis Foundation has been looking for someone to take over as the public face of the organization since Tony passed earlier this year, and they think I'd be a great fit for them. The head of the foundation told Davis based on my recent activities in the community, the board would be more than happy to meet with me. The Tony Mathis Foundation is huge. It's been around for decades and is basically a household name. It isn't exactly what I'd been looking to do, but it's a damn good alternative with little to no startup work. I told Davis I'd take the weekend to think about it and get back to him.

I'm just checking his latest email on my phone as I stand on the sidelines of the party. It's my teammate Malcolm's daughter's birthday, and the whole team and all their kids have turned out. I read Davis' email reminding me that I don't have all the time in the world to make a decision and he really thinks I should do this. They don't have much time to waste, and they want to have a set man for the job by Monday. Apparently, with the holidays coming up, they need someone to sign now so they can get things rolling for the new year.

Just then, Alex comes over with a cold Heineken for me, "Here's a beer, bro."

"Thanks, dude." I grab the beer while reaching into my pocket for my key ring, which has a bottle opener on it.

"What's on your mind, Tag? You look lost in your thoughts." He follows my line of vision over to the crowd of our teammates playing with the kids as they run wild through the indoor play facility. Pink and purple balloons float everywhere. There's a blow up castle-shaped bouncy house, trampolines galore, and even a face painter who's going around painting all the kids' faces. Squeals of laughter echo all around.

"Nothing. Just thinking about the Mathis deal and how I can't help but laugh watching our six-foot-four-inch, two-hundred-eighty-five-pound defensive tackle bouncing with a group of little princesses up and down on a giant trampoline. On a Friday night no less. It's one of the funniest things I've ever seen," I say, pointing to the group in front of us.

"Again, Daddy, again!" Malcolm's daughter yells as he jumps up again, causing her and her group of little princess friends to go flying into the air. There is so much joy on her face. "I love you, Daddy. You're best," she says hugging him something fierce when she comes back down from that last bounce into the air.

"I have so much respect for them," Alex says. "It takes a certain kind of man to give a child that much love. I once thought that you were that kind of man, Tag. But I guess I was wrong." He shakes his head, taking a long pull of his beer. Here we go again.

I take an equally long pull of my beer. "Dude, I don't want to have this argument with you again." We haven't really gotten into it too much since the night I first told him Ashley had claimed to be pregnant with my child. He's brought it up a few times but not in the hostile tone I hear in his voice right now.

"I just can't believe that my own best friend would abandon his child and the mother of that child. It really pisses me off. Especially when you're talking about becoming the front man for a charity for underprivileged kids. I'm sorry, bro, but you're a fucking hypocrite. I have a huge problem with the way that you're handling things. I thought you would've come around by now, but you haven't, and each day that goes by, it pisses me off more. Especially when I see how strong Ash is trying to be through this. I see the toll it's taking on her even though she won't admit it. I see the pain in her eyes. It makes me want to lay you out, honestly."

When he sees the pain in her eyes? When is he seeing her? More importantly, *why* is he seeing her? I don't want her anywhere near my life. Great best friend I have.

"What's wrong with you? I can't believe you'd side with that bitch over me," I accuse, moving to stand directly in front of him, not trying to hide the anger in my tone.

"What's wrong with *me*? What the hell is wrong with *you*, Tanner?" He shakes his head at me.

I hear the frustration in his voice, and it pisses me off. Who the hell does he think he is, getting all up in my face about this situation? He's the one who's keeping in contact with the woman trying to make a paycheck out of me.

"Listen, motherfucker, you may be my best friend, but I won't hesitate to lay *you* out. Who the fuck are you to take that tone with me? You're the one still talking to the woman who's trying to use me. If anyone should be pissed off here, it's me, you fucking traitor," I growl at him, getting close enough that we stand nose to nose. He's gone too far this time.

He doesn't seem the least bit fazed by me being in his personal space. He just cocks his head to the side and lets out a mocking laugh. "You really are a delusional dipshit, Tanner. Use you for what? Have you even heard from her since you walked out on her weeks ago? No, you haven't. And I'm pretty sure you won't ever again. She wants nothing to do with you, dickhead. Did you know that she got a second job? She's been working her ass off to prepare for the life of a single mom. Does that sound like someone trying to get a dime from you? I'm glad that you walked out on her. You don't deserve her. All the dumb shit you've done over the years has never bothered me or made me bat an eye, but this... this makes me ashamed to even call you my friend. Don't worry, bro. I'll keep my eye on your kid for you. I hope Ashley finds a real man that's willing to step up to the plate and be a father to your kid. Maybe he'll be a good role model and the kid will stand a chance of not turning out like his asshole sperm donor. Shame too. You had an excellent example of what a father is supposed to be, and yet here you are—a complete fucking moron. Hope you don't choke on that regret when it rears its ugly head, asshole," he says, tossing his now empty beer into the trash can. I watch him head over to Malcolm and his little family to hug them goodbye.

I stand there dumbstruck, watching the party continue around me. My feet are rooted to the floor as I reflect back on everything Alex has just said. She got a second job—so what? That could just mean the kid isn't mine, and she's finally realized that I'm not a sucker. It doesn't mean that she isn't guilty of using me. It just means that she's smart enough to know when the jig is up.

Even as I try to convince myself once again that I don't care about her, I feel a pit start to form in stomach. I'm pulled from my thoughts as someone sidles up beside me. "Hey, Tan," Kelvin, our cornerback, says clapping me on the back. "I know it's not my business, but I happened to overhear that argument between you and Alex. I want to say one thing, and then I won't ever mention it again."

"I really don't want to talk about this, man," I say, gritting my teeth. The last thing I need is another person knowing how Ashley is trying to screw me over.

"I hear you, but let me just tell you this one thing." The way his tone changes from friendly to forceful has me curious as to what he wants to say. I nod for him to continue before staring back at the bottle in my hands.

"My dad left my mom when he found she was pregnant with me—left her high and dry to fend for herself. We were poor, dude, and by poor,

I mean dirt poor. My mama's family disowned her and wouldn't help. We lived in a tiny one bedroom apartment in a building that should have probably been condemned. I got all the love I could ever need from that woman, but I know she had it super rough. She could've taken the easy way and got rid of me, but she didn't, and I have all the love and respect in the world for her. First thing I did when I made it big was buy her a huge mansion because she deserves the world for everything she did. Know what I would give my dad if I ever saw him?"

I look up from the label I've been peeling off of my now-empty beer bottle and shake my head.

"Not a second glance. I'd tell him to fuck off and keep it moving. Want that to happen to you someday when you decide that you made a mistake? If you think there's even a chance this kid is yours, you need to step up now. There ain't no going back. I had a shitty childhood—barely enough food to fill my stomach, holes in my clothes, and sneakers that never fit right because my mama couldn't afford to buy ones that would fit my big-ass feet. Do you really want your kid to go through things like that? I'm not saying that's how it'll be, but you never know, dude. What did this kid do to you? And FYI, your baby mama didn't wind up knocked up all by herself. Why should she have to deal with the results alone? Pretty shitty, if you ask me. There ain't nothing worse than listening to your mama cry herself to sleep every night—after she finished working her second shift of the day at the shithole diner down the road." With those words and another clap on the back, he's gone.

After that encounter, I need to clear my head. Between Alex and Kelvin, I'm all fucked up now, and I know I have to get out of here to figure out what's going on. I toss my beer bottle in the trash and follow the same path Alex did over to Malcolm and his family. I say goodbye and thank them for inviting me. I can't get to my Rover fast enough. All of a sudden, I don't feel all that well. I'm starting to sweat, and I feel my heart rate starting to pick up. Once I've hopped into my car, I pull out of the parking lot as fast as I can. My thoughts are all jumbled. Maybe Alex is right and I am a total fucking asshole. Fuck, fuck, fuck…

The sun is just starting to set when I finally pull to a stop. I don't remember deciding to drive to my parents' place or how I wound up here.

I stare up of the house that holds so many fond memories for me. This home was filled with so much love when I was growing up. Like a reel projecting in my head, all of my childhood memories flash through my mind: my dad tossing the football around with me in the front yard, my sisters and I running around playing tag, falling on the sidewalk and skinning my knees when I learned to ride my bike. I remember my dad telling me it was okay to not get it right the first time but to never give up. My parents have always been there for me. No matter what. I'd known that I could always count on them. If I were ever to be a father, I would want my child to feel the same sense of security I had growing up.

Thoughts swirl around so fast in my head that I can't make sense of them. I don't know what I think anymore. Old habits die hard, and I'm so used to people always trying to use me that it was my first assumption. It's not as though this is the first time I've found myself in this situation. Why couldn't Ashley have just told me what had happened when it happened? I don't understand her logic… And Google? What sane person follows medical advice from the Internet? Her choices still don't make sense to me, and they make me suspicious. I can't make heads or tails of anything right now, I'm pretty sure my subconscious has driven me here for a reason, even if I'm not sure what it is. Regardless, I'm not ready to talk about this with my parents yet, so I drive home, resolving to sleep on things

---

***"SAMMY, PLEASE GO** slow. Watch where you're running," a very familiar voice says behind me.*

I turn toward it just as a little body slams into my legs, making me stumble.

"Sammy, be careful. I told you to slow down. I'm sorry, sir." The woman pulls her eyes from the little boy who's trying to right himself at my feet and looks at me.

I'm frozen as I stare into the blue eyes I could never forget.

"Ashley." I gasp.

"Tanner."

There's a slight tug on the leg of my pants, and I look down to see a smaller version of myself. It feels as if I'm looking at myself twenty-five years younger.

"S'cuse me. Are you my daddy?"

"Sammy, come on. Let's go. Let's leave this man alone." She scrambles to grab the child's arm, but I'm faster.

"Yes, I believe I am."

"If you're my daddy, why didn't you want me? My mommy says I don't have a daddy like everyone else because he didn't want me. Why didn't you want me? Why don't you love me like the other daddies?"

I stand there, feeling as though someone has just ripped my heart out and stomped all over it. I can't formulate an answer for this beautiful little boy because I don't have one that will ever be good enough.

I look at Ashley and see tears streaming down her face.

"Let's go, sweetheart. This man isn't your daddy. You don't have a daddy, but don't worry. Mommy loves you enough for both a mommy and a daddy."

And just like that, they disappear.

I wake up from that nightmare covered in sweat, shaking violently. I need to fix this. I need to get to Ashley. I can't have that dream become my reality.

Chapter Five

TANNER

I **LOOK AROUND** as I try to catch my breath. It was a fucking dream. I keep telling myself that, hoping my heart will slow down. Drenched in sweat, I go to the bathroom to splash cold water on my face. I need to pull my shit together.

I check my phone and see I've missed a call from Davis. The Mathis Foundation wants to have a conference call to discuss my possible involvement. Davis says I'm the guy they really want, but they also have two other choices. They want to speak with all of us this weekend, and since today's Saturday, they want to speak with me this morning so as not to disturb my prep for tomorrow's game.

My nerves take over as the phone rings but I'm not sure why I was ever worried about being passed over. The feeling vanishes as soon as we start discussing the ideas I'd had for when I'd been thinking about starting up my own foundation. I tell the board about my plan to give video game systems to the local group homes, and they eat it up. They even offer to have the foundation match my donations with items that go along with the gifts, like controllers and games. By the end of our phone call—which may have been a meeting more than an interview, I'm not really sure—it's obvious that I'm all for hopping aboard and being the front man for the foundation, and they are equally eager to have me.

Thinking about being the next Tony Mathis is enough to distract me from the jumbled mess of things in my head—until I get to practice. Saturday practices are always easy and laid back, more like hanging out and tossing around the football than work, and I find myself wishing Coach had come up with some new plays or something for me to memorize—anything to distract me from my thoughts of Ashley. I guess the only way I'm going to work through this mess is to talk to the only people in the world who will tell me the truth and still have my back: my parents.

After practice, I find myself in their driveway once more, sitting in my car, reminiscing about childhood memories again before getting out and heading up the porch stairs. When I reach the top, Ma appears in the doorway.

"I was wondering how long you were going to sit out here in the car, honey."

"Hey, Ma, how are you?" I ask, hugging her tightly.

"I'm doing well. Better than you, it seems." She grabs my face and makes me look her in the eye.

"I'm fine, Ma. I've got news to tell you and Dad, some good and some not so good."

"Come in. I'll put on the tea kettle."

I follow her in, closing the front door behind me.

"Andrew, Tanner is here," my mom calls out to my dad, who's most likely back in the family room watching television.

Sure enough, Dad appears in the doorway of the family room a moment later before coming into the kitchen to greet me. "Hey, Son," he says, giving me a hug. "What brings you here this evening?"

"He needs to talk, dear," Ma answers, turning on the stove. She still thinks tea fixes everything.

Dad sits down at the table motioning for me to do the same. "What's going on?"

"I got the idea to start my own foundation for underprivileged kids, so I contacted Davis about it. After working his magic, he found out that the Tony Mathis Foundation is looking for a new spokesman and would love to have me. I spoke with the board this morning about everything, and we came to an agreement I'm comfortable with and I'll be accepting. They're working on the contract and whatnot with Davis now, but you're looking at the new face of Mathis," I tell them with a smile on my face.

"That's fantastic, honey." Ma beams at me.

"Yes, that's quite a role. They couldn't have found a better person," Dad says with a smile on his face that radiates pride. Let's hope that it's still there in a few minutes.

"That's not the only thing wanted to talk to you about though," I tell them.

"Okay, what else is going on?" Dad asks.

"Honestly, I think I screwed up something big… My mind is all over the place right now. I don't know what to believe, and I can't think straight anymore."

"Why don't you start from the beginning, dear?" Ma suggests.

I start with, "Ashley says she's pregnant." Where else is there to really begin?

Ma gasps. "Oh my."

"Okay," comes from Dad.

I look back and forth between them because I don't know what to say next. How do you explain a situation you don't understand yourself?

"You said that you think you messed things up. What does that mean?" Dad asks.

I take a deep breath and tell the rest of the story, "I kind of flipped out on her. I told her she was just like everyone else who thought they'd found their golden ticket in me. I said I didn't want any part of her lies and that I didn't believe her."

"YOU DID WHAT?" Ma yells at me from across the table while my father looks away from me, shaking his head.

"When I asked her how it could be possible when she was wearing the birth control patch, she said that the patch had gotten stuck to her sheets somehow. She *Googled* what to do and read on the Internet that she should just put on a new one and start over or something. It sounds so bogus!" I run my hands through my hair in frustration. "I told her she was an idiot for not calling a doctor. The whole thing sounded like a trap to me, and I told her I wanted a paternity test and that she wasn't getting any money from me until she proved it was mine. You know this isn't the first time someone's tried this shit with me. My gut said she's lying. With Carrie throwing me the same lines right after the draft, Ashley just happening to get pregnant during the best season that we've had in the last decade, it felt like a trap."

"Tanner Andrew Garrison, I never thought you could ever do anything that would make me ashamed of you, but you've just proved me wrong. Who are you, and what have you done with my son? The boy we raised would never have treated a woman with such disrespect. I cannot believe you said that to her." She shakes her head at me, her eyes filled with disappointment. "Carrie and Ashley are not the same person. Ashley is your girlfriend, not some random chick you picked up on a night out. Do you have any idea how scary it is to be pregnant? Never mind getting pregnant on accident and being left behind like a piece of trash by the man that helped get you in that situation… No birth control is foolproof, Tanner, and she definitely didn't end up that way on her own."

I avert my eyes in embarrassment, unable to handle my mother's scolding head-on.

"You know that I love you, but right now, I can't even stand the sight of you. I'm so disappointed. Excuse me," she says, leaving the table in tears. I can't help but get teary-eyed myself. My mother has never in my twenty-eight years looked at me like that. I don't think I'll ever be able to forget the look of disgust in her eyes or the fact that I put it there.

"I really fucked up, huh?" I ask my father while looking down at my hands. I don't think that I can handle seeing the same look of revulsion in his eyes.

"Tanner, look at me," my father says sternly.

I look up, expecting the worst, but I don't find disgust in his eyes. To be honest, I can't make out what emotion is there.

"Son, I have to say I'm pretty disappointed in the way you handled this situation, but that is neither here nor there at the moment. We can deal with that later. Where's your head at? If you were so sure this was all a lie and you didn't believe her, what changed your mind?"

"Alex," I tell him. "He's been pretty pissed at me about this for the last few weeks."

"THE LAST FEW WEEKS?" My mother screams from the other room and rushes back into the kitchen. "This happened weeks ago, and you left that poor girl all by herself to deal with this? This happened before Thanksgiving, didn't it? You lied to me about her being with her parents, didn't you?"

I nod my head, not wanting to lie to her anymore.

"I can't believe you right now. You just got done telling us that you're going to be the face of a huge foundation for underprivileged children. Don't you see the irony there? I can't believe you. You're being a coward, Tanner!" she screams.

"MARGARET! THAT IS ENOUGH!" Dad shouts, trying to cut her off.

I'm taken aback. I've never heard my father raise his voice to my mother.

"No," she says. "No, it's not enough. His actions are the actions of a coward, not the man we raised him to be. I can't believe you're defending him right now, Andrew." I've never seen my mother like this, and she's honestly scaring the shit out of me. I feel like a ten-year-old boy again.

"Margaret, you need a breather. I understand you're upset, but you standing here berating our son isn't helping things. He came to us for advice, not judgment. I think it's best you walk away now before you say something you'll regret," my father says calmly.

"You can sleep on the couch tonight. And don't worry—that isn't something I'll regret!" Ma shoots back before walking upstairs and slamming the door.

I sigh and look back down at my hands. "I'm sorry, Dad. Don't fight with Ma over this. This mess is screwing things up with everyone."

"Don't worry about your mother. I can handle her. She's looking at this from Ashley's perspective, and rightfully so, since well, she's a woman. But I can understand your feelings as a man. It's scary to hear a woman tell you she's pregnant. On top of that, you two aren't married and are still a pretty new couple." Dad stands and heads for the fridge. He opens it up and grabs two beers before turning back to me and handing me one. "Women automatically know that a baby's theirs, but we men don't have that same assurance. I also know you aren't always quick to trust, so I can see where you're coming from. Your mother can't right now. That being said, I'm still not proud of your actions. But you're second guessing your gut feeling now, right? Tell me why." Dad sits at the far end of the table before opening his bottle and taking a long pull.

Opening my beer, I take a deep breath before telling Dad about my conversation with Alex about what Ashley's been up to. I also recount what Kelvin told me and my dream about the baby, trying to make him see how confused I am and that I have no idea what to do. I explain how I feel betrayed and how I would have been more inclined to believe her if she had told me about the missing patch from the beginning.

Dad sits up and leans forward, resting his forearms on the edge of the table. "Has Ashley ever given you any indication that she's been anything but faithful and honest?"

I shake my head. "No."

"And can you honestly say that you can see her doing something like this on purpose?"

I shrug. "I guess not, but I don't know."

He sighs and then leans back in his chair. "Tanner, you've had trouble trusting people outside your safety net for a long time. You once told me that Ashley was different and special, that you felt an instant connection with her. I could see the love between the two of you clear as day when I saw you guys together. I think you're just scared, which is natural."

"Love? What are you talking about, Dad? Ashley and I weren't in love. I mean, things were great before this whole pregnancy shit happened, but neither one of us ever said anything about love."

"Son, that girl is head over heels in love with you—or at least she was. You may not have realized it, but you were in love with her too." He smiles at me.

"No, Dad," I object, peeling the corner of the label on my beer, which seems to be a new habit of mine lately.

"Answer me this: Would you have let anyone or anything hurt her?" He stands up and walks over to me, taking a seat beside me.

"No."

"Did you make her problems your problems and do what was needed to make sure they weren't problems anymore?" he asks, laying his hand over mine.

I sigh. "Yes."

"Did you feel the need to make sure that she was safe, secure, and happy?" He lowers his gaze to catch mine.

"Yes," I say, meeting his eyes.

"Did you find yourself thinking about her almost every second of the day?"

"Yes." Still do.

"You're in love with her. You just didn't recognize it because you've never been in love before, son. We men are blind, and sometimes we need something to slap us upside the head so that we take notice," he explains, squeezing my hand. "That's why you felt betrayed by her when you found out that she hadn't told you about the patch falling off right away. Love is a tricky feeling. It can sneak up on you out of nowhere and knock the hell out of you. But I can tell you that love is supposed to be unconditional. Am I happy about how your mother just acted? No, but I love her, so I'm going to forgive her and work this out. That's what love is all about."

"I don't know, Dad. I definitely had feelings for her, but I don't know if I would jump to calling them love," I argue even though I know he's right. I'd already tripped and started falling fast toward love when it came to Ashley.

"Okay, but think about it when you've cleared your head a little bit. Either way, from what you said Alex told you, I don't think that she has plans to use you. I want you to think long and hard about what you want to do. There are some things that you can't get back in life, Tanner. I would hate for you to miss out on some of those things. You kids are the greatest part of my life, and I'm glad I was there every step of the way. Now, if you'll excuse me, I have a couch that I need to go make up. Good luck, Son." He stands, pulling his hand from mine. He rests it on my shoulder for a moment before heading out of the kitchen.

Damn, I really have a lot to think about, and I don't know where I should begin.

"DICKHEAD," ALEX SAYS as a greeting when he opens the door. "You look like shit."

"I feel like shit. I didn't sleep well at all last night, and I've had a long fucking day." I push past him, inviting myself in.

"Oh yeah? Why's that? You decide to go back to hitting the bottle?" he asks as he closes the door.

Okay, I guess he's still pissed at me. Well, he can join the club. I'm sure my mom would have no problem hosting meetings at her house since she's practically the sitting president.

"You can drop the attitude. I know I fucked up. Why do you think I'm here? I don't know what to do, man," I tell him dejectedly. The nightmare I had last night combined with my mother's less than stellar reaction has me all twisted up inside.

"It took you long enough. What changed your mind?" he asks, heading into the kitchen.

I follow because I desperately need a shot of something. "You, Kelvin, my parents… Bro, my mother basically disowned me. I've never seen her look at me like that before, like she was disgusted. It was horrible. She went off on a tangent, and my dad had to yell at her to stop her. He never raises his voice with her, Alex. She told him that he could sleep on the couch for siding with me. That was after she called me a coward."

"Damn, dude. That's rough. I wouldn't want to be on your mom's bad side," he says, grabbing a couple of shot glasses and bottle a whiskey from the cabinet. "I know you don't want to hear this, but she isn't wrong. I'm not going to lie. What you did was probably the shittiest thing anyone could have done in that situation. I know that you've had issues since the whole Carrie thing, but honestly, why you let one crazy bitch control the way you look at every woman is beyond my comprehension." He shakes his head. "What did Kelvin say to you?"

I recount my conversation with Kelvin and proceed to tell Alex all about my nightmare. "Then Ashley grabbed him and told him that he didn't have a daddy, that he didn't need one because she loved him enough. It felt so real, man. I woke up sweating. I can't let that happen. I know I'm an asshole, but I need to fix this."

"All I can tell you is that she isn't going to take you back with open arms. This last month hasn't been easy on her. I had dinner with her and Quinn last weekend for her birthday, and I got to hear straight from the source what she's been going through. She's just starting to get over the nausea, and she's got the new job on her plate as well. Quinn also told me that she wants nothing to do with you. Ashley has no intention of ever seeing you again, man. You've got your work cut out for you. I don't know if you're going to be able to fix this." He sighs. "It might be too late."

It suddenly feels as if someone is sitting on my chest, and I can barely breathe. I remember how Ashley looked the last time I saw her—so sick and run-down. I'd wanted to take her to the hospital she looked so bad. To think that she's spent the last month sick like that turns my stomach.

"Why did she get another job? I have more than enough money to support them."

"Seriously, man?" he asks, shaking his head. "Have you been listening to me? She wants nothing to do with you, including your money. Jesus… Thank God you have an amazing arm because sometimes you're really stupid."

God, I really *am* stupid. How could I've fucked this up so badly that she'd rather work two jobs than come to me for help? Yup, the Asshole of the Year award goes to me.

"Any suggestions on where to start?" I ask.

"How about with an apology?"

Chapter Five

TANNER

THE MORE I think about it, the more I see that Alex has been one hundred percent right from the very beginning. I wish I'd been able to see it sooner. The only way back to Ashley will be on my knees. But how can I possibly begin to apologize for what I've done? I try to put myself in her shoes and think about how scared she must be. She's fucking pregnant and thinking she's going to be bringing this child into the world alone. When I replay the last time we spoke in my mind, I want to kick my own ass for the things I said to her. I was a fucking dick. Somehow I have to make this right.

I've spent the last few days thinking of ways to win her back, and I've drawn a blank every time I've tried to figure it out, so I decide to go with a simple "I'm sorry." Every second I waste trying to make up my mind on how to say sorry is a second longer that Ashley doesn't get to hear it, and this apology is long overdue. I try to think of what I would want to hear from someone if the situation were reversed, and I can't think of a single thing, so I decide on the truth.

I pick up a birthday card and some flowers on the way to her house, hoping that they'll at least get me in the door. I doubt they'll help much, but at least I have something to pin my hopes on. Better than showing up empty handed. I'm thankful the doorman doesn't stop me on my way in. I guess there isn't a no-admittance list anywhere. Either that or Ashley really thought I'd never show up here and never bothered to put me on it.

My palms are sweating profusely. I don't think I was even this nervous on draft day. I wipe my free hand on my jeans before exiting the elevator, and my heart rate picks up as I walk down the hallway toward Ashley's door. I don't expect this reunion to go over very well, but I hope I'm not being naïve in thinking there's a chance it could. I stand in front of the door for a minute or two, trying to gain some semblance of composure before realizing it isn't going to happen. I take a deep breath and knock. Everything seems quiet behind the door, and I'm just starting to think that maybe no one's home when I hear a slight shuffling. Then the door opens.

There she is, just as beautiful as I remember. Everything fades away but Ashley. I can't think about anything other than the sight before me. She's dressed casually, wearing a pair of black leggings and a long gray sweater. Her long brown hair hangs in loose curls. There's definitely a glow about her, but I also still see the effects of her recent illness. She's thinner and paler than when I last saw her but still stunning. She stands there, staring at me, her expression a mix of emotions. Her presence instantly makes my dick hard. I know I shouldn't be thinking about anything sexual right now, but I can't help it. It's Ashley, and she's always brought out the best in me when it comes to sex. I just hope my dick gets the message that he needs to calm down before he makes *his* presence known and this apology gets even more difficult for me.

"Hello, Ashley."

"What are you doing here?" Her mouth is turned down into a frown, and her voice is hard, a tone that doesn't match her beauty. The look in her eyes conveys nothing but contempt. Well, at least that helps alleviate my hard-on.

"I was hoping we could talk," I say, grateful my voice doesn't waver and give away the fact that the look she's giving me scares me shitless.

Call me stupid, but I wasn't excepting to be greeted with this much venom.

Her expression makes the look that Ma gave me the other night seem like a smile. I'd known she was mad at me, but I definitely hadn't thought she could hate me this much. I feel the weight of my guilt on my shoulders even more now. I really need to fix this, but it's going to be way harder than I'd anticipated.

"Talk about what?" she snaps.

"Us," I answer, straightening my spine, steeling myself for her anger and forcing myself to look her in the eye, knowing full well that I won't find any kindness there.

"There is no us, Tanner. Remember?" she practically growls at me, shaking her head.

"There will always be an us, Ashley. I'm so sorry that I lost my head when you told me. There's no excuse for how I have handled this, and I need you to know I'm sorry." I hope she can sense the sincerity pouring out of me. My empty hand reaches out to her almost instinctively. I just want to touch her, comfort her.

"You're sorry?" she asks with disbelief, her eyebrows arching with accusation as she steps out of my reach and eyes my hand as though she wants to break it.

"Yes, I'm sorry. I'm sorry for what I said to you. I'm sorry for how I acted. I'm sorry that I haven't been here for the last four weeks. I'm sorry for everything." Being here now, begging for forgiveness like this, is a huge reality check. I would've never thought it was possible for a person to experience so many feelings at one time. Guilt, shame, remorse, fright—they're all here, swirling around inside me. The only thing holding everything together is the little bit of hope I'm still clinging to.

"So you think that saying you're sorry and bringing me flowers is going to make everything better?" Her voice grows harsher. A coldness has taken over her gaze, and her body is tense. She looks down at the flowers in my hand with aversion, as if they're a rotting animal rather than a bouquet. Now I know for sure that this encounter isn't going to pan out well for me at all.

"I know it's not going to fix everything, but it needs to be said. I am sorry. There aren't enough words to tell you how sorry I am," I say, holding out the flowers toward her. "The flowers are for your birthday. I'm sorry I missed it."

She cocks her head to the side and studies me with a puzzled expression. "You're unbelievable," she huffs and turns away from the open door, walking farther into the condo. I don't know whether I should follow her or not, so I hover in the doorway, trying to figure out what's going on. She returns, her fist clenched around something I can't make out.

She points to the flowers and says, "I don't want that gift, and I don't want the last one you gave me either." She pushes her fist into my chest, and I realize she's holding the BMW keys.

"Ashley, I'm not taking those. The car was a gift," I tell her, gently pushing her fist back toward her. The sensation I get when I wrap my fingers around her hand, even for that brief instant, makes me feel alive again.

"I don't want it. It's been sitting in the garage for the last month rotting away. Take it or continue to let it rot there. I don't care either way, but I'm not driving it." She snatches her hand from my grasp and rolls her eyes.

"Your old car isn't safe. Please tell me that isn't what you've been driving around in." I'd bought her that new car because I'd been worried about something bad happening to her in that old piece of shit. Was she really carrying our baby around in that death trap now?

Our baby… Holy shit! For the first time, everything clicks together in my brain. *Our.* I want her, and I want our baby. I want this life with her. No matter what she throws at me, nothing will stop me from making things right. Not now. Not when I finally see things clearly.

"Tanner, please don't act like you care. Your time for caring is over, so if you're done making yourself feel better with this apology, I have things I need to do," she says, pushing me toward the door.

I lay the flowers and birthday card on the console table next to the doorway and stand my ground, forcing her to lean into me as she continues to try to push me into the hallway. "I'm not going away that easily, Ashley. And the car was a gift for you to do with as you please, regardless of what happens between us. I want you to have it. If you want to let it sit in the garage, that's your decision, but I want you to be safe. I *need* for you to be safe, so I'd prefer you use it." I hope the steely resolve in my voice masks my fear.

I'll stop at nothing to get her back, but based on everything I've seen today, it's going to be an uphill battle. She can barely stand the sight of me, and I'm scared to death she's just going to keep pushing me away. But I can't show her that fear. I don't want her to think that I'm ever going to stop fighting for her.

"What you want doesn't matter to me anymore. It was your decision to end our relationship. You should stand by your decisions. I stand by mine, which is to keep you as far away from my life as possible."

Seeing that things are going nowhere for now, I let her strong-arm me through the doorway at last.

She puts her hands triumphantly on her hips as I come to a halt in the hallway. "Oh, and please keep your little messenger to yourself. I don't need to be pushed out of your life. I left weeks ago, and I have no intention of coming back." She slams the door so fast I don't have the chance to question her about her parting comment. What messenger? What the hell is she talking about?

I know I shouldn't be surprised by her anger. I expected as much but damn… That did not go well at all. I guess it could've been worse. At least she didn't slam the door in my face right off the bat. I'm not going to let this get me down though. I didn't get to where I am in life by letting a little hard work get in my way. She's definitely worth the hard work. I created this mess myself after all. Now, it's time to fix it.

***"YOU THROW LIKE** a girl, Uncle Tanner," my niece tells me.*

"I don't throw like a girl, Maci. You just catch like one, so I can't put much force behind this Frisbee." I laugh at her.

"Throw it harder," she yells, running toward the other side of the little open field in the park. I give the disc a good chuck and watch her chase it down past a small building.

When Maci doesn't return with the Frisbee, I head over to help and make sure she's okay.

"Maci, did you find it? What's taking so long?" I ask, rounding the corner of the building, finding the bathrooms and water fountains there. On the far side, I see Maci crouched down, talking with a little boy who's sitting on the cement outside the ladies' room.

"Sorry, Uncle Tanner. He was sitting here by himself, waiting for his mommy to come out of the bathroom. I didn't want to leave him alone. They taught us in school that the buddy system is the best way to stay safe." My sweet little niece. She really is a special soul.

"That's fine," I tell her. "That's very thoughtful of you."

The little boy seems a little frightened. He gives me a wary look, and I can't help but stare at him. He looks as though he could be Maci's brother. Except, his face is ashen, almost dirty-looking, as though he hasn't had a bath in a while. His eyes are sunken in, making them appear almost too big for his little face. His pants don't meet his shoes, and he isn't wearing socks. Poor kid. Looks like he hasn't had an easy life. It breaks my heart to see kids like this.

Maci pulls a granola bar from her jacket pocket and asks him if he's hungry. He nods his head up and down, obviously excited at the thought of food.

"What's your name?" Maci asks.

"Sammy," he says, grabbing my attention. Why does that name seem so familiar? It's a common enough name, but I know that I've heard it recently.

"What's your mommy doing in there that's taking so long?" Maci asks innocently.

"It's bath day," Sammy tells her, his eyes never looking up from the granola bar.

"Okay, what's that got to do with the park bathroom?" Ignorance is such bliss, and Maci has no idea what he's telling her. I wonder whether they're homeless or just had their water turned off.

The bathroom door squeaks open, and I hear a familiar voice say, "Come on, Sammy. Your... turn."

The last word gets stuck in her throat when she notices Maci and I standing there talking with Sammy.

I gasp. "Ashley."

"Tanner... What are you doing here?" She asks, pulling Sammy behind her when he gets close enough for her to grab.

"My niece didn't want to leave Sammy sitting here alone. She thought the buddy system would be better." I smile at Ashley while I take in her appearance. She doesn't look much better than Sammy. They both appear too thin and seem beaten down by life. It dawns on me that Sammy must be about four or five—the same age Ashley's baby would be.

"Is he....mine?" I ask, needing to know if this impoverished kid is mine.

"He's mine," she answers. "Go away, Tanner, and forget that you ever ran into us. It's what you're good at."

"Ashley, is that boy mine?" I ask again more aggressively.

"What does it matter to you?" she spits back. "You made your feelings on the matter very clear five years ago."

"It matters when you're bathing in a park bathroom and it looks like you guys haven't had a decent meal in years. Why didn't you call? What happened to you, Ashley?"

"You happened to me, Tanner."

I bolt upright in bed, covered yet again in sweat. Not another fucking nightmare. I don't know how many more of these I can take.

Chapter Six

TANNER

THESE FUCKING DREAMS are really messing with my head, which in turn, is messing with my game. This is the worst possible time for me to not be on top of things. The playoffs start in two weeks, and I'd like nothing more than for us to clinch the division and give ourselves a week off. I can't afford to be distracted if I'm going to make that happen. I have an entire team riding on me to keep my shit together—not just for a few minutes but for an entire game. That's not going to happen if I can't sleep through the night because I'm having dreams about emaciated little boys. I guess you can't really call them dreams—more like slow torture. I know Ashley would never let something like that happen to our child intentionally, but if she doesn't let me into their life, I can't know for sure that it won't.

I drag my sorry ass into the locker room after the game and punch my locker. Fuck, I got my ass kicked today, and it's all because my head's not in the game. It wasn't as bad as my exceptionally shitty game last month, but it was bad enough—two fumbles and one interception that was almost run back for a touchdown. Thank God that guy stepped out of bounds right before the pylon. Saved my ass. Coach is lecturing us about how we all need to be present, and I can tell that all of his frustration is directed at me. He's going on about it being football and "on any given Sunday," things could change in a heartbeat. As if I need a reminder that we aren't guaranteed anything…

I've got a lot of shit to fix, and I need to fix it fast. It's the only way that I'll be able to get my head on straight. It's probably best to start with my mother. She'll most likely be the easiest—or maybe Alex, but I've already semi-fixed things with him. So, Ma it is.

I'm not sure if Ma came out to the game tonight, but I hope she did. I don't think she's catty enough to not show up just because she's mad at me. Either way, the game's long over when I pull into my parents' driveway and make my way up the stoop. Ma must have been expecting me to show up at some point tonight because the porch light is on. She opens the door just as I get up there.

"Hey, Ma," I greet her apprehensively. I'm not really sure what to expect. I've never been on the outs with her before, so I have no idea which way things could go. I stand at the door, waiting for an invitation to enter, not entirely sure if I'm even welcome. Well, I know I'm probably welcome. My parents would never turn their backs on me completely, but after my last encounter with Ma, I'm not assuming anything.

"Hi, honey." She sighs sadly, stepping out of the way to allow me in. "Have you eaten?" With Ma, an offer of food is as good as any invitation.

"Not yet," I say, feeling a little confused. I haven't spoken with my parents since last weekend, and I'd been expecting animosity if anything, not sadness.

"Come on. I'll fix you a plate," she says, turning toward the kitchen.

"I'm sorry, Ma," I lament, following her into the house. Disappointing Ma has been one of the lowest points in my life, and I want her to understand that.

"I know, honey. I'm sorry too." She turns away from the kitchen counter to look at me with a weak smile on her face and tears in her eyes.

I pull her into a hug and lean back, resting my butt on the counter. "You have nothing to be sorry for. You were right, as usual," I reassure her, giving her a bit more of a squeeze. She shouldn't be upset about what she said. It was the truth.

"I was angry, and I should've given myself time to calm down before I went off on you like that. I'm always telling you kids to think before you speak and be careful what you say. I should've practiced what I preach. I definitely could've handled the situation a little better. " She pushes away from me and turns to wipe a rogue tear from her cheek. "I'm your mother, Tanner. I should've never spoken to you like that. While I strongly disagree with what you did, I still shouldn't have reacted that way." she says, trying to collect herself.

I think I hear my heart crack. Ma shouldn't be carrying around this crap.

"Ma, don't cry, please. I needed to hear it, and you were the best person to deliver it. Without your extra push, who knows how much longer it would have taken for me to pull my head out of my ass?" I tell her, wrapping my arms around her tiny frame again. Her body shakes from the tears she tries to hide in my chest, so I rub her arms up and down, reassuring her again that there's nothing she needs to be crying over.

I smile at her and reach over to grab her a tissue from the box on the counter. "Ma, seriously, thank you. You gave me that last push I needed to realize that I'm a total dipshit."

"I'm not just crying because of that. I'm worried for you. This is serious. What if she never lets you see the baby? Even if you win a custody battle, you're still going to miss so much. I'm going to miss so much. You need to fix this." She sighs, wiping her eyes.

"I went to see Ashley this week."

"You did?" she asks, picking her head up and looking me in the eye for the first time since I got here.

"I did. See, I told you that you gave me the kick in the ass I needed."

"How did it go?" she asks, wiping away at her eyes for any moisture she might have missed.

"As well as could be expected—she told me to beat it. But I told her I wasn't going to give up that easy," I say, watching Ma head over to the counter to fix me a plate of leftover lasagna—her Sunday special.

"Good for you. She needs to see that you're serious now. You really messed up. What's your plan?" she asks, heading to the table with a plate piled high with food.

"Not a damn clue, any suggestions?" I shove a forkful of deliciousness into my mouth. Mmm … Ma's lasagna is always so damn good.

A sad look crosses her face as she takes the chair next to me. "You're going to have to prove that you're serious about this and in it for the long run. She isn't going to trust you again easily, sweetie."

"I know. She even tried to give me back the car I bought her."

"Damn. She is definitely a woman scorned." Ma chuckles. "I'm sorry. I know I shouldn't be laughing, but she must be seriously pissed at you to give back a BMW. Sorry to say so, but you're definitely going to have to think of something big."

No kidding. I wonder what Ma would say if she'd seen how Ashley looked at me. A dentist about to do a root canal has probably gotten a warmer reception than that.

NOW THAT THINGS are square with Ma, I need to make sure that everything's okay with Alex. Since we're on decent terms, he'll only require a phone call.

"Dickhead," he greets me when he answers the phone—seems to be his favorite nickname lately.

"How long are you going to keep that up? It's getting pretty old." I roll my eyes even though he can't see me.

He laughs. "That will probably be the last time. I heard you made a visit to see Ashley."

"Yeah, I think it's more than safe to say that she hates me, dude. I think she'd like seeing me strung up by my balls—or at least that's what I feel like her dirty looks were telling me." I sigh and flop down in the middle of my bed, which seems so empty nowadays.

"Told you, bro. You fucked this one up good." He laughs. The motherfucker actually laughed at me.

"It's not funny, asshole," I snap as I reach to grab a pillow from the top of the bed.

"It is when you're the one that gets to say 'I told you so.'" He laughs again, harder this time.

"Yeah, yeah. You told me so. Listen, I need to know if we're good. I'm trying to fix things with everyone one by one so that my head isn't one giant clusterfuck." I close my eyes, and my head begins to throb. I definitely feel a migraine coming on.

"We were always good. I just needed you to see how wrong you were. Every time you went into your little bubble, it pissed me the hell off," he says, easing one more worry from my mind.

AFTER SETTLING THINGS with Ma and Alex, Ashley is the only one left. I have no clue what to do. I've texted her at least a dozen times, trying to get her to agree to at least meet with me. I offer up dinner and lunch—hell, even coffee. Each time I'm met with a *go to hell* or a *fuck off*. Pregnancy has definitely made her feistier. My head is filled with thoughts of Ashley, once again, as I hop in the shower.

Am I fucked up for being happy about her sudden change in demeanor? Ashley has always been easygoing and hesitant to speak her mind. Now, she has no qualms about speaking it whatsoever. It makes me want her even more. Despite the fact the girl won't give me the time of fucking day, I can't stop thinking about her spread out before me with all that fire in her eyes.

My shower turns steamy, the hot water pounding my back as I stand there, thinking about fucking Ashley. My hand wraps around my cock of its own volition. The contact makes me hiss. The roughness of my hand is nowhere as arousing as the warmth and sweetness of Ashley's. I picture her in front of me, on her knees, begging me to fuck her. Her pleading in my mind turns me on even more.

"I want you, Tanner."

"Fuck me, Tanner."

"I need you, Tanner."

I stroke myself harder, faster, squeezing my engorged head with every pass. Fantasy Ashley leans forward and licks my cock from root to tip, "*Fuck my mouth, Tanner.*" Her words, even if only in my mind, send me over the edge. I fuck my own hand mercilessly as I picture each spurt of cum landing on another part of Ashley's body, marking her, claiming her as mine again. The relief of my orgasm only lasts a moment as the tension creeps back in.

It's as though I've gone back to the very beginning, before we were together. I'm stuck picturing all the ways I want to fuck her while rubbing one out in the shower. It's pure torture, and it's draining me slowly. At this point, everyone has noticed that something's off with me. The fact I've been a complete asshole hasn't helped, but I honestly don't know what to do or where to go from here. I wish I had someone other than Alex and my parents to help me navigate my way through this mess. It sucks to realize that you've fallen in love with a woman who absolutely hates you.

Chapter Seven

QUINN

"**WHERE ARE WE** going?" I ask Alex when I realize we're in the middle of a suburban neighborhood—nothing but tree-lined streets of enormous houses. I have no idea where we are. "I thought we were going to dinner."

"We are. I just need to check on the swelling in one of the guy's knees before we go." A devious smile takes over his face as he reaches over the center console of the car to place his hand on my thigh.

"Oh, okay. You could have mentioned that, you know." I smile back at him as I run my finger under the cuff of his jacket to get to the spot on the back of his wrist that drives him crazy. Seeing his smile reminds me how much of an easygoing guy he really is. Everything with Alex is fun and laid-back. I'd never thought I'd end up having a repeat guy, but with Alex, it's effortless. I've grown to like it, but I'd never admit it out loud. Being with him breaks all my rules, but the sex is so spectacular that it's definitely worth it—at least it will be until he turns out to be like every other shithead out there, lying and selfish.

We pull into the driveway of a beautiful mansion, bigger than most of the ones I've seen. But then again, the guy who lives here is a professional football player, so I don't know why I'd expect to see anything less than a towering monstrosity like this one.

Alex hops out and walks around to get my door. "Come on," he says, opening it.

"What? Why do you need me to come in? I'll wait here. It's fine," I tell him but immediately second-guess the decision. "Unless you're going to be a while. Is this going to take a long time?" I definitely don't want to be sitting in the car for an hour.

"Whether it takes five minutes or three hours, you aren't staying in the car. That would be very rude of me, don't you think?" He offers his hand to help me out of the car. There's a weird expression on his face I can't decipher. It could be annoyance at me for wanting to wait in the car… or maybe nervousness about introducing me to the person inside. We don't do things like meeting friends and family, which makes me wonder why he's so hell-bent on me coming in.

I grab my purse from the floor of the car and take his hand apprehensively, following him through the garage to a door. My mind is going a mile a minute trying to figure out what in the world Alex is up to with this 'meet the player' game.

He punches in a security code on a keypad before opening the door. "Hello," he yells as we enter.

There's no answer, so we walk farther into the house, stopping in a massive black-and-white marble-filled kitchen. Everything is quiet, and it seems as though no one is home. I follow Alex to the other side of the house, and he stops in front of a doorway hung with heavy blue floor-length curtains.

"Before we head in here, I need you to keep an open mind. Can you do that?" he asks, a very serious undercurrent in his tone.

Things seem to have just taken a hard turn into weird. "What the hell is this, Alex? The velvet curtains to your sex dungeon?" I ask, taking a step back.

"No, you dirty-minded little diva. It's a screening room. I have a feeling that this is where he is." He laughs as he wraps his arm around my shoulders, but he quickly turns serious again. "I'm serious, Quinn, can you keep an open mind until I explain things a little better?"

"Sure, I guess," I say, clutching the straps of the purse slung over my shoulder. "But I have to say that you're freaking me out."

"That's what I'm afraid of—you freaking out." He pulls back a curtain and ushers me inside.

The room is dark and very theater-like, except there are couches instead of chairs and a huge flat screen hangs on the wall. I look around, trying to figure out why Alex brought me here and why I need to keep an open mind. Then I spot the answer.

"Why would you bring me here? To *his* house? " I demand, doing my best to keep my voice low so as not to draw Tanner's attention to me. I don't know why Alex has brought me along, but I want no part of this meeting. I don't want to talk to him, so I turn to head back into the hallway.

He stands in the entrance, blocking my escape. "Because he needs your help, and I'm asking you to do this for me… for Ashley… for the baby," he says in a tired voice, his hands folded as though he's begging. All that's missing is the pout and a *pretty, pretty please*.

"What the hell are you talking about?" Now I understand all the weird shit back at the car. He was nervous about me kicking his ass for bringing me to Tanner's house.

"Things are pretty pathetic over here. He's a mess, and before you get all defensive, I thought he deserved what he's been getting in the beginning too. What he did to Ashley was fucked up, but look at him." He sighs, throwing his thumb over his shoulder drawing my attention toward Tanner. "He hasn't even noticed that we're standing here arguing, and I know as much as he's trying to focus on that game film he's watching, his mind is busy trying to figure out how to win back Ashley. He's a freaking train wreck, and I need him to see a little light at the end of the tunnel. I thought maybe if you talk to him and see that he's really trying to make things better, then you might help me help them."

He can't be serious.

"You think I'm going to help you by going behind my best friend's back and selling her out to him?"

"Please?" he asks, but *he* isn't Alex. Tanner has finally acknowledged us. He must have overheard our argument. "Please, Quinn. I need to fix this."

I take in his face, and even in the dimly lit room, I can tell that things have been wearing on him. He doesn't look very much like the superstar I met back in September. His face is thinner. His eyes are bloodshot, and he's sporting some serious bags under them. There's no happiness radiating from him anymore. He looks like a man who's had his world ripped away from him. It's sad, but he's done it to himself. I've seen Ashley look worse over the last month and a half, but the difference is that she didn't ask for it.

I take a step back and put my hands on my hips. "Tell me why I should care that you want to fix this, Tanner. Why? So your conscience can feel clean and you can focus on football?" I ask in my most irritated tone. I'm irritated with Alex for bringing me here and with Tanner for being an asshole and now wanting my help.

"Because I love her, Quinn," he says, looking me directly in the eye. There's no hint of bullshit reflecting back at me, and that realization knocks me for a complete fucking loop.

"Fuck! Did you just finally say that out loud?" Alex asks, looking shocked. "Took you damn long enough…"

"You have a funny way of showing love, Tanner. If you treat all the people you love the way that you've treated Ashley, remind me to never get close enough to you for you to love me," I say sarcastically.

"Excuse me," Alex says, smacking my ass.

"Shut up," I tell him. "I'm trying to make a point here."

"You think that I don't know how bad this sounds?" Tanner asks, his hands burying themselves in his hair. Everything about him radiates frustration. "I do. I made a mistake. Hasn't something from your past ever made you question everything and react badly? When she said she was pregnant, it felt like I was right back in a place I swore I'd never end up again. It didn't matter to me that it was Ashley. I couldn't see that. I spent that entire drive back to your place that day worried to death about her. She was so sick, and I just wanted to make her feel better. Then she didn't even want my help because she didn't want me to get sick. I knew she was different and that I was sunk even then. I knew I was falling in love with her…" He sighs, sounding defeated. "Then she dropped one of my worst fears in my lap. I know I was wrong, and I'm trying to make it better. I don't want to only be able to see my child every other weekend and holidays. That's not a way for a family to live. Are the three of us supposed to suffer forever because I had a temporary lapse in judgment?" His voice is the saddest, most pathetic one I've ever heard a grown man use before.

He's playing to my weaknesses too, whether he knows it or not. I know what it's like to have one person ruin the way you look at things—to have your judgment clouded by one stupid asshole. And he just said the three of us. He's including the baby—a baby that means the world to Ashley and a baby that I'm looking forward to meeting. That baby shouldn't have to grow up without a father, especially if he has one that wants nothing more than to be a part of his life.

"Fine, I'll help you." I say, taking a seat on one of the couches. "But only because you admit that you were wrong and I know that before everything went haywire, Ashley was very much in love with you. Every child should have their father." I probably shouldn't have mentioned Ashley being in love with him… Oh well!

Tanner's eyes are suddenly full of hope. "She loves me?"

Yup, I definitely shouldn't have told him that…

"Loved. She loved you until you broke her heart. Now? Now she hates you." I feel bad saying it, but the truth is the truth, and he's the one to blame.

"Hate is good. I can work with hate because that means that she still feels something for me. Just help me get her to realize that she doesn't hate me, that it's just anger. She has every right to be angry, but she needs to let me back in so I can make up for everything. I'll make up for it forever if she just lets me," he pleads.

Jesus, how can I say no to this?

"Okay, what do you have in mind?" I ask, conceding to the fact I'm now plotting against my best friend behind her back. I can only hope this is for her own good.

"I have no idea." He sighs. "I don't even know where to begin."

"I'll tell you this—that baby means everything to her. That might be your way back in. But I swear to God if you hurt her again, I will make a hat out of your penis and wear it to your funeral." And I'd wear that bitch proudly.

"I like my penis where it is, thanks. I promise I won't fuck it up again, Quinn," he says earnestly. "When's her next appointment? Does she have insurance? Is everything okay so far?" He asks his questions in such rapid succession it's as if he's afraid I'll clam up and stop talking to him at any moment.

"I believe her next appointment is in two weeks, but I'll have to check. I've been to them all so far, and yes, everything's fine. Yes, she has insurance, but I'm not telling you anything more about the pregnancy. It's not my place. You're going to have to get her to open up to you about it. There are some lines that I won't cross with this, Tanner," I tell him. There's help, and then there's betrayal. I'm already tiptoeing along that fine line, and I don't want to do that to Ashley.

"Can you at least tell me if she's still getting sick like she was the last time I saw her?" he asks, giving me those pleading eyes that pull at my heartstrings. No wonder Ash has never been able to say no to this man… until recently, anyway.

"Not anymore. They gave her medication for it."

"Medication? Is that safe for the baby?" he asks, his voice laced with concern.

"Yes, Tanner. I just told you that everything was fine," I answer, mildly irritated because he's doubting my, Ashley's, and the doctor's abilities to make sure she's properly cared for, but it's hard to be mad when he looks so concerned.

"Hey, Tag. I brought dinner!" A familiar female voice yells out from the other side of the house. I couldn't forget that nasal voice if I tried. Why is that bitch here? And why is she bringing Tanner dinner if he's pining away over losing Ashley?

I stand up and step toward Tanner. "You love her, huh? If you love her so much, why is that twat bringing you dinner?" I snarl at him as I cross my arms over my chest and shoot him a look of disdain.

If he's trying to win Ash back, he'd better not be anywhere near Melissa or Ash will never take him seriously. I still can't believe that bitch had the nerve to come to our place and tell her to abort her baby. After talking with Tanner, I don't think the message came from him. I never really had, especially after hearing Melissa had claimed she and Tanner were together, but I wasn't going to tell Ashley that.

"I didn't know she was coming by. I haven't talked to her all week. And she's just a friend," he answers with a slight panic to his voice.

"Well, here's your first piece of advice: get rid of that bitch. She isn't who you think she is, and Ashley will *never* consider taking you back with her in the picture," I tell him before heading back toward the door we came in. I need to leave. The longer I'm near her, the more likely I am to break her lying face.

I round the corner into the kitchen just as Melissa lifts her head up from the bag she's unpacking and smiles, but the smile fades when she sees that it's me.

"What are you doing here?" she asks, looking like a deer caught in headlights. I have a feeling that look of fear has something to do with her visit to our place, and seeing it confirms my suspicions that she went to torment Ashley of her own accord, not to deliver any messages for Tanner.

I know I should tell Tanner and Alex about the visit now, but if I stick around any longer, I'll probably end up shoving my stiletto up her ass, and the last thing I need is a night in jail because of some skank.

"I was asked to help Tanner win back the girl he loves, and she isn't you. Your little game is up. Did you honestly think anyone was going to believe that Tanner would send *you* to our house? Who the hell are you? You were never more than a piece of ass to him. You'll never be on the same level as Ashley. You're pathetic, and I can't wait until your friends figure you out for the fake bitch that you are." I smile as sweetly as I can at her before turning back toward the hallway I've just come from. "Alex, can we go to dinner now?" I call out to him. "All of the cheap perfume in this room is giving me a headache."

Chapter Eight

TANNER

I DIDN'T SEE Melissa's encounter with Quinn before I walked into the kitchen, but I know something must have happened. Melissa tried to hide the worried look on her face as soon as Alex and I came into the room.

I'm annoyed that she's just shown up unannounced. Thank God Quinn didn't change her mind about helping me because of it. I still can't believe she agreed to help in the first place. I don't know what Alex was thinking bringing her here, but I'll have to thank him later. Now that they're gone, I ask, "What are you doing here, Melissa?"

"You haven't answered my calls all week, so I figured I'd pop by with dinner and check in on you," she says with a smile as she grabs forks from the drawer and sets them on the counter.

"I don't need checking on," I tell her. Why does she think she can come over without any warning? She's never done it before. That's not how things have worked between us—ever. Her audacity could've derailed everything I'm trying to do to get Ashley back. Quinn is my best chance at fixing this mess, and Melissa could've fucked it all up.

"I remember how you were after the Carrie incident, and I figured you might need me." She sidles up next to me, molding her body to my side.

I step away from her. "The two situations are not the same," I say frustrated. I don't like the way she's comparing Ashley to Carrie, and I don't care if I sound like an asshole.

"How are two gold-digging whores trying to trap you with a baby not the same?" She drops the Styrofoam container on the counter, where it pops open and pasta spills everywhere. Even with the mess, her attention is one-hundred-percent focused on glaring at me, the anger evident in her eyes.

"First of all, I know I was angry with her, but Ashley is not a gold digging whore, and that better be the last time I hear you refer to her as such," I bark, slamming my hand on the counter. "Second, she isn't trying to trap me with anything. She hasn't even contacted me since she first told me about the baby. She isn't out for any money or whatever it is you think she's after. Third, I *will* be doing whatever is necessary to fix our relationship and get her back." Melissa had better get that through her damn head now because I don't need her making this situation any worse with her misplaced anger.

She throws her hands into the air in frustration. "Get her back? Are you insane? Have you forgotten that she got knocked up, most likely on purpose, and hid it from you?" she asks, her tone laced with hate. Melissa has never reacted this way before. It's completely out of character. What the hell happened to the girl who's always been drama-free and sensible?

I know it's my fault she thinks Ashley has some ulterior motive, but I don't give a shit if she's not going to listen. Either way, Melissa's feelings on the subject really aren't important. I'm starting to realize I should never have told her about anything that happened between Ashley and me.

"She didn't get pregnant on purpose, and she didn't try to hide it from me. I was wrong," I admit.

"How you can seriously be so naïve about this situation? Have you forgotten everything that happened, Tanner?" she asks in disbelief, clearly still thinking Ashley is setting me up.

"I'm not being naïve. I'm finally pulling my head out of my ass and seeing the truth. The woman I love is pregnant, and I was a complete asshole to her."

Melissa's expression turns cold and she looks at me with a rage that I've never seen before. "The woman you *love?*" She says the word *love* as if it's poison in her mouth. "Please, Tanner. You don't love her. She's brainwashed you into thinking that you do. That's what lying bitches like her do. You'll see eventually." She grabs her purse from the counter. "Call me when you take off the blinders you're wearing. I can't hang around and watch this girl make a fool out of you," she spits before storming out and slamming the door behind her.

Wow, I definitely didn't see that coming, but it's not my fault if she doesn't understand. Based on what Quinn said to me earlier, Melissa's only going to be a hindrance in getting Ashley back anyway, so it's probably for the best she stays away for a while. That's fine with me. Football, Ashley, and our baby are the only things I'm concerned with right now.

IT'S CHRISTMAS, AND this is the last week of regular season games. We've already clinched our playoff spot, so it'll be an easy week. Since we're leading the division, we don't have a game next week. Coach has given us the usual speech about not expecting anything and still needing to play this last regular season game like it matters. Even so, everyone's basically treating this week as a glorified practice, but none of us would dare say that to Coach. We don't want to lose, but we all want to take it easy and enjoy the holidays with our families.

I'd spent the beginning of the week orchestrating Ashley's Christmas gifts with Quinn's help. The day after she and Alex had been at the house, I'd called her and begged her to help me. I want to show Ashley that I'm invested, and I'd thought getting her what she—no *we*—needed for the baby would do just that.

Quinn hadn't thought it was the best idea to buy all the baby stuff for Ashley because she might want to do it herself, but I got her to come help pick out things that Ashley would like in the end. Since she'd pointed out that she knows nothing about baby things, so we also brought my sister along to make sure we got everything important. We practically cleared out Babies "R" Us, and I'd arranged for it all to be delivered to her on Christmas morning.

I've told Quinn that Ashley is more than welcome to take everything back and get what she wants if she doesn't like what we've picked. It's more about the statement to me than anything else. I want her to understand I'm ready to be a part of this family with her. I want to be a part of this and support her in every way possible. Apparently, that was the right thing to say to Quinn because she got all teary-eyed when I did.

I've also called an organic specialty store and set up weekly deliveries of organic fruits and vegetables to Ashley's house as a way to show her that I care about her health and what she's eating. I want the best to be available for her and the baby. High-quality food is expensive, but I know even without asking she would never take money from me, so I'm hoping this will help.

The third and final gift I've set up is a delivery of some pregnancy books. One of the books I ordered was one of those scrapbook things that women can write in about all the things they go through while pregnant—doctor's appointments, sonograms, cravings, and whatever else pregnant women think about. That gift has a dual purpose. While I want her to be able to keep track of all of her feelings and appointments and the like, I also want to be able to read all about it when things finally settle down and she lets me back in. It kills me that I'm missing out on all of those things. I pray to God that my efforts don't all go to waste.

Yesterday, after making all the necessary arrangements for all of my gifts to be delivered to Ashley, I gave out a very different collection of presents. I gave out PlayStation 4s and new computers to ten different children's homes. The Mathis Foundation bought accessories to include in the packages, like controllers and video games. The looks on the children's faces were more than worth the money spent. Watching the boys and girls go insane over the new video game systems and freaking out about being able to go online on decent computers was all that I needed this Christmas. Well, aside from a certain woman's forgiveness.

I'm on my way over to Ma's for Christmas dinner and presents, daydreaming about the way things used to be between Ashley and me, when my phone rings. Seeing her name flash across the screen makes my heart speed up, and I can't help but think she might be calling to say thank you and finally accept my apology.

Those hopes are squashed the moment I answer the phone and she starts screaming at me.

"Merry Christmas, Ashley," I answer.

"How dare you? Who do you think you are? You don't get to go AWOL for weeks and then decide you now want to play daddy," she yells so loudly I have to turn the volume down on the radio as she echoes through the car.

"I'm not 'playing daddy,' Ashley. I am the daddy." I hope that her hearing me take responsibility will soften her rage.

"You aren't shit, Tanner. You gave that up the minute you called me a lying whore and claimed you didn't believe the baby was yours. You lost your right to be daddy then and even more so when you sent over your little messenger. I don't give two shits who you are, Mr. Garrison. You can't buy your way out of this."

Tapping my thumbs on the steering wheel, I try to figure out who this messenger is she keeps talking about. It's the second time she's said something about it, and I still have no clue what she means.

"Ashley, I have no idea what you're talking about. I never sent you any messages. Anything I've wanted to say to you, I have said myself. But this is my baby too, and like it or not, we're raising it together." I don't want to take it to a legal level, but I do want her to understand just how serious I am about being in my child's life. I wish she could see I'm trying to be involved, not simply trying to buy my way back in.

"No. We're. Not!" she says, her voice strained in anger. "I don't want your gifts. I can and will get my own stuff for *my* baby. I don't need your organic fruits and vegetables either, and I already bought my own books. Thanks for the reminder that you think I'm an incompetent moron who doesn't know how to take care of herself."

Wow, this is really backfiring in my face.

"Ashley, calm down," I say gently. I'm pretty sure that her being this upset and yelling can't be good for her or the baby. "I don't think you're a moron, and I know you're more than capable of taking care of yourself. I just wanted to do something nice for you. I know the way I reacted at first has pushed me out of your life. I fucked up, but I'm trying to make up for it. I want to be there for you and our baby, and since you won't physically let me near you, this was the only thing I could think of. I have no hidden agenda…"

"Don't tell me to calm down! I don't need you to do shit for me, Tanner," she says before hanging up on me.

Well, there goes that.

Chapter Nine

ASHLEY

*"**DO YOU LIKE** that, Ashley?" he asks, blowing on my nipple. He covers my stiff peak with his mouth again and swirls his tongue around it in the most delicious circles.*

"Mmm," I hum as he kisses along the valley between my breasts, making his way over to my other nipple, all the while kneading my breasts with his hands.

"I know you do. I haven't found anything that you don't like," he murmurs against me, sending vibrations through my entire body and lighting my core on fire.

"Please," I whimper. "Please, Tanner. I need you."

He smiles up at me before starting his descent down my body. "I know you do, baby."

Goosebumps cover my body as he leaves no spot unkissed. He worships me with his lips, setting me ablaze. When he reaches my center, he kisses and licks everywhere except where I need him to most.

"Stop teasing me," I growl at him in frustration. I weave my fingers into his hair and try to direct his mouth where I want it.

"You want me to eat your pussy, baby?" he asks, nuzzling his face further between my legs and running his nose up and down my slit. "It's all pretty and pink, glistening with your juices."

"Yes! Yes!" I pant out. My whole body is overly sensitized, anticipating the warmth of his mouth, wanting the pleasure it knows only Tanner can give.

Tanner replaces his nose with his tongue and runs it up and down my slit, dipping inside me. Screams of pleasure leave my mouth as involuntarily as my breath. There's no holding back. He has me hanging on edge. The tiniest nudge and I will fall, fall into the sea of nirvana that is better than any other feeling known to man.

He abruptly stops and moves away before bringing his eyes up to meet mine. "I'm sorry, Ashley, but I only make genuine people come—not lying gold diggers like you."

My eyes pop open as I jackknife up in bed. My heart is racing, and I'm covered in sweat. My panties are fucking soaked. Again. This bullshit has to stop. I can only take so many cold showers in the middle of winter.

"SOMETIMES BEING PREGNANT sucks," I whine to Quinn as I plop myself down next to her on the sofa and put my feet in her lap. I lean my head over the arm of our overstuffed blue couch and sigh. I've really come to love this couch. I like to rub my cheek on the soft micro-suede, and lately I've found myself preferring to sleep here rather than in my bed. If only it were bigger so I could sprawl out more.

"Your ass hasn't gotten that big, and you haven't been sick in weeks. You even get to sleep in the middle of the day, and no one questions it. What's wrong now?" Quinn asks, pausing whatever dumb reality show she's watching from her DVR stash.

"Well, first, my boobs are killing me. I've gone up a whole cup size. Normally, I'd be grateful for the free boob job, but these babies hurt," I tell her, my hands unconsciously rising to rub my sore breasts. "Second, my nipples are super sensitive, which is sensory overload when you add in the fact that I'm hornier than a frat boy in a whorehouse. I had to replace the batteries in my vibrator last week, and they were still practically brand new. I'm seriously considering going back to that shop and buying one of those purple vagina killers."

She laughs as though I'm kidding, but I'm completely serious. My vagina has been one greedy bitch lately. Nothing seems to satisfy her.

Quinn grins and says, "You burnt through those batteries already? Damn."

I don't know why, but the comment really pisses me off. "Don't laugh at me, bitch," I snap. "Just because you've got Alex fucking you into next week doesn't mean you get to make fun of my lack of sex like you're the Queen of Cocks." I feel tears welling behind my eyes.

"Queen of Cocks?" she asks, laughing even harder.

The tears have risen up, brimming on my lower lids. One blink will surely cause a tidal wave.

"Yes, Queen of Cocks, you know—the gatekeeper of all the cocks. She's the bitch who decides who gets some and who doesn't and then gets her rocks off mocking the poor pathetic fools like me who don't get to enjoy any of it," I explain, tears now streaming down my face.

"Hold up. You're crying because, in your delusional mind, you've made me Queen of Cocks and I'm supposedly the one denying you a good fuck?" she asks in a confused tone.

"No. I'm crying because I'm a hormonal wreck and I'm sex deprived. I was getting superb sex on a regular basis, and then I was cut off cold-turkey. On top of that, my sex dreams are always with him, are way better than the reality ever was, and I always wake up before I come. EVERY. FUCKING. TIME. Then I wind up needing to finish what my dream started, requiring me to use said dream to finish the job, and then I'm angry at myself for thinking about Tanner while making myself come. Or I have to take a cold shower. Who the hell enjoys cold showers?"

Quinn stares at me, speechless, as I continue my tirade. I'm having a full blown meltdown at this point, so I might as well let it all out.

"Then there are the cravings! I want Cherry Garcia Ben and Jerry's like all the time. Plus, I saw at least ten very pregnant women this week, and they all—each and every one of them—had their significant others by their sides, fawning all over them. I'm never going to have that, and it makes me really, really sad." I drop my head into my hands and let the sobs out.

"Aww, Sweets, I'm sorry. I didn't mean to make you more upset, but come on, Queen of the Cocks? It's funny, and you know it." She pulls my feet together in her lap and massages them. "How long have you been having these dreams and when did they start?" she asks, focusing on rubbing my left foot.

I sigh in pleasure as she hits a sweet spot in the middle of my foot. "They started after his impromptu apology visit."

"You've been this horny for two weeks?" She gives me a look filled with sympathy as she moves on to the right foot.

"Don't look at me like that, and yes, I have. It wasn't nearly as bad until I saw him in person. In my mind, I'd convinced myself that he'd morphed into Quasimodo after we broke up." I laugh. "All that work down the drain with one stupid visit. I could smell his cologne for two days after. Why does he have to be such a good-looking, good-smelling prick?"

"You know what you need?" she asks, moving her still-massaging hands from my feet up to my calves.

"Whaaat?" I moan out, enjoying the calf massage.

"Are you seriously going to orgasm just from me rubbing your calves?" she asks in disbelief.

I chuckle. "Hopefully, because that would be really nice. You'd be a better lover than almost all of my past boyfriends." All but one. Of course, he would be the only one who knew how to play my body like a fiddle and could fuck me six ways to Sunday.

"I know that I promised to be here for you throughout this entire thing, but I draw the line at making you come. That's weird even for me." She pushes my legs off her lap and onto the floor with a laugh.

"Ha, ha, ha… You were saying?" I give her a glare for disrupting my comfort.

"You need a night out. You know, Alex asked me to go to that upcoming fundraiser with him. Why don't you come with us?" she suggests excitedly. "We have an extra ticket. You need to get all dolled up and feel good about yourself. It'll make you feel like a million bucks." She does make a good point. Nothing makes a girl feel better than getting all dressed up for a big party.

"Why the hell not?" I have a feeling that somehow I'm going to regret this.

"You need a new dress," she says enthusiastically.

"No. I'm not buying a dress that I'm literally only going to be able to wear once," I tell her as my hand roams over my slowly growing bump. She opens her mouth to say something, but I stop her before she has the chance because I know exactly what she's thinking. "And neither are you."

"You're right. We'll go consignment. There's a place down in Hudson Square," she says before going off on a tangent about colors and accessories.

Lord help me.

"YOU LOOK ABSOLUTELY stunning," Quinn says when I open my bedroom door.

"Gorgeous," Alex agrees with a wide smile. Over the last month, he's become a very good friend, even if his taste in other friends is completely questionable.

"Thank you," I say, smiling genuinely. I think I look great as well. The dress Quinn and I found is fabulous—metallic silver and covered in beading. With its flowy style, it's great for my expanding midsection, and it's impossible to tell that I'm pregnant. I can't remember what Quinn called it—empire something or other. With a slit on the left side that goes to mid-thigh, it's still quite sexy. Quinn had me pair it with simple black Jimmy Choo heels, but she'd insisted I need party makeup, so I'm a bit more done-up than usual. My hair is swept over to one side and hangs down over my shoulder in a bevy of curls. Quinn had been right. Getting dressed up was just the pick me up I needed.

"Are you beautiful ladies ready?" Alex asks, flashing his most charming smile at Quinn and I.

"I just need to change out my purse really quick," I say, heading to my closet to grab my black clutch. I move everything I might need from my everyday purse and then make my way down the hall toward the coat closet for my dress coat.

As I reach the end of the hallway, I hear hushed murmuring from the entryway.

"Did you tell her?" Alex asks in muted tones.

"No," Quinn answers.

"You know she's going to be pissed, right?"

"I don't care anymore. She needs this. They need this push."

I have a feeling I'm not going to like whatever it is that they're talking about, so I choose to ignore it as I make my way toward the front door, resolving to find out tomorrow. I'm all dressed up and ready to go, and I don't want anything to ruin my night out.

As we pull up to the Waldorf Astoria, I'm starting to wish I'd asked more questions regarding this event before agreeing to go. They don't let just anyone host an event at the Waldorf on New Year's Eve. Whatever charity is hosting this, they've certainly gone all out.

Quinn and Alex get stopped near the entrance by an acquaintance of Alex's, but I keep walking, taking everything in. I wish I would've known the event had a gold theme. I feel as though my dress clashes with everything… Oh well! I look damn good.

The table linens are white and covered with sparkly gold tulle. The square centerpieces are bowls with floating candles and glittering ornament-like balls in them. A huge sign over the stage area reads, "A New Year, A New Face." Underneath, smaller gold letters spell out "The Tony Mathis Foundation."

Now I know what the whispering must have been about. I'm going to kill those two—just as soon as I find them. How could they do this to me? Scanning the crowd, I try to find them, but I end up finding him instead. Of course, he's in a fucking tux… and he's laughing it up as though he doesn't have a care in the world. Fucking asshole. As much as I hate him—and I really fucking hate him—I can't tear my eyes away from him. That is until I catch a flash of teal in my peripheral vision and beeline it toward my traitorous best friend and her date.

"Are you fucking kidding me?" I growl out between my gritted teeth.

"I'm guessing you figured out where we are, huh?" She looks down at the floor to hide from my murderous glare. At least she has the decency to look remorseful.

I'm seething. "After everything I told you the other day while crying my eyes out, you decided this is exactly what I need?" On what planet did she think this was a good idea?

"Yes, I did. You need a night out while looking absolutely fabulous, and he needs to see it. And you need to see him too. I think you should hear him out, Ash," she says, a slight wariness in her voice. Quinn is never timid or wary, so she must really be worried about my reaction.

"This is the last thing I need. I'm horny twenty-four seven and getting off to my dreams of him fucking me, and you think I need to see him in a tux? He's wearing a fucking tux, Quinn. My vagina doesn't give a shit how much I hate him right now," I spit at her, not caring that Alex can hear every word. Thankfully, he's smart enough to keep any smart-ass comments to himself.

"Why don't you just try to have a good time, Ashley? Hang out with us, and if Tanner tries to talk to you tonight, hear him out. What can it hurt?" she asks, shrugging.

"Everything. It can hurt everything. Thanks a lot." I turn to head to the bar before I remember I can't even get drunk. Fucking great!

Once he's spotted me, it takes Tanner about twenty minutes to make his way over to me. I try so hard to move in opposition to him, but he must be more determined than I've given him credit for. As I feel him closing in on me, I make my way closer to the bar, where there's a high concentration of people. Better to be near others than secluded with him.

"This is much different than the last time we were at one of these functions," he says, appearing at my side. "You couldn't get close enough that night, but now you can't seem to get far enough away from me," he says with his panty melting smile and I know I need to get away from him now.

"I don't have anything nice to say to you, unlike last time, so it's better that we keep our distance. Wouldn't want to make a scene, no?" I say before I walk away. He just had to bring up that night, didn't he? I've been doing my best to ignore the fact that the last time we were at one of these was when he made our relationship official and public. This is going to be a long night if this is how he plans on playing things. A trip down memory lane will do me absolutely no good. I know what we had then, and I know what we don't have now. I don't need him reminding me. He's got a lot of nerve.

I do my best to keep as far away from Tanner, but that means I have to keep an eye on him—watching him schmooze for hours, chatting everyone up to get donations for the kids. The irony isn't lost on me. He's raising money for other people's kids when he can't accept his own… He may claim he wants in now, but how can I believe that after the things he said?

Tanner heads toward the stage for his speech, and that's my cue to make sure I'm not around. I can't bear to listen to him babble on about helping to save these strangers' kids when he wanted me to get rid of his own. I don't think I'd be able to keep down the chicken that was served for dinner.

I head into the hallway behind the ballroom and stroll along it, admiring the artwork on the walls until the faint buzz of Tanner's voice over the sound system turns into an applause and I'm sure he's finished with his hypocritical speech. Making my way back into the party, I stand on the sidelines, watching everyone enjoy their evening. Quinn and Alex are having a great time out on the dance floor. They look as though they've never been happier. I'm jealous for a moment when the music slows down and Alex wraps his arms around her, drawing her close for the dance. I'm taken aback by the sadness of the song. It seems an odd choice for a New Year's party, but whatever.

Closing my eyes, I listen to the lyrics Christina Aguilera's melodious voice is belting out. She's sorry for hurting someone and wishing she had just one more chance. I guess I can see the correlation to the starting of a new year when I think about it—washing away the sadness and mistakes of the old year. If only it were that easy.

"I asked the DJ to play this song," a strong, familiar voice says from behind me.

“Congratulations,” I say sarcastically. I’m not sure what someone says to something like that except to ask why, but I don’t want to engage him. I want him to go away, so there’s no way I’m asking that question. His cologne invades my nose as he gets closer to me, and it does nothing to calm my libido.

“Don’t you want to know why?” he says, standing close enough that I can feel his breath on my neck. It makes me shiver. Fuck! The last thing I need is for him to think he still has an effect on me, which he doesn’t—just on my fucking uncontrollable hormones.

“Not even a little bit,” I spit out as harshly as I can. “Now, if you’ll excuse me.”

I don’t even get a step away before he wraps his fingers around my upper arm, stopping me. The moment his skin touches mine, the familiar and undeniable jolt of electricity buzzes through me. I hear his gasp, so he must feel it too… and know that I’m still affected by him. Just what I fucking need. Why the hell can’t I get my body on board with the hate in my heart?

“Because almost every word of this song applies to me and you. Because I’m sorry for hurting you, and I’m sorry for the things I said that definitely weren’t true. I’m sorry for blaming you,” he says.

I sense him staring at me, but I’m not ready to look at him just yet. I take a deep breath, straighten my spine, and meet his gaze. “Good for you, Tanner.” I pull my arm away from him and head back toward the hallway I’d hidden in earlier. I remember seeing a restroom there, and I need somewhere to pull myself together. My pussy really needs to get the message that she shouldn’t get turned on by that asshole.

As I reach the bathroom, I’m relieved to find it’s empty. Grabbing a paper towel, I run it under the cold water, and blot the back and sides of my neck with it, hoping to cool myself down. The door opens and closes behind me and then there’s a click, like that of a lock sliding into place. I lean back to look around the partition that separates the sitting area of the bathroom from the facilities area only to find Tanner striding toward me as though he’s on a mission.

“Don’t you understand?” he asks, shaking his head.

"What? That you're a grade-A asshole? Yes, I understand that better than most," I say, cocking my head and flashing him a snarky smile.

"No, Ashley. I made a mistake. I've apologized for that mistake. I'll keep apologizing for that mistake, because I'll do anything to make things right between us. What's it going to take for you to realize that we belong together? Don't think I didn't notice that little shiver back there," he says, invading my space again. He's so close he's shorting out all my mental circuits. The tux, the cologne, the apologetic rasp of his voice—I need to get away from him.

"Nothing, because we don't belong together. If we did, you would've never treated me the way you have," I say, trying to sound strong as I ignore his comment about my reaction to his touch.

He closes the last bit of space left between us. "I recall you liking all the ways I treated you, Ashley. I've felt your beautiful eyes following me all night, and I could practically hear all the dirty thoughts running through your mind," he says in that tone he always uses when he's trying to convince me of something. He hasn't lost using it yet. "You look absolutely beautiful tonight." He runs his nose down the side of my neck, from my ear to my collarbone.

I don't have enough resolve to fight him off, but maybe if I can give in to this feeling on my own terms, I can make it out of here with my heart still intact. I hate him. I know that. But right now, I want to hate him while he's buried inside me, making me forget everything including my name.

"Yes, I know. I've been told. Repeatedly," I say, baiting him. If I'm not leaving here unscathed, neither is he. Two can play at this game. The only difference between us is that I don't give two shits what he thinks of me after I get what I need.

He grips my hip. "Who's been telling you that?" he asks, his tone hard and jealous. Perfect, exactly what I want.

"None of your concern." I push his hand away but don't quite let go of him. My eyes stay glued to our connected hands.

Tanner must see whatever it is he's looking for in my reaction because his expression becomes harder, more possessive. "Everything about you concerns me, Ashley," he says, gripping both of my hips now.

"Not anymore," I say, sounding breathier than I'd wanted to. My traitorous body caves to his touch, and my lower half has molded itself to his.

"I bet your body thinks otherwise, baby," he says, sliding his hand from its spot on my hip to the slit of my dress. He drags his fingers up my exposed thigh to my panties, where they pause as if he's expecting me to stop him, but I can't formulate a coherent thought with the way he's touching me. The way I've been dreaming of for weeks. The way my body has been begging for.

He finally slides his hand up farther and his fingers find their prize. The small contact between his fingers and my clit, even over my thong, sends my overly needy body into a sensory tailspin. I know doing this with him is wrong, and I'm sure I'll regret it tomorrow, but I want it so badly right now.

"Just as I thought, Ashley," he whispers into the air. I close my eyes and try to tune him out as best I can but he has other plans. He wants me to say something back, engage him. He has always liked dirty banter during sex, but he isn't going to get it today. "You're so wet, baby. Your pussy misses me, doesn't she?" he asks, gliding my panties down my legs and pulling them off. He drops to his knees and buries his face between my legs.

I hear him inhale deeply, taking in the scent of my arousal, and the sound makes me even wetter. The first lick along the seams of my folds sends my senses spiraling out of control. He licks me again and again in rapid succession, taking me to the edge as he assaults my flesh in the best of ways and pushes me over in record time. I try to hold my scream at bay, but I can't. My orgasm rocks me to my core, sending me soaring to the highest of heights. I'm so high up that it seems impossible for this sensation to be wrong.

"Fuck," he growls, standing and unbuckling his belt. His pants and boxers hit the floor with impossible speed. Stepping out of them, he roughly grabs me and pushes me toward an upholstered chair in the sitting area of the bathroom. He sits down and pulls me between his legs. Using the slit in my dress for easy access, he pulls the skirt over the sides of my legs, exposing my lower body.

When I glance into the mirror in front of us, I see the moisture dripping down my legs, and I'm sure he must see it too. My suspicions are confirmed when he gathers my juices with a finger and brings it to his mouth, licking it clean.

"Mmm, exquisite as ever." He moans. "Sit on my cock, Ashley."

I don't want to oblige any order of his, but old habits die hard. I hate to let him think he's winning, that he can still boss me around. If I didn't want to ride his cock as badly as I do, I'd tell him to fuck off, but I want him so much it hurts. Without further hesitation, I impale myself on his hard, rigid length.

"Ahhh…" I moan out, enjoying the burning stretch of having him fill me.

He grabs my legs and drapes them over his, spreading me wide. "See that, Ashley?" he asks, nodding toward the full-length mirror on the wall in front of us. "Watch me fuck you."

Like a car accident on the side of the road, I don't want to look, but I can't pull my gaze away. I have a front row seat to the show. He digs his fingers into my hips, giving him the leverage he needs to bounce me up and down, and I watch his cock slide in and out of me as if its sole purpose is to please me.

"Your pussy knows my cock belongs in it, Ashley," he growls. "She didn't forget me. Your body knows we belong together, that we fit together perfectly."

"Will you please just shut the hell up and fuck me?" I demand, tired of hearing his voice. Hearing him talk takes away from my pleasure. In silence, I can close my eyes and pretend the man I'm on top of isn't him, pretend he's someone else who actually deserves to be fucking me right now.

He finally shuts his mouth and does what I want him to—fuck me. In and out. Over and over. I feel my orgasm brewing on the horizon, so close I can taste it. Unfortunately, the asshole under me is the only one who's ever been able to get me to this point. I've missed it, and it's almost within reach.

"Harder, Tanner," I order. "Stop dragging this out."

Again, he does what is asked of him with no comment, fucking me harder, faster, and deeper. My orgasm barrels through my body, making me lose all motor and cognitive function. I scream out his name from force of habit and dig my nails into the hands that are gripping my hips with punishing force.

He's still thrusting into me when my body collapses into a heap in his lap. He comes roaring my name along with every curse word in the book and a few that might be new.

I don't want this to be mistaken for anything other than a quick fuck, so I stand as soon as I'm able to, causing his cock to fall from my body. I quickly head over to the sink area to clean myself up, trying to make it look as though I haven't just had my brains fucked out.

It doesn't take Tanner long to follow suit. He pulls up his pants and boxers, getting dressed with a smile on his face. His eyes meet mine in the mirror, and he steps up to stand behind me. "I'm so glad you were listening, Ashley. I've been so miserable without you," he says, smoothing my hair back into place.

I look at him for a moment before letting him know exactly where I stand. "I don't know what you think just happened, but let me enlighten you. That wasn't me coming around. That was me needing to be fucked. Contrary to what you may think, I'm not a dirty whore, and I won't be fucking anyone else while pregnant with your child. That's disgusting. So basically, I wanted something that, unfortunately, only you can give me. Nothing has changed. I still loathe you."

The look on his face is priceless, and I know I should feel bad but I just can't.

"Come on. You can't deny that we belong together, especially after that," he says, running his hands through his hair in exasperation.

I give him a sad smile and push away from the counter. "I thought we did at one time, but that time seems like it was ages ago."

"What can I do to get you to understand that I'm sorry and didn't mean all those things?" he asks, watching me pull open the door to head into the hallway.

A song drifts in from the ballroom, and it couldn't be more perfect, "You hear that song, Tanner? I didn't request it, but it most definitely describes how I feel about you."

He stands there, staring at me with devastation on his face. I can't bring myself to care though, because like the song says, it's too late to apologize.

Chapter Ten

TANNER

"TAG, YOU NEED to get your head straight," Alex reminds me—as if I could forget.

"I know, man." I sigh into the phone. "I've been trying. I don't know what else to do." My head has been in even more of a disarray since New Year's Eve, which I hadn't thought possible. I can't help but think that Ashley letting me inside of her—hell, even near enough to touch her—means there's a chance for me to fix this. It has to. No matter what she says, she isn't the type of girl to use someone for sex. I know that it meant something. Unfortunately, these thoughts have occupied every part of my mind not dedicated to subconscious functions.

"Try harder. The playoffs start Sunday, so you don't have much time," he says, being completely unhelpful.

"You think I don't know that? My head doesn't seem to really give a shit." I used to be able to forget about anything when it came to football, but even the playoffs aren't helping get my mind off Ashley and the harsh sound of her voice saying it's too late to apologize. I refuse to believe it. Even the mere thought of it guts me.

"I wish I could help you fix this, but I've got nothing, man. I'm sorry."

I sigh again—I find myself doing that a lot these days. "I know. This is my fight and I'm going to have to figure out how to put things back together on my own."

"You know I'm always here if you need me," Alex says. "I need to head out, though. I'm meeting Quinn for dinner."

"Just Quinn?" I ask, an idea forming in my head. I feel hopeful for the first time in two weeks.

"Yeah, why?"

"Let me come with you. Please. Maybe Quinn will tell me what's going on with Ashley."

"I don't think that's a good idea," he says wearily. "She doesn't like being in the middle of this any more than I do."

"But she helped me before. I'm sure she would again," I say, trying to coax him into agreeing with me.

"Fine, but if she gets pissed at me, it's your ass." After giving me the name of the place, he says they'll be there in an hour.

I move faster while getting ready than I have in the last two weeks, even on the field, and I get there before Quinn and Alex do. Anything that might help get Ashley back is the only motivation I need. I wish Ashley would just tell me that winning the fucking Super Bowl would get her to take me back. I'd be on top of my damn game then.

Quinn gives me a sad smile when she and Alex arrive at the restaurant, and I guess Alex must have filled her in on the way over here.

"You look as shitty as she does," she says, pulling me into a hug.

My heart drops instantly, worrying that Ashley's sick again. "Did something happen? Is everything okay with the baby?" I ask, filled with concern.

Our conversation is momentarily disrupted by the hostess telling us our table is ready. It's hard not to press Quinn for an answer, but I wait until we're seated to continue.

"What's going on, Quinn?" I ask as I take my seat. "You're killing me here."

"Everything with the baby is still fine," she says as she does the same, finally giving me a little reprieve.

"Are you sure?" I ask skeptically. "Has she been back to the doctor recently?"

She grabs a menu. "Yes, she had an appointment earlier this week. Everything was good." A warm smile spreads across her face, as though she's recalling a fond memory.

"What did they say?" I ask, craving more information than she's giving.

"That's all you're getting out of me on that, pal. Nothing has changed on my part there." She gives me a stern look over her menu.

I sigh in exasperation. I know I should be happy Quinn's willing to give me any information at all, but it's my baby too. It's not fair that I'm being kept in the dark, especially considering that I want to be part of this experience. There are probably thousands of women who would give anything for their babies' fathers to want to be involved.

"I know. I'm grateful for you keeping me somewhat in the loop, but it's still hard." I bring my gaze to meet hers, hoping she sees my earnestness there.

"It's a shitty situation for all of us," she answers, looking toward Alex. It really must suck for them to be stuck in the middle, but that doesn't mean I won't try to exploit our friendship to get all the info I can.

"If everything is fine with the baby, then why does she look shitty?" I ask, coming back to her initial comment.

"You sure as hell did a number on her at that party," she says. Her non-direct answer makes my stomach plummet again. She walked away from me, not the other way around. How could I have done a number on her? Unless, I physically hurt her…

"What do you mean? I… I didn't hurt her or the baby, did I?" Fuck, I hope not. I wouldn't be able to stomach that news. I'm suddenly reminded of the night in my kitchen when I'd thought I had pushed Ashley too far.

"No, relax. That bitch needed to be pounded out." She laughs—fucking laughs as though she hasn't just given me the heart attack of all heart attacks.

Alex's eyes go wide. "Dude, you didn't! Tell me you didn't bang her out in the bathroom." He shakes his head in disbelief.

Quinn grins before taking a sip of the wine I didn't even notice the waitress had brought over. "He sure did. He worked her over like a two-dollar whore."

"I…I didn't mean to, I swear. I only had intentions of trying to talk some sense into her, but then I got all sidetracked. I don't know what came over me. I just needed to connect with her again," I explain and realize how lame I sound.

"You thought a quick fuck in the bathroom at a charity event was the way to reconnect with her?" Alex shakes his head again. "You really are a moron."

"Quinn," I snap. "What do you mean I did a number on her?" I'm getting really tired of having to repeat myself.

"She was a hot mess before that night, but it's even worse now—I suppose in kind of the same way it is for you." She gives me a pointed look.

"She told me she hates… no, *loathes*… me, and that it's too late for apologies." Repeating Ashley's words out loud leave a bitter taste in my mouth. "I think she made it out of that bathroom far better than I did."

"She doesn't actually hate you, Tanner. She only thinks she does." Hearing that should fill me with hope, but it doesn't.

"You didn't see her face. She meant it."

"She wants to hate you. If she actually did hate you, you wouldn't affect her the way that you do. It's when she hits indifference that you need to worry," she says just as the waitress comes to take our order. I haven't even looked at the menu yet, so I just order the first thing that catches my eye—a sirloin.

"What do you mean by indifference?" I ask once our food has been ordered and the waitress has left.

"You've heard the saying that the opposite of love is indifference, right?" she asks, sounding surprised.

"No."

"Love and hate go hand in hand, Tanner. If she didn't love you, she couldn't hate you. If she didn't care about you at all, she would be indifferent, not caring one way or another. She still loves you. I know it. That's why she's trying to convince everyone, herself included, that she hates you. I guess she feels like the more she says it, the truer it will become." She still loves me? Those words fill me with optimism even though I shouldn't let them.

"What am I supposed to do then? I have no fucking clue."

Quinn looks me in the eye. "Take a step back—"

"No." I shake my head. No way. It'd be too easy for her to shut me out further if I weren't around trying to earn my way back in.

"Hear me out," Quinn demands. "She's a hormonal mess right now. She cries over everything. Last night, she cried hysterically over that damn animal welfare commercial—the one that plays that stupid Sarah McLachlan song. You being all up in her face isn't going to help her sort shit out. It's just going to make it worse."

"I don't like it," I say, not believing any good can come from this plan.

Quinn lays her hand on my arm. "I'm not telling you to back off completely. Just be less in her face. Send her flowers, simple messages telling her you miss her… Remind her of the things you guys used to love doing together—other than fucking her brains out. She definitely remembers that. I promise you it's a better game plan."

I hadn't really factored in the fact that Ashley's hormones are all over the place, and I should have. I remember how my sisters were when they were pregnant and how my brothers-in-law, Dillon and Tony, complained about never being able to do anything right.

"Okay, you make a good point," I concede. "No one knows her better than you do." From what I've seen and what Ashley has told me, Quinn has always been a straight shooter, so I don't think she would give me bad advice. "You really are a great friend, Quinn. I'm glad that even if she won't depend on me, she has you. Are her parents helping her at all?" I know Ashley isn't really close to them, but maybe that's changed too.

"She hasn't even told them, but that's for the best. Trust me. Her mother's a real piece of work. I can't stand the bitch," she says, irritation all over her face.

"So I've heard." I wish Ashley had more people to rely on, but it's not my place to get involved in her family dynamics. If I'm going to gain my own entrance back into her life, I can't be worried about them too.

OVER THE NEXT two and a half weeks, I take Quinn's advice to heart and back off a little. I do my best to physically keep away from Ashley, but I make sure that she knows I'm thinking about her, sending sweet texts to wish her a good day or to remind her of our time together. I text her whenever I see something that makes me think of her. I have one sided text conversations with her. At least the nasty responses stopped coming after the first few days. I take that as a good sign.

I send flowers and little gifts—massage packages, spa days, and the like. I've continued to have the organic fruits and vegetables delivered to her every week despite her initial protests. I have no idea what she's doing with all of them, but I'm content in being able to say that I'm trying.

I've decided it's best I keep myself busy with the foundation and practice while I'm waiting for Ashley to come around. If I'm not practicing, I'm organizing something or other for the kids. I've come up with a daily plan to keep my mind focused. I'm focused on all the prizes: Ashley, the kids, and the Lombardi trophy. Crazily enough, it's actually working! We've just won the AFC championship and earned our spot in the motherfucking Super Bowl for the first time since 1969.

It feels good to have something to be proud of finally, like a light at the end of the tunnel reminding me that hard work always pays off. I just need to keep it up, and I'm sure I'll get what I'm aiming for.apologize.

Chapter Eleven

ASHLEY

I'M SO TIRED. I have no idea how much longer I can keep up with two jobs. If this is how tired I am at twenty-two weeks, I can't imagine I'll be able to keep this pace up for much longer. Tonight, in particular, was super busy, but what else can you expect from a sports bar on Super Bowl Sunday when one of the hometown teams is playing?

It was bittersweet for me to watch Tanner play the game of his life from the bar. Even though I'm still infuriated with him, I'm happy and proud for him and the team. I don't even know if I really am infuriated anymore. All of his texts and deliveries have been starting to soften my anger. He's clearly playing right into my current hormonal state, and whether I'm angry or not, I can't deny he deserves the win. He's put in the work.

Most towns in the area have been decked out in Jets regalia for days already, and there hasn't been a corner to turn lately without finding a Jets flag waving or Tanner's picture on display. All the bandwagon jumpers have been out en masse, and even some of the Giants fans are Jets crazy right now, local pride trumping team loyalty.

I'm pretty sure all the bars were just as packed as Legends was tonight with everyone out drinking and celebrating. Naturally, the more alcohol people drink, the faster they drink it, so the later it got, the more I had to run around like crazy. My ever-growing bump makes it hard to squeeze between the packed tables and crowds of people. On top of that, my feet hurt from all the extra walking, and my back is killing me from carrying trays.

I can't wait to get home and fall asleep, and I can't get to my car fast enough after my shift. It's freezing even for February, and I really need a new coat. This one is getting way too snug in the belly area.

It's bar policy that Colby, our 'bouncer', walk all us girls to our cars at the end of our shifts at night, but I'm too tired to wait for him. Even so, I don't get two steps out the back door before I hear him calling after me.

"Ashley, stop your fine ass there right now!" he yells from across the parking lot as he jogs toward me. He's always making comments about me being a MILF. Me a MILF? I find it completely hilarious—almost as hilarious as watching him slide about the parking lot, trying to avoid the icy patches on his dash over to me. It looks as though he's doing some weird dance as he skips and hops around them.

"Well then, move your big, scary ass a little faster," I yell back. Colby's a scary-looking dude. You would never know by looking at him that he's the biggest softy ever. Not many men who are six-foot-five and about two-hundred-ninety-pounds seem cuddly. Colby's biceps are bigger around than my thighs, which we know for sure because we measured them once on a slow night for shits and giggles.

"Ashley Mama, you know you can't come out here at this hour alone—especially after a night like this one," he says in an exasperated, winded tone. "You're no match for all the drunken idiots that see your baby mama hotness and want to try a piece for themselves."

"Yeah, all the guys are tripping over themselves to get a piece of this." I roll my eyes at him, waving a hand over my bump.

"They are, and we don't need some drunken asshole not taking no for an answer. So from now on, please wait for me," Colby admonishes, grabbing my arm and escorting me the rest of the way to my car.

I sigh. "I'm tired, Colbs. I just want to go home and go to bed."

"Okay, next time, just come get me and tell me you're ready, and I'll get you to your car immediately. Deal?"

"Deal," I agree, unlocking my door.

"Okay. Drive safely, and I'll see you next shift, Mama." He smiles as he opens the door of my ancient Honda for me.

I've been thinking about getting a remote starter for this piece of crap so I don't have to freeze my ass off waiting for it warm up. I'm starting to hate the cold, and I can definitely see why people move south. There's nothing appealing about scraping ice off your windows or sitting your ass down on a frozen seat.

As I pull out of the parking lot, I'm surprised to find the roads so empty. I would've thought lots of people would still be out. The game did end almost two hours ago, but still... My mind wanders to thoughts of my warm bed as the light I'm stopped at turns green. Just as I push down on the gas pedal, the car behind me beeps loudly, his horn an endless wail. I look around, trying to see what the reason for his beeping is since I'm already moving. When I look to the left, I see a pair of bright lights coming at me. I brace myself in the little time I have. As I slam on the breaks, I throw one arm over my growing tummy in a last ditch effort to protect my baby. *Hold on, little one. Please hold on!*

PAIN. ALL I register is pain. I can't move, I can barely breathe, and what little oxygen I manage to suck in smells like sulfur. I can taste it. My eyes won't open, and there's an awful ringing in my ears that's making my head throb. I think I hear voices over the ringing, but they sound as though they're miles away and underwater. I don't understand anything they are saying. My hazy brain only recognizes a few words that don't make sense.

"You...Okay...Move...Help...Coming..."

I try to pull myself together and figure out what's going on, but as I struggle to speak, I realize my words aren't making sense either.

"Help," is the one word I think I manage to get out clearly, but I can't even be sure of that.

"Don't move," a voice says when I try to lift my arm to the warm liquid dripping on my face. Those words come through at least, and it seems as though the blur is starting to clear. Then I remember my precious little boy.

"Baby..." Please God, let my baby be okay. "Baby…." Everything in my field of vision blurs again as I attempt to move, needing to get out of this car. I need to help my baby.

"Stop...moving," Oh no! The voice fades again as the pain registering all over my body swells once more. "Help…coming…what….baby?" The voice asks.

"Pregnant." I'm certain I've gotten that word out clearly before the searing pain takes over, and I can't hold on to consciousness any longer. It hurts too much. The banging in my head, the stabbing pain in one of my arms, and the lack of feeling in my legs make it impossible to stay awake.

Please hold on, little one, and know that Mommy loves you no matter what... so much. The black takes over. Nothing hurts once it's black.

Chapter Twelve

ALEX

I STILL CAN'T believe the team's done it. It's not that I hadn't believed they could, but holy shit! We've just won the Super Bowl. Granted, I've never played a down in a single game, but being a team trainer and a main PT makes me a member of the team regardless.

The smile Tag has on right now is the biggest I've ever seen. It's awesome to see him smile after how hard these past two months have been for him. Watching your best friend beg repeatedly for redemption is never easy, even when he deserves what he got in the first place. The poor dickhead's been completely consumed with regret and remorse, and it's been painful to watch. Seeing him this lit up is nice for a change.

The club the guys have picked for the after-party has a tropical beach theme—palm trees, surf boards, beach balls, and white Christmas lights are everywhere. Oddly, the combination works. The place is packed, but I wouldn't have expected anything less in Miami. Everyone says that New York is the city that never sleeps, but after partying it up here, I have to disagree. I love New York, but I don't think the nightlife there compares to Miami's at all.

A huge crowd has formed around the team, and they're eating up the attention, enjoying the accolades of a big win. Good for them. It's taken a lot of hard work for all of them to get here, and they deserve to celebrate like rock stars. Knowing that most of them have someone waiting on them at home, I hope the guys don't fall into bed with any of the star struck beauties swarming like bees to honey.

My phone starts vibrating in my pocket once again. It hasn't stopped ringing for the last five minutes. Someone must be dying to get a hold of me. Jesus Christ, my team just won the Super Bowl! We're celebrating. What asshole thinks I'm going to answer the phone right now? I've called everyone important tonight already.

I pull my phone out just to check who's so determined. It could very well just be a fuck-ton of text messages. I swipe the screen, and my phone lights up to reveal that I have four missed calls from Quinn. Having talked to her earlier, I have no clue what could be so important that she's blowing up my phone. Before I have the chance to consider whether I should call her back now or wait until later, my phone buzzes again. What the hell?

I pick up. "Quinn, baby, this isn't the best time. It's really loud in here. Can I call you back?"

"You…you…need to get Tanner and come quick," she sobs out — and I mean *sobs.*

"What's going on? Are you okay?" Panic rises inside me. It's obvious that something's very wrong.

"It's Ash. It's… it's... bad, Alex. Real bad." She's so hysterical that her words are almost impossible to understand.

I scan the crowd looking for Tag, and it doesn't take me long to spot him.

"Quinn, I need you to calm down and tell me what's going on. Can you do that for me, baby? Take a deep breath." If she can't pull herself together, there's no way I'll be able to understand what the fuck is happening. It's already hard enough to hear her over the din of the club.

"It was a drunk driver. He… he blindsided her." She hiccups. "I don't know much else. Right now, she's unconscious and has some broken bones, probably internal bleeding too. The guy who was driving behind her followed the ambulance to the hospital. He said they had to cut her out of the car, Alex. CUT HER OUT!" she screams.

It takes her a second to regain her composure and continue. "The impact was on the driver's side. They aren't telling me much and I don't understand doctor talk." She starts to cry again but holds herself together enough to tell me, "The guy from the car behind her also said she came around for a minute after the accident, just long enough to tell him she was pregnant."

"We're on our way. Hang tight, baby," I tell her before I end the call and head toward my best friend. I really don't want to be the one to wipe that luminous smile off his face. I was happy to see it there a few minutes ago, and I have a feeling it'll be a long time before I see another one in its place.

Chapter Thirteen

TANNER

I SEE ALEX heading toward me with a look of devastation on his face, which I can't comprehend. With this huge party going on all around us, it's almost impossible to be having a bad time. My backup quarterback had just done a body shot off some bar girl. According to him, that's the only way for him to get some action since he doesn't get any on the field. I'd almost choked on my own shot when he yelled that out! Who knew the kid had a sense of humor? The entire offensive line is currently singing "We are the Champions," which I wish I was recording. Things couldn't possibly get any better at the moment. Alex should be ecstatic, not looking like his puppy has just died.

"Hey, buddy! Wipe that frown off your face. We won! Let's celebrate!" I shout, holding a bottle of champagne out toward him.

"Umm, sorry, but I really need to talk to you, Tag," he says, his eyes shifting nervously. They dart around the room as though he's looking for an escape route.

"Right now, asshole? I just had the game of my life. I don't want to talk right now. I want to celebrate. Now smile and drink with me." Alex is always down for a party, so what the fuck is his problem?

He grits his teeth at me. "Listen, no one wants to see you celebrate more than me, trust me. But right now, you need to come with me so I can tell you something. This isn't the place, and we need to talk now!" he says with an attitude as bad as if I'd just pissed in his Cheerios or something.

"What the fuck could possibly be so important right now?" I throw my hands up into the air to bring his attention to the huge party going around us. Can't I have five minutes of fun with no drama? Is that so much to fucking ask for?

"Ashley," he answers, and that's when everything around me except Alex and his words fades away. The music goes silent. The people disappear. My attention is focused solely on Alex and whatever he has to say.

"What about her, Alex?" What in the world could be going on that Ashley is what he wants to talk about right after the Super Bowl?

"Let's take it outside," he says, turning toward the front of the club and heading to the exit. He's left me no room to argue. My only choice is to follow.

"We're outside," I say as soon as we've stepped through the front entrance. "What the hell is going on?"

"There's been an accident," he says calmly, not taking his eyes off me for a second.

"What?" My stomach sinks, and the buzz I'd been enjoying a few minutes earlier is completely gone, replaced by fear. Whatever he's about to say can't be good.

"There's been an accident, and Quinn says we need to get on a plane right now."

It feels as though the floor has been pulled out from under me. "How bad?"

"Really bad," he answers with a look that tells me he would rather be doing anything else right now than relaying this information to me.

"Like alive bad or dead bad?" *Please let her be alive. Please.*

"Like alive-for-now bad."

"We need to go now. How far is the nearest airport, Alex? What are we waiting for? We need to get moving." I need to get to New Jersey. I need to be there for her. My whole body has gone numb but is somehow buzzing with energy at the same. I need to get to her—that's the only thought running through my head. I. Need. To. Get. To. Ashley. Those six words are the only ones that exist. My body is moving, I think, but can't make any headway. None of the parts of my body are working together right now.

"Tag, stop pacing. Chill for just a minute. You're not helping right now," Alex yells, slamming his hand down on my shoulders to hold me in place.

"Chill? I can't chill," I scream. "We need to fucking go."

"You need to slow your roll for a second. Get your shit together. We can't get a damn thing in order with you acting like a fucking lunatic. I know you're scared, but give me a minute to form a plan, please. I need you to calm down for just a few minutes."

Calm, he says? Calm? That's the last thing I could possibly be right now.

I HAVE NO idea how Alex has pulled it off, nor do I really give a shit, but when he comes back out of the club with our wide receiver, Darren, he tells me we're heading to a private airstrip. I'm more than ready to get the hell out of here and get to my girl and my baby.

Alex isn't getting any more information out of Quinn before we take off, but she's said that she'll email updates if there are any. There haven't been yet… It's pure torture.

My mind hasn't slowed down since Alex told me about the accident. What on Earth was Ashley doing out that late? Why did that drunk fuck have to hit her? Of all people, why Ashley? Hasn't she been given enough shit to last a lifetime? What if she doesn't make it? What if the baby doesn't make it? Oh God, the baby!

"Tag, you need to breathe, buddy," Alex says, coming over to sit next to me as soon as the pilot tells us we're free to move around the cabin. "We have no idea how bad things are yet. I'm sure that when we get there, they'll have her stabilized and everything will be fine."

I give him a look that says something between "Are you fucking kidding?" and "Do you really believe the shit that you just said?"

Alex seems to understand my glare immediately and says, "I don't know what to think, but I have to hope, man. I have to believe everything will be okay when we get there."

"And what if it's not?" I ask through gritted teeth. "Do you not remember what Quinn said? They had to use the Jaws of Life, man. When has that ever resulted in everything being okay? I can't lose either one of them." I'm on the verge of tears. "I just can't."

"Just try to stay positive. That's all you can do for right now," Daren says from his chair across from us. I'd totally forgotten he was here. I should probably thank him for leaving early and letting us catch a ride with him on his flight home, but I can't focus on him right now.

"He's right, Tag," Alex chimes in.

I shake my head, thinking about how much I've really fucked everything up. "She should have never even been in Jersey today, Alex. She should have been in Miami with us. She would've been if I wasn't such an asshole. Anything happens to either one of them, it's on me, man. It's all on me."

"Tanner, it was an accident. It's not your fault at all. It's the fault of that motherfucker who got behind the wheel drunk."

"You can tell me that all you want, but we both know the truth, bro. If she had been with us, she would be perfectly fine right now. Why wasn't she with us, Alex? Me—that's why. Because I was such a blind bastard."

Alex continues to argue his point, but his reasoning falls on deaf ears. He can keep on until he's blue in the face; I know that this is my fault. And if something happens to either one of them, I'll have no one to blame but myself.

ARRIVING AT THE hospital does nothing to calm my nerves. If anything, it makes them worse. The sun is rising, and it feels like judgment day. Going into that building might rip my world apart, and I don't know if I'm ready for that. I've spent the twenty minute drive from the airport to the hospital terrified of what I would find when we got here. The time had gone faster than I'd expected, not giving me much time to steel myself—unlike the three-hour flight that had felt like a year. It's been over four hours since we found out about Ashley's accident, but it already feels like a lifetime ago.

"Come on, buddy. We need to head in. Quinn needs us, and we have to find out what's going on," Alex says, ushering me through the revolving door into the emergency department. Alex stops at the reception desk to ask where we need to go. As the desk clerk is giving him directions, his phone rings.

"Hey, baby, we're here. Okay… okay… We'll be there in two minutes. Ask him to hold off just a second, okay?" Alex hangs up, turning to grab my arm and pull me down the corridor I'm assuming, based on the signs, leads to the ICU.

"The doctor just came out to give an update on Ashley, and they're asking for the baby's father. We need to move it."

Those words snap me out of my trance, and I pick up the pace, forcing Alex to do the same. If they're asking for the baby's father, that has to be a good sign, right? I know it could mean anything, but I'm hoping—praying—it means everything is okay with both of them.

We round the corner into a larger waiting room where we find Quinn. She's hard to miss as she paces in circles, her face splotchy and eyes swollen. It takes Alex less than a second to rush to her side and wrap his arms around her—like I wish I could do for Ashley, but Lord knows where or how she is in this godforsaken place.

When the doctor appears, Quinn informs him I'm the baby's father, and we all wait to hear what news he has.

"First of all, Ashley has sustained many severe injuries."

Quinn gasps audibly, and her eyes fill with tears. None of us wanted this conversation to start that way. Alex pulls her into his side as he grabs a hold of my arm in support for what is about to come next. Taking a deep breath, I give a nod for the doctor to continue.

"Ms. Taylor, as you know, Ms. Mitchell has given you medical power of attorney, so all healthcare decisions are your responsibility for the time being."

Quinn gives a halfhearted nod. "That stupid form wasn't ever supposed to matter," she whispers. "I only signed it because she said over her dead body would she allow her mother to make important decisions in her life…" A few tears slide down her cheek.

After giving her a moment, the doctor continues, "As I said, Ashley has several severe injuries. Let's start with the least complicated first. Her spleen was ruptured in the accident, causing a large amount of internal bleeding, which led to hypovolemic shock. That's typical with a lot of blood loss. We removed her spleen due to the rupture and gave her several units of blood. She has also sustained a punctured lung from a broken rib, which subsequently led to a collapsed lung, so we inserted a chest tube to remove the excess air. Right now, Ashley is on a ventilator to help her breathe while her lung recovers. She shouldn't need it for more than a day or two, but we'll monitor her progress closely."

Good God, please let that be all.

"Ashley's left arm was also broken, and an orthopedic surgeon was needed to repair it due to the severity of the break, which required screws and pins to be set. Her arm will be monitored for signs of infection, just in case any debris from the accident was missed during surgery. Her right knee was also partially dislocated but was repaired after her arm, and she won't require any major reconstructive surgery for that. For now, she just needs to keep it elevated and free from pressure. All of the injuries I've mentioned should heal just fine, provided there are no complications. Our main concern right now is the injury to her brain."

Quinn can't hold back her sobs any longer, and I can't say that I blame her. My poor Ashley. She's so broken. I wish it were me in here. I would give anything to trade places with her. Based on everything the doctor's said so far, I know deep down there's nothing good left to say. It sounds as though he hasn't even given us the worst of the news yet, and he hasn't even mentioned anything about the baby.

Once Alex seems to have Quinn calmed down, the doctor continues once more, "Ashley's brain went without a sufficient amount of oxygen for a while and also suffered trauma from the impact itself. There's some swelling. We'll be watching closely to make sure that the swelling doesn't get to a point where we need to alleviate the pressure by opening her skull. The brain hypoxia is more of a concern right now. We won't know the extent of the damage it caused until she wakes up—if she wakes up. More often than not, people with extreme hypoxia have severe to permanent brain damage. We've done what we can, but from this point on, it's all on her."

Hearing those last words, my knees buckle, and Alex struggles to guide me into a seat on my way down. I don't care that everyone can see the tears freefalling from my eyes. All I can think about is that my beautiful, vibrant Ashley may never be the same. I'd rather have her hate me forever than wake up with brain damage—if she wakes up at all. God, this can't be happening. No. No. No. A sudden loud sobbing pulls me from my thoughts of Ashley. I open my eyes to see Quinn and Alex kneeling in front of me, trying to comfort me, but I don't hear anything other than the gut wrenching sobs all around me.

"Tag, calm down. She's going to pull through. I know it," Alex says, fighting back his own tears.

"She's too stubborn to go like this, Tanner. She's going to wake up," Quinn adds.

It's then that I realize the loud sobs are coming from me. They're trying to console *me*.

"What about the baby?" I ask, looking back up to the doctor.

The grim expression on his face is all I need to confirm my worst fears.

"The force of the accident caused the placenta to detach from the uterine wall. There wasn't anything that we could do by the time Ashley arrived. He was stillborn. We're just thankful that the abruption didn't cause us to lose Ashley as well, which is very common. Part of the reason I was asking if you'd arrived is because we can allow you to spend some time with the baby and Ashley before we have to take him away," he explains apologetically.

"Him?"

Ashley had never told me if she'd found out the sex of the baby. She'd barely told me anything at all about the pregnancy. She'd been too busy telling me it was too late and that they didn't need me. I'd gladly step away now if it meant life for both of them.

"Yes, the baby was a boy. If you like, I can have the baby brought to Ashley's room so that you may spend a little bit of time with the two of them. I'm so sorry that this is all I have to offer you," the doctor says sincerely while motioning for me to follow through the double doors behind him.

I look back at Quinn and Alex before heading through the doors. Quinn cries into Alex's chest as he rubs her back. His eyes, filled with sympathy and sorrow, never leave mine. I would gladly take the look of disgust that he'd been giving me for weeks instead if it meant that this wasn't really happening. Maybe this is one of my god-awful nightmares, and I'll wake up soon to realize that this was nothing but my subconscious telling me to get my shit together once again.

I know that isn't the case as soon as the doctor leads me into Ashley's room. She looks so small and broken, lying in the middle of the bed, hooked up to tubes and wires and machines that are keeping her alive. There are so many wires.

God, this isn't fucking fair! Why Ashley? Couldn't this have been anyone other than her? Why her? Why me?

The doctor is explaining to me how she's getting fluids, antibiotics, anti-inflammatories, and pain medication when there's a small knock on the door. A nurse enters, carrying something small bundled in a blanket—my son. She gives me a grim smile while gingerly handing over this special little man. He's barely as big as my hands.

I choke on a sob at my first glimpse of his perfect little face. He's a handsome devil, despite his purple color. His head is smaller than my fist, and I'm terrified that the slightest movement will break him. Then I remember that I can't break what's already broken.

Placing my forehead against his, I let it all out. I cry for everything that he's lost, everything that he'll never experience because the world is an unfair place. I cry for the things that I'll never get to tell him, the lessons I'll never get to teach him, the love he'll never feel for anyone—

the sort of love I feel for him and his mother. I cry for Ashley and the fact that she'll never get to see him, never get to hold him, and never get to smell him. I cry because, unlike me, she'll never get to tell him to his face how much she loves him.

"I love you, buddy. I'm so sorry I couldn't protect you. I know Mommy tried though with everything she had. I know she would have done anything in the world to save you. *We* would have done anything. I'm so sorry that you'll never get to meet her. She's amazing, you know. You got really lucky in the mommy department. You couldn't have asked for a better one. She's smart and beautiful and a pain in my ass, but I love her, and you would've too. I'm sorry that because I was an idiot, you had to pay the price," I can't help but weep as I lay the beautiful boy on his mommy's chest, careful not to snag the blanket on any tubes or wires.

Looking at the two of them together makes me cry harder. My beautiful little family. Well, it would have been my beautiful family if I hadn't been such an asshole. I sit there beside them, cataloging every detail of the moment, so I can tell Ashley all about it and all about him when she wakes up—from his thin white eyelashes to the curve of his lips that's the same as his mother's. My moment is cut short by a knock at the door, and the same nurse that brought him to me has returned to take him back, to take him from us forever.

"Please," I plead with her.

"I'm so sorry, but I have to," she whispers, tears in her eyes.

"Can't I just have a few more minutes?" I ask, suddenly unable to contain my sobs again.

She slowly makes her way closer to me. "I'm sorry. I can't imagine how hard this is for you, but it's only going to be harder the longer you have him."

"I never really got to have him, did I?" I ask as I hand my son over to the woman, knowing full well it will be the last time I ever set eyes on him.

"No, I guess not," she answers with a little sniffle, and I know that she at least understands some of my pain.

I lay my head on the bed next to Ashley and hold her hand. I hear the door click closed behind me, telling me that my son is now gone forever. How do I come back from this? How on Earth do I go forward without him? Without Ashley? What if she never wakes up? She already hated me before today. I can only imagine how she'll feel if she wakes up.

Chapter Fourteen

TANNER

"**WHY HASN'T SHE** woken up yet?" I ask the doctor when he comes around to check on Ashley the following afternoon. "She hasn't even moved or twitched."

"These things take time, Mr. Garrison," he says, trying to placate me. "Everything looks good. Ashley's vitals have been stable all night and all morning. Her arm doesn't show any signs of infection, and the sutures from the splenectomy look like they've begun healing well. I'm ordering the removal of the chest tube. She just needs time right now. It's only been a little over twenty-four hours since her surgeries."

"The longer it takes her to wake up, the worse it is, right? The brain damage?" I ask, knowing fully well I don't really want the answer.

"The brain is a miraculous thing, but nothing's a guarantee when it comes to it either. Ashley could wake up completely fine in ten days, or she could wake with severe brain damage in five minutes. But yes, typically, the longer it takes Ashley to regain consciousness, the more damage there might be." He squeezes my shoulder before leaving the room.

I squeeze Ashley's uninjured hand and beg her, "Please, baby. Please wake up. I need you to open those beautiful eyes. It's been too long since we've seen them. You need to fight. Fight like hell from wherever you are, and come back to us."

Laying my head down next to our joined hands, I send out a silent prayer. *Please, you've already taken my son. Don't take the love of my life too!*

I must have fallen asleep after that because the next thing I know, I'm being woken up by a knock on the door. When I look up, I see a gentleman introducing himself to Quinn, and I wonder when she and Alex got back from going home to shower and change.

Alex had tried to talk me into going with them, but I'd refused to leave Ashley's side. I need to be here for her when she wakes up. She's going to be devastated when she learns the news of the baby, and I don't want her to be alone for that.

"Ms. Taylor, I'm Detective Wallis. I just wanted to come down and give you an update, regarding Ms. Mitchell's case." He shakes her hand.

After everything that's happened over the last thirty-six hours, hearing the detective refer to Ashley as Ms. Mitchell only makes me angrier at myself. She shouldn't be Ms. Mitchell anymore. I should have done right by her, by my son, and married her the minute she told me she was carrying my child. She should have a giant sparkling ring on her hand, not a cast that's helping hold her bones together. If I had done that, she wouldn't even be in this bed.

"The driver of the other vehicle will be released from the hospital into our custody today. He only sustained minor injuries from the crash," the detective informs Quinn.

"Of course he did," she scoffs.

"He'll be booked on charges of aggravated assault with a motor vehicle and vehicular manslaughter. We'll hold him until arraignment."

The charges don't sound severe enough for the catastrophic damage he's caused. He still gets to breathe—hopefully in a cell for the rest of his life—while Ashley fights for her life, while my son will never get a chance at life or even the chance to breathe. The world really is a cruel place.

"We received the preliminary investigative report of the scene of the accident about an hour ago. I'm not sure how much information you were given originally, but you probably already know the accident was a side collision, and the point of impact was on the driver's side, near the front fender and door. Older vehicles like the one Ms. Mitchell was driving don't withstand this particular type of impact the way newer ones do, especially at the speed the other car was travelling. The frames crumble more easily, and the lack of side airbags make crashes like this much worse. Thankfully, Ms. Mitchell was able to make it out alive. We'll make sure that the prosecutor knows the extent of the injuries, so please rest assured that we'll get Ms. Mitchell the justice she deserves. This city has zero tolerance for driving while intoxicated, and the other driver was at almost double the legal limit."

The conviction in his voice is great, but at the end of the day, none of it matters. What's done is done, and nothing will change what we've lost.

"Here's my card," Detective Wallis says, handing Quinn his business card. "If you have any questions, please don't hesitate to call me. Again, I'm truly sorry for all that you've been through."

None of us says a word as Detective Wallis leaves the room. There's really nothing to say. The three of us sit in the unbearable silence, listening to the beeping of all the machines hooked up to Ashley and the whooshing of the ventilator as it pumps oxygen into Ashley's lungs. Then Alex's phones rings, grabbing our attention.

Alex picks up. "Hello?" His face grows stern.

"Not now," he says to the person on the other end of the line. "Don't you think there are more important things that need his attention right now?" He grits his teeth. "I understand, but it'll have to wait." His voice rises in frustration. "Yes, okay. I'll keep you updated." He sighs, disconnecting the call.

Certain the call was about me, I look at him expectantly.

"That was Davis. They want to know when you'll be back to do all the press conferences and the parade. Word's gotten out about the accident, but nothing's been released about the baby. He's been calling me since last night, but I didn't want you to have to deal with it yet," he explains with sympathy in his eyes. He clearly doesn't want to add anything to my already-full plate.

The audacity of these people. "Do they honestly think I give two shits about parades and interviews right now? If word about the accident has gotten out, then they should know why I'm too preoccupied to give a damn about anything else."

"I know, Tag. But in their eyes, the team just won the Super Bowl, and their main man has dropped off the grid."

"I don't give a fuck what their thought process is. I'm not going anywhere until I know that Ashley's going to pull through this. I give these people everything they want, no questions asked. The least they can do is stand behind me right now." I glare at him. "I need you to make them understand how serious I am."

"Okay. I'll relay that to Davis," he says as a nurse enters the room to check Ash's vitals again. "You might want to consider taking a shower, though."

"What part of 'I'm not leaving until she opens her eyes' don't you understand?" I ask, annoyed.

"There's a shower in the bathroom you can use, honey," the nurse says while checking Ashley's IV bag of antibiotics—well, I think they're antibiotics. There are so many different things being injected into her at this point that it's hard to keep everything straight.

I like this nurse. She's older, maybe in her early fifties, with graying hair. She's motherly, unlike the younger two nurses who were here yesterday. They had been staring at me with stars in their eyes, despite the fact that my girlfriend is lying here, fighting for her life, and my dead son is down in the morgue.

"You can use that one. No one will say anything to you. If they do, you tell them that Darla said it was okay. I think it's wonderful that you don't want to leave her side. You don't see that kind of dedication much these days." She smiles sadly.

"Thank you, Darla," I smile back. It's probably a good thing she doesn't know I'm the reason Ashley is even in this bed and under her care.

I turn to face Alex and Quinn after Darla has left. "You know, if she had been driving the BMW instead, she might not have been so badly injured. I can't believe she hates me so much that she won't even drive a perfectly safe, brand new car… It might've saved her a lot of agony."

"You don't know that, Tanner," Quinn says.

"You heard the detective. Older cars crumple in those types of collisions more often than not. I wish she hadn't been so damn stubborn. I knew something bad was going to happen in that shitty-ass car of hers." I know that I shouldn't be angry with her about not using the BMW, but how many times had I told her that damn car wasn't safe?

"What's done is done. There's nothing we can do about any of it now. Let's just concentrate on what's coming next, concentrate on Ashley," Alex says, trying to be the sensible one.

I sigh. "This is going to be a long road."

Alex claps me on the shoulder. "You don't need to tell me. I'm a trained physical therapist. I know how long and grueling that road is going to be better than most. She's going to need everyone on her side."

"I'm on her side. Someone just needs to convince her of that."

Chapter Fifteen

ASHLEY

W*HAT THE HELL* *is going on?* Everything is fuzzy. Pain... Oh my God, my entire body hurts like a bitch. I try to open my eyes, but I can't. What the hell is wrong with me?

"How much longer until she wakes up?" a voice that sounds like a garbled version of Tanner's asks. What's he doing here? Who is he talking to?

"When she's ready, Mr. Garrison. Everything's still the same, and that's a good thing."

Whose voice is that? It doesn't sound familiar at all. Then again, nothing seems familiar right now.

Something warm rests on my forehead. Suddenly, one of my eyelids is pulled up, and a blinding light shines into my eye.

"Argh!" I moan. At least my voice works.

"Ashley?" Tanner's voice is much closer now.

I try to shake my head to get the light out of my eye. "That hurts." I push the words past my lips even though my throat is sore as hell. My whole damn body is in pain. What the hell happened to me?

"You're hurting her," Tanner snaps at the person shining the light at me.

"I have to examine her. I'm sorry, Ms. Mitchell, but I need to check you over. How are you feeling?" the stranger I'm assuming is a doctor asks.

"Everything freaking hurts." My voice sounds as though someone is squeezing my throat as I try to talk.

"Why is she in pain? I thought at least one of those million tubes sticking out of her was for pain medication," Tanner asks, sounding more annoyed than I feel.

"We lessened the dosage because we needed her to regain consciousness. Sometimes the pain medication keeps patients asleep. We needed to know whether she was still unconscious because of her injuries or the medication. I'll increase the meds again after I finish my assessment," the doctor explains. "Ashley, can you open your eyes for me?"

Sure, no problem. Take the fifty-pound weights off of them.

"They're really heavy," I say, trying to open them anyway. Who would have ever thought it would be a struggle to open my eyes? With some effort, I'm able to open them slightly, but all the lights are blinding. "Can you shut off the lights?"

"Sure, baby," Tanner says, presumably rushing to turn them off. Why is he calling me baby? Why is he the only one here right now?

"Can someone tell me what the hell is going on?" I ask, expending far more energy than I normally would to speak the simple sentence.

I hear a quick intake of breath from the side of the bed that Tanner's on. "Doctor?" he questions, panic in his voice.

"What's the last thing that you remember, Ashley?" the doctor asks.

"Umm..." The last thing I remember? I don't really know. Everything is hazy. Something next to me starts beeping quickly, making me feel even more alarmed. "I don't know… Why don't I know? What's going on?" The beeping gets faster as endless questions swirl in my mind.

"Ashley, take a few deep breaths for me and try to calm down. Everything's okay. I promise. You're working yourself up right now," the doctor says gently. "Why don't we start with some simple things? Do you know your full name?"

"Yes, Ashley Marie Mitchell. Can I have some water, please?" If I'm going to continue talking, I need something to make my throat stop burning.

I hear water pouring. Through narrowed eyes, I see Tanner hold out a cup to me.

"Here, baby," he says.

I try to reach out with my left arm, but I can't. It hurts like a bitch. The shooting pain prompts me to pry my eyes fully open. Now I have to know what the hell is happening. My arm is encased in a white cast from my wrist all the way up to my armpit. What the fuck happened?

"Why is my arm in a cast? Someone please tell me what's going on. Tanner?"

His face is covered by a mask of sorrow, and it frightens me. That stupid machine beeps faster again as I look him over. Tanner's gaze meets the doctor's, but he doesn't say anything until the doctor nods.

"You were in a car accident," he says slowly, as though it physically pains him to say the words.

A car accident? I try to sift through my memories, but everything's still cloudy. I certainly don't remember an accident. I try to conjure the last thing I can remember before waking up here, and I can't. It's all just a jumble of incomplete thoughts and blurry memories that don't fit together. My heart races, and it becomes harder to breathe. What happened to me?

"Why don't I remember it?" If I don't remember, then something must be wrong with me. How can I not remember being in an accident? My freaking arm's broken, for Christ's sake. How can I not remember my arm breaking?

"Given some time, I think you will. You hit your head pretty hard, and you had a collapsed lung. Because of that, your brain was deprived of oxygen for a little bit. Why don't we start with what you do remember?" Doctor Whoever asks.

I rack my brain for memories. So many things are whirling around there, but nothing makes sense.

“Do you know who this is?” he asks, pointing to Tanner.

“Yes,” I answer, but I’m still trying to figure out why he’s here. I try to sit up, but my damn legs aren’t working right either apparently.

I feel panic setting in again, and that fucking beeping speeds up once more, making my already-pounding headache worse. Looking down, I notice the blanket spread over my lower body for the first time. I can’t see any damage, but if I can’t really move my legs… am I paralyzed? No, wait, I can’t be paralyzed. I can feel the awful pain in one of my legs, and it hurts like a motherfucker.

“What’s wrong with my legs? Why can’t I move them? Why does it hurt like crazy? Someone please tell me what the fuck is going on!” I try to shout, but my throat still feels as though it’s on fire. Why won’t anyone tell me what the hell happened to me?

“Shh,” Tanner says, running his hand down the side of my head, smoothing my hair out of my face. “It’s okay. You have a dislocated knee. There’s a big immobilizing brace on it.”

“Take a minute and give yourself some time. What’s the last thing you remember?” the doctor asks yet again.

If I knew, I’d fucking tell him. Even so, I try again, thinking for a minute before the memory of a crowd comes back. “Work,” I say at last. “It was cold.” I think so anyway. There are vague little blips in my recollection, but I don’t know what they’re from.

“Okay, that’s good. Anything else?” he asks as he grabs a clipboard and pen. He writes something down quickly on what I assume is my chart.

“You,” I tell Tanner. His face on all the televisions at the bar.

“Me?” He looks as though that’s the last thing he’d expected me to say.

“Yes, you… were all over the TV.” He nods, seeming sad. Why would that make him sad?

I close my eyes, willing myself to remember—cold, work, Tanner… “Bed,” I say. “I wanted to go to bed.”

“Good, Ashley. Good. Take your time,” the doctor says.

My eyes are still closed, but I hear him writing.

“You’re doing great, Ash.” Tanner continues running his hand through my hair.

I instinctively lean into his touch. I feel like I shouldn't be doing that, but for some reason, I can't stop it.

"Beeping… I remember a car horn." Like a hole in a dam, memories are trickling in. "Lights, bright lights… Oh my God!" I gasp as the mental dam bursts, and I'm unable to stop the flow of images flooding my mind. My mobile hand instinctively moves toward my stomach, and I look at Tanner in shocked comprehension.

His eyes are locked on my hand, and I see the tears welling in them. He must know I've just remembered the most important thing ever.

"NO!" I shake my head, despite the excruciating pain. "No! No!" I shout, knowing the truth without having to ask. The baby. Oh my God! How the hell could I have not remembered him the second I woke up?

Tears run down Tanner's face as he stares at me. I continue to shake my head as though denying it will make it not true.

"I'm so sorry, baby," Tanner says, choking on a sob.

I turn toward the doctor, hoping he'll tell me that Tanner and I are both wrong, but he has on the same sad face Tanner had been wearing a few minutes earlier.

"Can you turn the pain medicine back up?" I ask, knowing full well it'll knock me back out. "Everything hurts." Maybe I'll wake up and this will have been a bad dream.

"Sure," the doctor says before heading out of the room.

He'd better get back with the medication quickly. I don't want to remember anything anymore. I want to go back to five minutes ago, when I had been blissfully ignorant—when my world had still been intact.

The accident might as well have killed me. What do I have left to live for now? Why? Why couldn't God have taken me too? What have I ever done to deserve this? How am I supposed to go on after experiencing the first joys of being a mom—even if he hadn't been here yet—and then having it all ripped away from me? What's the point?

I HEAR THEM talking about me, but I don't let on that I'm awake.

"Why didn't you call me?" Quinn asks.

"She was only awake for about ten minutes before she asked them to up her pain meds. I was more concerned with her lack of memory at the time," Tanner snaps. "There was no point in calling you back after they gave her the meds. The doctor said they would probably knock her back out for at least a few hours."

"What do you mean 'lack of memory'? Like brain damage?" She sounds scared.

"No, she remembered who she was, who I was. When he started asking her questions about what she remembered, things came back slowly," Tanner explains.

"Did she remember the baby?" Quinn asks.

"Not at first. It took her a few minutes, but then she did."

I hear the sadness in his voice, and it angers me. I remember so much more now. The dreams I've had since waking up here have been like a reel of the last few months.

"How'd she take it?" Alex asks. I hadn't realized he was here too.

"As soon as she remembered, she asked for the meds. I can't say I blame her. I wish I could get something to knock me the hell out."

I could help him with that. I wish I could knock him out with my new cast.

"So you didn't get to tell her about him?" Quinn asks, piquing my interest.

Tanner sighs. "No, we didn't get to tell her much at all. She knows about the accident, her arm, her knee, and her head injury. I don't know how I'm going to tell her about him. I memorized everything I could about him, but I don't know how to relay it all back to her."

My blood boils hearing his words. "You mean you got to see my son and I didn't?" I practically growl, but I don't open my eyes. I don't want to see his face right now.

"Sweets?" Quinn says.

I hear her move toward me, and it's only a few seconds before I feel her hand grasp mine, squeezing. "How are you feeling?"

"Answer my question," I demand, finally opening my eyes to glare at Tanner with all the contempt I feel right now.

"Yes," he says, sounding defeated.

"Get out!" I tell him.

"Ashley," Quinn says gently.

"No!" I cut her off before turning back toward Tanner. "I remember everything now. Being knocked back out wasn't the sanctuary I'd been hoping for. GET OUT!"

Alex pats him on the back. "Come on, Tag. You could use a little fresh air. It's been awhile," he says, trying to lead Tanner toward the door.

I know I should feel bad that his eyes are swimming with pain and hurt but too fucking bad. The asshole got to see my son, and I won't ever be able to say the same. I'm not sure how long I was out for, but I know it was long enough that there's no way I'll get to see my baby.

Even though I'd expected him to, Tanner doesn't argue. He just sighs, accepting his defeat, and heads toward the door.

"That wasn't very nice," Quinn says. "He hasn't left your side for four days. He didn't even celebrate his big win. He dropped everything, came running, and hasn't left since."

"I don't give a shit, Quinn. I don't need to hear about him right now. Tell me everything that happened."

Quinn relays the details of the accident back to me, and they sound like the plot of a horrible movie. I don't know why I'm surprised. This is the way that my life goes. Of course, Tanner would be the only one who got to see my son—ironic, considering Tanner didn't want him in the first place. Yet somehow, I'm the one paying for his bad karma.

I'm surprisingly glad the doctor comes in just as Quinn finishes recounting my horror story. He's a welcome distraction from my thoughts.

"Glad to see you awake, Ashley," he says. "How are you feeling?"

"My whole body feels like it was hit by a car," I answer sarcastically. I mean, how does he think I feel? What a stupid question. It reminds me of the conversation Tanner and I had about the dumb questions reporters ask during their interviews.

"Well, I guess that's pretty accurate." He doesn't seem too fazed by my wit. "I assume you've been given some information regarding your injuries." He looks back and forth between Quinn and me.

"Not really," Quinn answers. "I only gave her the rundown of the accident."

"Okay, well, let's start with your head injury. All of your scans look fine. I don't expect any permanent damage. Your memories are coming back, but expect things to be a little muddled for a bit. You may also notice some trouble paying attention and difficulty making decisions. All normal. You'll probably notice some trouble getting your mind and body to work together—also normal.

"As for your arm, the upper bone—your humerus—was broken in the crash. It punctured your skin and required surgery. There's a metal rod and screws holding it all together now. Due to the severity of the break, expect to be in that cast for eight to twelve weeks," he explains.

"Twelve weeks?" I ask, shocked and pissed off. Twelve fucking weeks with this fucking cast on?

The doctor nods and continues, "We've been monitoring you for signs of infection, and you've been receiving antibiotics through your IV as a precaution. You also have two broken ribs—one of which punctured your left lung. We had to make a small incision near your left breast, where we inserted a chest tube."

I look down, wondering how the hell I could've missed a tube sticking out of my chest. There's no tube there, and I look back up at the doctor in confusion.

"It was removed yesterday because you were breathing much better. We expect no complications there. As for the broken ribs, you're going to be very sore and may notice some pain with breathing."

Well, at this point everything fucking hurts, so I probably won't notice shit.

"Your knee was dislocated, but it wasn't as bad as it could have been in a crash like yours. The orthopedic surgeon will explain the recovery process in more depth to you, but for now, the knee has been set back in place, and the ligament damage was repaired. You'll be in that brace for about eight weeks. Your leg, like your arm, will require significant physical therapy—probably about nine to twelve months' worth before your leg feels back to normal. Well, as normal as it will after this kind of injury."

"How the hell am I going to do a goddamn thing with only one arm and one leg?"

First, I lost my son, and now I'm basically an invalid.

"You're alive," Quinn says softly. "It could have been much worse."

"Maybe for you. Starting to seem like it would've been best for me if the damn accident had just killed me," I say in complete earnestness. Why not just let me die? Why take my son and then leave me in this hell, for at least a year based on what the doctor is telling me? "So what else is all fucked up, doc?" I don't care whether or not he thinks I'm a complete bitch.

"Well," he responds with some attitude of his own. Fuck him. "We had to remove your spleen, which will make you more susceptible to infection from now on, but all in all, you'll be fine without it. After that, we delivered the baby by caesarean. The procedure went fine. There was no permanent damage that would prevent future children. The OB will also give you more information on that procedure when he comes in."

"Anything else?" I ask, entirely done with this conversation. I want to drift back off into the darkness, where I can hopefully dream about life as though it hadn't just been completely ripped away from me.

"No. Do you have any questions?"

"Can I have another dose of whatever you're giving me for pain, please?"

He nods and looks toward Quinn, silently asking if she has any questions.

"How long does she have to stay?" Good question. Funny that I hadn't thought to ask it.

"I'd say at least a few more days. We'll reassess everything at the end of the week."

Great! I get to stay and look at the same ugly walls for a few more days. Wonder if I can just stay in a drug-induced coma until I have to face the real world—or better yet, for the rest of my now-miserable life.

"What day is it?" I ask, not feeling up to the effort of counting the days out in my head.

"Thursday," Quinn says in unison with the doctor whose name I still don't know. Not that I really care.

"Oh…" Yep, four days. That's right.

"I'll have a nurse administer another dose of medication for you," the doctor says before leaving the room.

"Do you want to talk about it?" Quinn asks.

"No, I don't want to fucking talk about it. I don't want to talk about how my life has been torn to shreds or how I didn't get to meet my son but the asshole who helped create him did. Why the fuck is he even here anyway?" I know she's just trying to be a good friend, but I don't have it in me to care.

"Because I called him. He had every right to be here, Ashley. I know you're pissed, but do you realize we didn't know if you'd even make it? We had no clue if you were going to wake up, and if you did wake up, we didn't know if you would be you or some mushed up version of yourself. Be mad all you want, but the only thing I care about right now is that you're alive and you're you."

I hear the anger in her voice and see the fear still lingering in her eyes. I shouldn't be mad at her for calling people to lean on, but I can't stand the thought of Tanner getting to see my baby when I won't get to.

"Am I me, Quinn? Look at me!" I yell. "I'm a fucking invalid. I can't even wipe my own ass! I'm stuck in this fucking bed like a useless piece of shit. You heard him—almost a year of recovery! Yeah, I'm really alive, and I'm really me. Tell me what the fucking point is. Huh? It would've been easier for you to plan a funeral instead of having to wait on me for the next several months, and it would've been easier for me to have never woken up! At least one of us is happy I'm alive…" I turn my head away from her since it's the only part of my body I have any control over right now, ignoring her tears.

Thankfully, a few moments later, the nurse comes in with my ticket to oblivion.

Chapter Sixteen

TANNER

I'M RELIEVED TO find Ashley sleeping when I get back to the hospital in the afternoon. She might as well have reached into my chest and ripped my heart out when she kicked me out of the room. I know she hates me—I hate myself—but that doesn't make the sting of her anger hurt any less. I have countless battles to look forward to with her from here on out, and the road ahead is going to be hard, but nothing will stop me from being here for her, not even Ashley herself.

"Hey," I greet Quinn as I take the empty seat next to her.

She smiles sadly. "Hi."

"How's she doing?" I ask, unsure whether or not I want to know the answer.

"Worse than expected." Tears well up in her eyes.

"What happened?"

"She said the accident should've just killed her too," Quinn says.

"Goddammit." I'd known her reaction would be bad but I hadn't expected her to wish she were dead.

Quinn sniffles. "She's mad I called you too." Quinn has always been the strong one, so I hadn't thought about how hard all of this must be on her.

I suddenly wish I hadn't told Alex to take a night off. He'd wanted to come back with me, but I'd told him I'd be okay, completely forgetting about Quinn.

"Let her be mad at me, Quinn. Let her pin it all on me." I've been preparing myself to take the blame anyway.

There had been a glimmer of hope that she might have forgiven me when she woke up. She'd seemed to be looking to me for answers. I should have seen her attention for what it was though—I was just the only one in the room she knew. I see that clearly now, and it was a reality check.

"But it's not your fault. You have every right to be here," Quinn argues.

"It's okay. I knew this was coming. I've done wrong by her, and because of that, she's landed here. It's on me. You're the only one she'll lean on, and she needs you. We know that she'll pull through now, so why don't you go home and get some sleep in a real bed? You're going to need it."

"She's going to be pissed if she wakes up and you're the only one here."

I have no doubt that Quinn's completely correct in that assessment, but I've spent the last few hours preparing myself for the oncoming storm. Alex has tried to convince me to give Ashley some more time apart, but I can't do that. I need to be with her, even if she doesn't want me to be.

"I can handle it," I tell her.

Quinn can't deal with Ashley all on her own. Plus, Ashley can't run from me here, so we might as well start hashing things out now. I'd felt the anger radiating from Ashley as soon as she heard I'd gotten to see the baby, and I understand her rage. I'd be more than angry myself if I hadn't gotten to see that little miracle. Ashley didn't have that chance, and she's heartbroken. I can't fault her for it. I can't imagine what it must feel like to wake up blissfully ignorant only to find your entire world has been ripped out from under you. At least I was conscious for it.

"Call me if she gets too unruly," Quinn says, vacating her chair. "I really could use a good night's sleep in my own bed."

"Sure," I say, watching her leave the room, knowing full well I won't call. I want Ashley to lean on only me for a little bit, even if she doesn't want to.

I take a look around, really taking everything in for the first time. Before, my focus had always been strictly on Ashley, but now that I know she'll make a full recovery, the tunnel vision has subsided a bit. Of course, I'm only assuming she'll make a full recovery. Hopefully, Quinn would have told me if anything had changed in the time I was gone.

There are several vases of flowers by the window I haven't noticed before. Checking the message cards, I see one is from the paper, one is surprisingly from the Jets' organization, and one from her friends at a place called Legends. I don't know what Legends is, but they clearly know Ashley well enough to send flowers. The last arrangement is from a "Jason." There's no note with it, just the signature.

I can only think of one Jason who Ashley has ever mentioned, and that asshole has a lot of nerve to send her flowers. He'd better not show up here, at least not while I am… and I don't plan on being anywhere else.

A knock on the door interrupts my thoughts of taking my aggression out on Ashley's awful ex-boyfriend. I glance over and see the friendly nurse, Darla, standing there with a box in her hands.

She smiles despondently. "Hi, Tanner." Darla had insisted on calling me Mr. Garrison during her first two shifts with Ashley, but after that I'd told her enough was enough and that she should call me Tanner.

"Hi, Darla." I smile back.

She glances at Ashley's sleeping form in the bed. "I know she's not awake at the moment, but I thought she might like to look at this." She lifts the box in her hands.

"What's that?"

"It's a box of things regarding the baby we put together," Darla says as she lays the box on the little rolling tray beside the bed before heading back out into the hallway.

I really want to know what's in the box, but I decide it may be better for Ashley to get to do something before me. I've already taken the most precious moment from her, and I know she's never going to let me forget it.

Taking a seat on the uncomfortable reclining contraption in the corner, I close my eyes, hoping to get a little bit of sleep. I'm sure I'll need it once Ashley wakes up and finds me here instead of Quinn.

THE SOUND OF someone crying softly startles me from my sleep. My eyes slowly open to find Ashley weeping over the box Darla left on her food tray.

I attempt to rise quietly from my chair, feeling certain as soon as Ashley realizes I'm up, she'll demand I leave again. The stupid chair creaks, and Ashley looks over at me, but surprisingly quickly directs her attention back to the contents of the box.

"Did you already get to see this?" she asks, sounding more sad than hostile.

"No. I thought you should get to see if first," I say, glad she hasn't decided to attack me the way she did last time. I make my way slowly toward the bed, hoping to get close enough to see what's in the box before she goes on the defensive again.

"Hmpf." She ignores my approach, never taking her eyes off the box.

I get close enough to see that she's looking at a picture, a picture of the baby. In it, he has on a blue crocheted hat, and he's wrapped in the same blue striped blanket I held him in. The nurses must've taken the picture of him for Ashley.

"He's so beautiful." She sobs, dropping the picture back in the box.

How she was able to reach the box with her limited range of motion is beyond me, but with the urge to comfort her as overwhelming as it is, now isn't the time to try and figure it out. I sit down next to her good leg, afraid of accidently bumping into her injured knee. At least her arm has a plaster cast to protect it. Even though I know she's going to push me away, I pull her to me as gently as I can so she has someone's shoulder to cry on right now.

"I know he is. He's the most beautiful baby I've ever seen—not that I expected any less. Look at his mom." I know those aren't the right words to say as soon as they leave my mouth, but that doesn't make them any less true.

She pulls away from my grasp and glares. "Since you're the only one who got to see him, tell me about him." It's not a request. It's a demand.

I spend the next five minutes recounting everything I possibly can about my short time with our son. Tears flow from my eyes even though I'm trying to stay strong, and we both cry together until her mood suddenly flips from sad to angry again.

"How can you sit there and play the brokenhearted father?" She sneers at me as she scoots farther away. "You didn't even want him. Don't think I forgot about that little message you sent over with Melissa."

"What are you talking about? I did want him. I never sent you any message through Melissa," I say, honestly having no clue what she's talking about.

"Please. You're really going to deny you sent her over to tell me to abort the baby?"

What the fuck? "I *never* sent Melissa anywhere, and I would never suggest that. *Ever*." I have absolutely no idea where this is coming from, but I have a sick feeling that I'm not going to like it.

"Melissa came to the condo the week of my birthday. She said you two were making plans for your future—*together*. She told me all about how you were going to take over her daddy's company when you retired from football. She also informed me that you would never accept the baby and neither would she—since the two of you were going to wind up married anyway. She said I should consider doing everyone a favor by getting rid of him," she says, her voice filled with rage and sadness.

Holy shit! I can't wrap my head around what Ashley's telling me. How could the woman I've considered one of my best friends for the last seven years stab me in the back like this? Melissa sure is lucky she's in France at the moment. Otherwise, I'd probably end up in jail for killing her.

"Ashley, I swear to you that none of that's true—not one bit of it. She made one joke one time at dinner about me taking over her father's company. I never ever agreed to it or even considered it, and I *never* thought about marrying her. Not ever. I may have lost my mind for a little bit there in the beginning, but I never once thought about asking you to abort our baby. There's not a chance in hell I'd ever think about doing that, let alone sending Melissa over to try and bully you into it."

"This is all your fault!" she screams. "God's punishing you for not wanting this baby, but I'm the one who is paying for it."

"Ashley, I swear to you I did want this baby. How can you doubt that after the last few months?"

We don't get any further into the conversation because Nurse Darla suddenly appears.

"I'm so sorry to interrupt," she says sheepishly when she notices the open box on the bed. "I just came to see if you happened to have a name picked out. I need to finish his certificate, and all that's missing is a name to put on it." Her face is filled with anguish as she asks, and I can't imagine how hard this part of her job must be. Well, I guess I don't have to since I now know the pain of being the parent in this situation.

"Daniel," Ashley says without hesitation, and Darla nods before leaving. She must have already known the baby was a boy and been considering names without me.

He had always been Sammy in my dreams, but Daniel's nice too.

"That's a good name," I say, our argument momentarily forgotten.

We sit in silence, staring at the box containing the blanket and hat from the picture, as well as the picture itself.

Darla comes back about five minutes later, holding some kind of certificate in her hands. I immediately notice the footprints on it and can't tear my eyes away from them—those tiny little footprints, no bigger than half my pinky finger. I feel the tears trickling down my face.

Without warning, Ashley lets out the nastiest snarl I've heard. "You bastard!"

I stare at her, having no idea what I've done this time. "He wasn't a Garrison. He was a Mitchell."

It's then that I notice the name at the top of the paper she's holding in her hand: Daniel Garrison.

"I had nothing to do with this… but he was a Garrison, Ashley." Was she really not going to give my son my last name?

"No, he wasn't," she growls at me. "He was mine! MINE!"

"Whoa! What the hell is going on?" Quinn asks, appearing in the doorway.

"This asshole had them give Daniel his last name." Ashley sobs as Quinn approaches the bed.

"No, he didn't," Quinn says with a soft sternness. "I was the one who filled out the paperwork while you were still unconscious. I listed him as the father. They'd probably written Tanner's last name as the baby's in the paperwork before you'd even woken up."

"How could you do that to me?" Ashley cries into her hands and mumbles to herself.

Quinn leans closer to Ashley, whispering in her ear, but I honestly don't think Ashley hears a word she's saying.

Quinn nods toward the door. "I think you need to give us a little bit."

I shake my head as I mouth out, "Waiting room." I'm not going home to my comfortable house while Ashley's stuck here during the worst thing that's ever happened to her. I'll give Quinn the space she needs to get Ashley calmed down, but I'm not going anywhere.

Chapter Seventeen

TANNER

IT'S BEEN TWO days since Ashley's meltdown over Daniel's last name. When Quinn had come out of the room after calming Ashley down, she told me Ashley doesn't want me here. It wasn't a surprise, but I could see how hard it was for Quinn to say that to me. No matter how many times I insist it's not her fault, she keeps apologizing.

Since being banned from her room, I've taken up residency in the waiting room, which is thankfully pretty empty most of the time. The hospital staff has been really good at keeping the attention swirling around my presence here from generating a crowd. Apparently, Alex asked Davis to get in touch with some head of something or other, and so far, the extra security staff he hired has kept any crazy super-fans out, which is impressive since I'm in such a public place.

The waiting room is quiet but covered in fucking Valentine's Day decorations. This is the first Valentine's Day on which I've ever been able to say I love someone… and she wants nothing to do with me. I would love nothing more than to fawn all over her today and celebrate our love, to see her face covered in the same delight as that of the nurses who've been receiving flowers all day. Some have gotten balloons, some candy.

One even comes back to the nurses' station with a big-ass teddy bear from a patient, holding a heart that reads, *I love you.* It reminds me that our love is one-sided. I love Ashley, and she hates me. Even so, while she might not want me here, there's nowhere else I want to be. If I'm being honest, I have to admit I'm holding out hope that she'll break down and want me by her side. It won't happen, but I need to hope for something, or I'll go insane.

Her parents came to see her yesterday, and reality sunk in a little for me. I'm really screwed if she'd rather see her mother than me. Not knowing what Ashley's told them about us, I made myself scarce so her parents wouldn't see me and ask questions. Quinn had already told me that Ashley never mentioned the baby to them, and I didn't want to make things worse by accidentally saying something I shouldn't. They didn't stay long, but I avoided the waiting room for a while in case they decided to hang around. Instead, I hid out in the little coffee area meant for the nurses where I could covertly keep an eye on things since it wasn't a good idea for me to go roaming the hospital. They never did head to the waiting area though. They just stood in the hallway outside Ashley's room, only two doors up the hall from the coffee cove, criticizing her, and I finally got to see firsthand why Ashley doesn't speak with her mother. I'd been close enough to catch quite an earful.

"I just don't understand what she was doing out that late at night. Why did she get that job as a waitress? If she would've just listened to me years ago and chosen a different career, she would've never had the need for another job," her mother had said to her father, her voice full of disdain as she finished her little tirade. Then the two headed down the hallway and didn't come back.

Now, I'm back in the waiting area, sitting amid the paper hearts and streamers, thinking about how those people are the polar opposite of my parents. I can't wrap my head around how Ashley's mother could be so awful to her. She's a great person who's great at her job—a job she really loves.

When I look up, I see my own wonderful parents walking toward me.

"What are you doing out here?" Ma asks before pulling me into a hug.

"She doesn't want to see me. What are you guys doing here?" I ask. I hadn't been expecting them to come.

Ma holds up a large brown paper bag that looks as if it holds enough food for the entire floor. "I wanted to bring you something to eat. I know you most likely haven't been eating." She smiles softly. "I'm so sorry she won't let you see her, honey."

"I admire your will to stay here and wait it out in case she changes her mind. You're a good man, Son," my father says proudly.

Somehow, I don't feel as though I've made him very proud though.

"Not good enough. This is all my fault," I tell him, choking back the sorrow. I'm not ready to break down again. I need to be strong for Ashley, even if she doesn't think she needs me. I need her, and focusing on her gives me something to do.

"It is not," my parents say in unison.

"This was the fault of some asshole who thought he was better than calling a damn cab," Ma says with so much disgust in her voice it startles me.

"That asshole just pled guilty," a voice I don't immediately recognize says from behind us. I turn around and find myself face-to-face with the detective handling Ashley's case.

"Detective," I say, shaking his hand. I can't remember his name for the life of me.

"I've already informed Ms. Mitchell and Ms. Taylor. Mr. Michaels, the driver of the other vehicle, pleaded guilty early this morning on the advisement of his attorney. He was offered a deal of ten years. The evidence was there. He wasn't getting out of it, but the prosecutor didn't want to take any chances. It's ten years flat, no possibility of parole," he says.

"That's it?" Ma asks, sounding appalled.

I can't say that I disagree with her.

"There was a chance he could've gotten less time with a trial. This was also to prevent Ashley from ever having to set foot in a courtroom to relive that night," he explains.

"Well thank goodness for that, but it still doesn't seem like enough. That man killed my grandson," Ma points out as if we all hadn't already known that.

"Margaret," my father chides.

"Sorry, sweetie," she says as she rubs my arm.

"It's okay, Ma," I say before returning my attention to the detective. "Was Ashley okay with the plea bargain?"

"She was once I explain it saved her from court," he says.

"Okay, then. Thank you," I say, offering my hand to him again.

"My pleasure," he says, taking my hand. "If it were up to me, people like him would never see the light of day again."

I nod, watching him walk off down the hallway. My sentiments exactly.

"Tanner," Ma says. "You're allowed to feel, too. Ashley isn't the only one who lost him. You can't keep everything all bottled up. Make sure you take time to grieve."

"I know," I say, even though I don't agree.

"Okay, well, we'd better get going. You call us if you need anything," Dad says, wrapping his arm around my shoulders and giving me a squeeze.

"Yes, I will. Thanks guys." I smile grimly at their backs as they walk away.

"Oh, and honey," Ma says, turning back to face me once more. "Melissa's been trying to get in touch with you. She's worried. You should give her a call."

"Ma, don't take any more of her calls. She's not what she seems," I say, my tone serious.

Ma furrows her brow. "What does that mean?"

"She went to Ashley's and told her I wanted her to have an abortion," I explain, my suppressed anger rising to the surface. I still haven't decided how I want to deal with Melissa, but I will. Oh, I will…

"You've got to be kidding me!" Ma gasps.

I sigh, a feeling of sorrow washing over me. "I wish. Ashley spent the last two months thinking I wanted her to get rid of him." I can't help thinking that if Ashley had just confronted me sooner about it, things could have turned out differently.

"No wonder Melissa kept asking about the baby." Ma sighs. "I'm sorry, honey. I didn't know."

"It's okay, Ma," I say hugging her. "Just don't take any more of her calls,"

"I won't." She nods and takes my father's hand before they head off down the hall again.

I find my way back to the chair that practically has my ass-print permanently ingrained in it and wait. I'm not sure what I'm waiting for. In the silence, my mind goes blank, which I'm grateful for. It's nice to hear nothing from time to time in the midst of all the chaos. II should probably get back to handling all the mundane details of my life, like dealing with Davis, but I'm not ready yet. Right now, I just want to sit in silence.

I'm not sure how long I've been enjoying my solitude when Quinn appears. Every time she comes out to talk to me, I hope it's to tell me that Ash has changed her mind and is asking for me, but that's never the case.

"As long as everything stays the same through the night, they're going to let her leave tomorrow," she informs me.

I nod. Sensing there's more coming. I ask, "And?"

"We need to start planning a service for Daniel," she says sadly.

"Okay, whatever Ashley wants. I'll take of everything," I say.

"Okay, I'll keep you posted," she says before heading back into Ashley's room.

Chapter Eighteen

ASHLEY

I **TRY TO** avoid Tanner and his family the best I can, but with them making up about eighty percent of the people at Daniel's funeral, it's pretty hard. His parents are both here, along with two small families who I assume are his sisters'. There's woman with her husband and daughter, and there's another couple next to them with two older children. Alex is also a part of the group. Hell, the whole football team probably would have shown up if it wouldn't have brought the paparazzi down on us like a swarm of locusts.

I just wish I could have a break from him and his guilt-fueled concern for me. I hate him and everything he reminds me of, and every time I have to look at him, all the pain comes flooding back.

The only people here for me are Quinn and some co-workers from the bar and the paper. I never bothered to tell my parents when I found out about the baby, so why tell them about losing him either? Quinn knew not to mention anything in front of them, and I'm sure that she said as much to Alex and Tanner.

I suppose I'm lucky that I've been in a painkiller coma since being discharged from the hospital earlier this week. Everything relating to this funeral has been a blur. When Quinn had told me Tanner said he'd cover anything I wanted for the service, I couldn't be bothered to fight him on it. I vaguely remember being asked questions about burial plots and caskets and brunches and churches until I snapped and said I had enough, that whatever Quinn thought best was fine.

I still don't want to deal with anything related to burying my precious baby boy in the cold, hard ground forever. Alone. Without me. If the world was a fair place, he'd be here with me… or I would at least be with him. I just don't understand why we had to be separated when life seems so meaningless without him.

The priest makes his way toward the front of the group, next to the hole that's been dug for my son's casket. I'm sadly relieved to see him take his place. It means I can get away from all these people without having to be rude—not that I really give a shit about being rude. This is my son's funeral for Christ's sake. I have no desire to speak to anyone, and I don't want any condolences for a pain and loss that most people will never understand.

I squeeze Quinn's arm, hoping she'll get the hint that I want to move closer. Since I can't move well on my own, I need her help. She wraps her arm around me, and we maneuver me very slowly toward the grave. Thankfully, my broken arm and busted leg are on opposite sides, so I can use one crutch at least. I feel everyone's eyes on me as I make my way forward, but I refuse to look up, concentrating on limping forward one leg at a time.

The only specific order I'd given Quinn was that I didn't want a huge production. I wanted everything done at one place. My body can't handle all the traveling right now, and quite frankly, neither can my emotions. I'm grateful she was able to find that for me. There's a chapel on the cemetery grounds, and it was big enough for Daniel's mass. Mass and burial—that's all I wanted, no get together after. It's not as though people could sit around telling stories about him, so what would the point be? There is no life to celebrate. Daniel never got a chance at life.

My eyes refuse to move from the small baby blue casket. I stare at it, not paying the slightest bit of attention to anything happening around me. The cold wind whistles, but the winter chill doesn't register in my already numb body. The rain splatters on my shoes, but I don't feel any wetness. The priest is speaking, but I can't focus on the words. Sniffling and crying fill my ears, but I don't look to see who's shedding tears. Whispered prayers sound miles away, as though I'm in a bubble—a bubble of sorrow. My son is so close yet so far away. Never to come back. I feel a lone tear slide down my face.

I watch the line of people walk by Daniel's casket, dropping flowers on top of it before exiting the cemetery. I make no move to follow them. I want to be the last one with my child after everyone has left. He'll know, wherever he is, that his mommy didn't want to leave him.

How the hell am I supposed to leave? How am I supposed to turn my back on my son, my flesh and blood, and leave him all alone?

"Sweets?" Quinn asks, giving my arm a little squeeze.

"Hmm?" My eyes are still glued to Daniel's final resting place.

"Ready to walk up?"

I answer with a nod and adjust my crutch, readying myself to move forward. Good leg. Bad leg. Good leg. I repeat in my head until I reach Daniel. Quinn doesn't rush me as I stand there, staring into the ground. I imagine him in that casket, his sweet little face, all alone. He shouldn't be alone. He should still be nestled in his warm little home in my belly, not freezing out here.

Why? Why him?

I bring my hand to my lips and kiss my fingers before leaning over as far as I can to place my kiss on the casket. "I love you." Straightening back up, I say, "I'm sorry." Sorry that I have to turn and walk away, leaving him here. "It should have been me."

As Quinn helps me walk away, I look back over my shoulder, not acknowledging the tears trailing down her face. They do nothing to me. My emotions have been shut off, and that's fine with me. I don't want to feel anyway. I'd be happy to never feel anything again. There's no joy left in my world, nothing good left in my life, so what's the point of feeling at all?

Chapter Nineteen

TANNER

DURING THE SERVICE, I can't take my eyes off of Ashley. It's like looking at a robot. Not a single emotion plays across her face, and she doesn't once notice me watching her like a hawk. I watch her every move. Having not seen her in five days, catching sight of her is like finding a single sip of water in the desert. It isn't enough.

I want to be the one she leans on, her support system. There's no reason why we shouldn't be going through this together. He was our son. My son too. There's nothing that can be done to change that. Yes, I have Alex and my parents, but they don't understand how I feel. They don't understand my pain. I need her too, dammit. Can't she see that?

When it's all over, my body instinctively moves in her direction, but Ma stops me.

"Come on, sweetie," she says, her eyes rimmed with red and small smears of black from her makeup. "You're not going to be able to get through to her today. She didn't make eye contact with anyone. She needs time."

"I need her." I sigh, refusing to take my eyes off of Ashley as she stands with Quinn next to the grave, her lips moving soundlessly.

After a moment, Quinn helps her turn away from the hole in the ground, but before she's taken a full step, Ashley looks back over her shoulder. I hear her say, "It should have been me."

My heart cracks in two at those words. It shouldn't have been either one of them. They both should have been in the warm Miami sunshine with me.

Watching Ashley shut down little by little is harder than I could have imagined. I understood when she shut me out after seeing Daniel's "Certificate of Life." I even understood when Quinn came to me to ask me to help plan the services because Ashley had wanted nothing to do with it. But seeing the emptiness in her eyes has me more than worried about her emotional stability. Despite the fact it's been raining steadily all day, she hasn't seemed to notice. Instead, she's soaked through. Quinn has tried a few times to get her under an umbrella, like everyone else at the service, but she's made no effort to get out of the rain or even wipe the moisture from her face. I'm not sure worried begins to cover how I feel about her well-being at this moment.

I follow my parents over to where our driver stands beside his Town Car, and we say goodbye to my sisters and their families. I tell Alex I'll see him later and slide into the back seat beside my mom and dad, more than ready to head home. I can't wait for this day to end. I can't imagine that anything is harder than burying your own child, but I don't want to find out if that's true. Nothing could really make this easier, but I honestly believe that if Ashley and I had been a unit through it all, this nightmare could be slightly more bearable

I must really zone out because I don't remember dropping off my parents or the subsequent drive to my house. I don't even realize I've arrived home until the driver has come around the side of the car to open my door. Being out of it is fine by me, though.

This suit needs to go. On my walk to the door, I consider throwing it in the fire place since I'll never wear it again. It will forever remind me of saying goodbye to my son. I probably sound like a psycho teenage girl debating on burning an outfit because it reminds her of an awful ex-boyfriend or a night out, but I don't care. My eyes will be drawn to it every time I walk into my closet, reminding me of everything I lost that terrible night—not just my son, but Ashley too.

Once inside, I walk straight to the den and strip out of my suit, throwing it piece by piece into the fireplace—jacket, pants, shirt, tie. I never want to see any of it again. I turn on the fireplace and sit on the oversized ottoman in the middle of the room in nothing but my boxers and dress shoes, watching my clothes burn. I wish all my pain and sadness could burn away with them, that the weight I've been carrying around on my back would dissipate too. I wish I could turn back the hands of time, but I can't, and none of my troubles are going to burn away with the charred remains of my clothes, so I decide to hit the shower.

Standing under the warm spray of the six built-in shower heads, I try to shake away the haunting vision of Ashley at the burial. Hollowed out, broken, dull—words I would've never thought to use to describe Ashley, but they're accurate nonetheless. For the first time since the accident, I'm seriously wondering if there's any way for her to come back from all the trauma.

She was always the bright light in my darkness. There was always an aura about her that made me want to be near her, but right now that light is so dim. There's been so much tragedy, and the last thing I want to see her light swallowed up by it forever. She may not have died in the accident, but a part of her is gone, and it breaks my heart to see her living as a shell of her former self. It almost makes me glad that she didn't get the chance to see and hold Daniel. It was almost impossible for me to give him up, and I can only imagine it would've been a million times harder for Ashley.

After I fail at attempting to wash all my sins away during my hour-long shower, I throw on some sweats and head downstairs, thinking that maybe some time in my gym can help me work through my feelings. I convince myself it's a better choice than drinking, until I find Alex sitting at my kitchen table with a beer in his hand and an open one waiting for me next to him.

"How long have you been here?" I ask, sliding into the chair across from him and grabbing my beer. So drinking it is.

"About half an hour. I was getting ready to check to make sure you didn't drown in that massive oasis you've got up there," he answers with a smile that doesn't reach his eyes.

"It's been a long day," I offer in explanation of my lengthy shower.

Alex's phone chirps and lights up on the table. After checking the message, he looks up at me and says, "Quinn."

"How's she doing?" I ask. "It was kind of hard to talk to her today."

"As well as can be expected. She's got a lot on her plate with helping Ash. You know how bad things are between Ash and her family, so that puts everything on Quinn. She's the only family Ash has right now, since Ash doesn't want her mom anywhere near this whole thing." I'm not surprised Ashley doesn't want her mom involved. She was almost intolerable at the hospital. "She actually just asked me if I would swing by," Alex says.

"Okay, go then. She could probably use someone," I say sincerely. Quinn will definitely need someone to help, and there's no way Ashley will let that person be me.

"Wanna come?" he says, taking another sip of beer before going back to his phone. "I don't think you should be alone either. You don't need to suffer in silence." He glances up from his phone with a concerned look on his face. He knows me too well.

Being alone is exactly my plan.

"It's not a good idea for Ash and me to be in the same room. She doesn't need anything else to set her off right now," I say as I stand to toss my empty beer bottle in the trash. Damn, I downed it fast.

"Already checked with Quinn. Ashley took a bunch of meds, and she's out for the night. No reason we all can't spend tonight together. You both need me, and I want to be there for the two of you."

"Okay," I say only to make the situation easier on him. I don't want him to have to choose between being here for me and being there for Quinn.

Besides, Quinn wouldn't lie. If she says Ash is out for the night, then she's out for the night.

The drive over to Quinn and Ashley's goes by more quickly than usual. I guess it must always seem that way when you don't really want to reach your destination. There are so many memories waiting for me within the walls of that condo, and most of my recent ones are bad—telling Ashley I didn't believe her and ruining everything, asking her for forgiveness and having the door slammed in my face… Add to that all the wonderful memories I have there, and nothing great can possibly be in store for me there.

"Hey, baby," Alex says enveloping Quinn in a hug when she opens the door.

Quinn's hair is in a messy pile on top of her head, she has on no makeup, and she's wearing sweats. I don't think I've ever seen Quinn in attire this casual. She's usually so put together, even while sitting vigil at a hospital bedside. This day has clearly taken a toll on her.

She wraps her arms around Alex's midsection and burrows into his chest as if the answers to all her problems are buried in there. He guides her backward a step inside and squeezes her harder, allowing me in and giving me room to close the door. When she lifts her face from the crook of Alex's neck, her eyes land on me, and she smiles sadly.

"How are you holding up, Tanner? I'm sure today was really rough for you."

"It was. I'm dealing," I don't really want to focus on me. "How's Ashley?" I ask as we all make our way into the living room and sit down on the couch.

"A freaking mess." She sighs. "Or at least I'm assuming she is. She's not really talking much, and when she does, it's just one word answers."

"She looked like a zombie, an emotionless pod person," I say. "It's really sad to see her so lifeless."

"I know. I was waiting for the breakdown, but it never came," she says, curling her legs beneath her. "She just stares out into space. She's not eating or drinking. I had to force her to shower today. Do you have any idea how hard it is for her to shower lately even when she wants to? Forget about me having to force her! I just don't know what to do. I know it's only been three weeks, but I'm worried, guys."

"You don't think she'd do anything stupid, do you?" I ask, needing to voice the possibility. "I heard what she said when she was leaving the casket."

Quinn shakes her head. "I don't think so... I'll definitely keep an eye out for that, but I don't know how much longer I'll be able to stay home with her. My father's already getting on my case about when I'm coming back to the office, and I only have one week of leave left."

"I'm more than willing to help," I offer. "Especially with her current behavior the way it is. Clearly, depression's setting in fast. Don't hesitate to let me know if you need anything. You can't do this all by yourself, alright?"

"Absolutely. Thank you for that. I know it can't be easy for you to be around her with the way she blows up at you all the time." Quinn says as she reaches for a bottle of whiskey on the coffee table. "Who wants a drink?"

"Make mine a double," I say, not wanting to admit that I'll stay no matter how badly she treats me.

Chapter Twenty

ASHLEY

"I HAVE TO go back to work on Monday," Quinn says, plopping down next to me on my bed.

"Okay?" I let my tone rise, wondering where the random comment came from.

"I tried to see if I could get another week off, but HR said I've used all my vacation time, and Daddy dearest said he would be setting a bad example if he allowed me to take more than a month off," she says with venom in her voice. The way she gets worked up over her father always cracks me up.

"Okay, so go back to work on Monday. What's the big deal? Did you and Alex plan on doing something?" I ask even though I'm not really interested in hearing about how she and Alex are busy enjoying life.

"No, I can't leave you here alone, Ashley," Quinn informs me as though I'm a child who's never been left home alone before.

I love her, but she's really getting on my nerves. Last week, she yelled at me for sitting around silently all the time, saying it wasn't good for me. Then she sat there talking incessantly, going on and on about nothing of importance until I told her to shut the hell up. She said if I don't start interacting with people again soon, she'll continue to sit next to me and talk my ear off until I start talking back.

"I'm a grown-ass woman. I don't need a babysitter," I snap at her.

"You only have one working arm and one working leg. How the hell do you to expect to stay here by yourself for eight hours?" she points out as though I've forgotten about the itchy plaster cast and the cumbersome monstrosity on my knee.

Quinn's only concerned, but it's fucking annoying. I'm tired of everyone treating me as though I can't fend for myself. It's suffocating, as though I'm on suicide watch. While I can't say putting myself out of my misery doesn't seem slightly appealing, I don't have the nerve, but I do wish she'd just leave me alone sometimes.

"Quinn, I'm fine!" I say, struggling to sit up straight and waving her off. "I have all day tomorrow to rearrange anything I need to. I don't need someone up my ass twenty-four seven. In case you haven't noticed, I've been doing just fine this last month." It's true. I've gotten pretty good with the one crutch I can use.

"Seven days of that month you were in a damn hospital bed. They don't count. You can barely get to the fucking bathroom alone, and you don't get out of that bed unless you have to. I don't think it's a good idea for you to be all alone," she says, gesturing wildly, the tone of her voice now matching mine in annoyance.

"So I'll fucking go to the bathroom before you leave, and I'll continue to stay in bed all day. The bathroom is less than ten steps from my bed. I can move everything I need to in my room, and I'll manage until you get home. I *want* to be alone. It's not the end of the fucking world." I didn't ask her to stop her life for me. I didn't ask for any of this. I don't need someone to tell me what I can and can't do.

"I still don't think this is a good idea," she says, skepticism in her voice. Quinn has always been the fun one, and I've always been the cautious one. When did the tides turn so much?

"When did you become an overbearing mother? I already have one of those, in case you forgot. There's a reason she's not here," I tell her pointedly, narrowing my eyes in warning. I don't need another person telling me I'm doing everything wrong, which is exactly why I didn't want my mother here.

She was bad enough at the hospital… *Why were you working so late? I told you being a reporter wasn't a good enough career! If you just listened to me, you wouldn't have needed another job.* Blah, blah, fucking blah. Imagine if she knew about the baby… Christ that would have been the be-all and end-all.

Quinn shakes her head in frustration. "When you almost fucking died! That's when. Don't like it? Too bad. You scared the hell out of me, and I don't want to be in the position to see something bad happen to you again," she said, her tone falling from hostile to sad.

She walks out of my room. A few moments later, I hear the sound of slamming cabinets and glasses clinking from the kitchen. When she comes back, she has the biggest wine glass we own filled to the brim with a red wine, most likely a cabernet—her favorite. She sits down next to me, leans back against the headboard of my bed, and sighs.

"I can't go through that again. I've watched enough bad shit happen to you. I'll do whatever I can to never see anything like that happen again."

I'm grateful for everything Quinn has done for me, but it's hard to give a shit at this point. She wants to make everything better, as though I'm just going to move on with my life when there's no healing from this kind of hurt. I lost my child. He's the first thing I think about when I wake up. Every time I move and feel the pain that has taken over my body, I'm reminded he was ripped away from me. It's a pain she'll never be able to empathize with. She's worried about bad shit happening to me, but there's nothing God can do to me that would be worse than what he's already done. I'm living in hell, and it doesn't get worse than that.

"Nothing bad will happen, Quinn. If anything goes wrong, I can always call you," I say, grabbing her hand, hoping to placate her into moving on, but, of course, it doesn't work.

"We can totally rearrange this room," she says as she brings her wine glass to her mouth. "If we move the bed over to that wall there, you'll be as close to the bathroom as we can get you. I'll stock you up with food and drinks and magazines and whatever else you want before Monday morning. How does that sound?" She suddenly seems more hopeful.

"Sure. Sounds perfect," I reply, knowing that all the planning and rearranging will give her something to do other than hover over me like a fucking mother hen.

"OKAY, DO YOU need anything else before I go?" Quinn asks, pacing. "I filled the basket with water, soda, snacks, and a sandwich—which you need to make sure stays on the ice pack or it's going to get warm and taste like shit. Your medication's in there too. I put some mail on your nightstand—magazines and other stuff that's piled up. Do you have the remote?"

If she doesn't stop pacing, I'm going to throw the fucking remote at her head.

"Too many questions for eight o'clock in the morning, Quinn. I'm fine. Go," I growl, trying to get comfortable again so I can go back to sleep.

"Okay, call me if you need me alright. Or call Tanner. He said he'd be around if you needed anything today."

Tanner. Always back to Tanner with her.

"When are you going to get it through your thick head that Tanner is no longer a part of my life? My baby is dead, buried in the cold ground. Tanner and I are nothing but a bad memory. Go back to fucking work, and leave me in peace."

"I almost liked it better when you weren't talking," she huffs.

"Quinn…" I warn.

"Okay, okay… Have a good day."

Ha! A good day? I'm trapped in this fucking bed. Yeah, it's going to be a great day.

After she goes, I manage to sleep until about ten, which is good. I wake to find about ten messages from Quinn, all asking how I'm doing and why I'm not texting her back.

I tell her I'm fine, that I was sleeping, and not to have a damn heart attack. I haven't had this much solitude since my mini-coma. I may have bitched about someone always being around and never having alone time, but I've kind of gotten used to it, and now it feels weird being by myself.

I grab a few of the magazines that Quinn has piled up and start flipping through them. As I'm skimming the first one, a card falls onto the bed from between its pages. It's a generic blue envelope with my name and address scrawled across it in girly handwriting—no return address. Strange. I open it to find yet another one of the sympathy cards I'm so damn sick of. I open it to find a message and signature.

My future mother-in-law filled me in, and I understand condolences are in order. Funny how little problems always seem to work themselves out.

-Melissa

Stupid fucking cunt! How dare she refer to my son as a "little problem". I rip the card to pieces, hoping to feel some of the anger leave my body. I want to throw things, scream, punch her fucking face in, but I'm sure that's what she wants, and I won't let that dumb bitch get the best me. Her future mother-in-law? Really? I wonder whether she's trying to convince herself or me since I don't give a rat's ass what Tanner does. I'm not keeping him from her. I wish she would come take him away. I look down at the scraps of paper in my lap before gathering them up and tossing them in the trash can beside my bed. I'm not going to give that bitch or her games another thought. I've let her wreak enough havoc in my life with her stupid little messages.

Needing something to distract me while I'm stuck in bed, I decide to catch up on some TV. I'm not normally a TV person, so I google some hot shows. *The Walking Dead*? Nope. I'm not into the whole zombie trend… *Sons of Anarchy*? Hot bikers and debauchery. Lots of death and destruction. Sounds good to me. Seven seasons to catch up on. That should keep me busy for the week.

By the middle of the third episode, my leg is throbbing, and my head is pounding—probably because I haven't gotten out of bed yet and I'm buried under a mountain of stress thanks to that twatface, Melissa.

I grab my bottle of pain meds from the nightstand and take one. My stomach growls as soon as the pill and water hit it, and I realize I haven't eaten anything yet today, which is probably not the best idea when I'm taking such strong pain killers. I grab the sandwich Quinn made and go to town.

Damn, I hadn't realized I was so hungry. I'm apparently pretty thirsty too because I down a bottle of water and a can of soda in about two seconds.

My pain killers kick in pretty fast, and I suddenly have to pee like a race horse too. I had been planning to see if I could hold out until Quinn got home, but I hadn't been thinking about that while I was guzzling all that water and soda. Pushing myself up with my good arm, I sit up before swinging my good leg over the side of the bed. It takes a minute but I get my injured leg over the edge as well, and my lovely immobilizer makes it stick straight out. I grab for my crutch, which Quinn left leaning against the wall, perfectly in reach with my new room arrangement.

When I finally get myself to a standing position, the ground moves. I swear to God it does. I feel completely drunk. Making this trek on my own for the first time fun. I'm high as a kite, probably shouldn't have had pain killers for breakfast, but it's okay. I can do this. I don't need help. One step at a time. I got this.

After what seems like an hour and a hundred hobbling steps, I've made my way to the toilet. Walking with one crutch, a broken arm, and a banged up knee had seemed pretty feasible in my head, especially with the injuries on opposite sides, but it was much harder than I'd anticipated. Even so, I've done it.

Peeing has never felt this good before. I moan as I relieve myself and then break into giggles at my own reaction. I'm grateful my left arm is broken and not my right because it would be so much harder to wipe my ass with my left hand. I laugh even more, picturing the awkwardness. I'm so giddy that I'm sure as soon as my head hits the pillow again, I'll be down for the count.

Glancing over at the sink, I know I need to wash my hands but it seems like so much work. What if I get my cast wet? Then it'll reek, and that's the last thing I need right now. Deciding to pass on the cast washing, I gimp my way back to my room.

As I limp along, my crutch catches on the carpet. I feel myself going down as though it's happening in slow motion, but there's nothing I can do to stop it. Fuck, I should've paid better attention.

I let go of the crutch and try to soften the impact with my good arm, but in the process, I wind up twisting, and my bad leg takes most of the force of the fall.

"Owww," I cry out.

Pain radiates through my entire lower body and then through my right elbow as it smashes into the floor as well. Holy shit, it fucking hurts. Sobs rack my body, and I lie on the floor crying for a few minutes. When I try to move, it's no use. My wrist buckles as soon as I try to push up off the floor, and I scream out in agony. My bad knee throbs so badly it feels as though my heart's pounding inside my leg. I'm in too much pain and too hopped up on meds for the working parts of my body to move properly. The pain's excruciating, and I can only imagine what it would feel like if I didn't have any medication in me. As much as I don't want to, I know I have to call Quinn.

Shit! My phone's on the bed.

A new wave of sobs takes over as I realize I'm going to be stuck on this floor until Quinn gets home. That's hours from now, hours of laying on the floor in pain, crying because I can't stop the tears—tears of pain and frustration and sadness because I've become helpless. I close my eyes, feeling sorry for myself and hoping to just pass out.

I've almost cried myself to sleep when I hear a door open and close.

"Ashley?" A voice that sounds like Tanner's calls out.

I must already be asleep if I'm imagining him being here.

"Ashley?" he calls again, sounding closer this time.

Why does my subconscious always come back to Tanner?

"Ashley? Holy shit! What the hell happened?" he asks from right next to me.

Opening my eyes to see his face, I burst into tears again. "I had to pee. I tripped. Everything hurts," I tell Dream Tanner.

"Okay. It's okay, baby. Let's get you off the floor," he says. Could he be the real Tanner?

His arms reach under me and wrap around my midsection to pick me up. As soon as his hold tightens around my ribs, pain shoots through me.

"Oww," I cry. Yup, this is definitely not a dream.

"Shit. I'm sorry. I forgot about your ribs." His grip loosens, but then he says, "There's no other way to pick you up. I'm so sorry." That's his only warning before he scoops me up off the floor, causing me to scream out in pain again.

He kisses my hair. "I know. I know. I'm so sorry."

Normally, I'd yell at him for even thinking about kissing me, but I'm in so much pain that I don't give a shit right now.

He lays me down on the bed and helps me with the covers while I bury my head in my pillow to cry some more.

"Where are you hurting? What happened?" he asks, his voice full of concern.

"My crutch caught the freaking thingy in the doorway and I fell. I tried to fall on my good arm, but somehow I fell on my leg. My legs and elbow hurt. Now my ribs too," I say, keeping my face in the pillow.

"Why didn't you call someone, sweetheart?" he asks, his voice so soft and sweet that it warms my heart, even if just for the moment.

"Because my stupid phone was on my bed."

"Okay, well you're back in bed now," Tanner brushes the hair away from my face. "What can I do for you? Want something for the pain?"

"I took one before I went to the bathroom."

"How long were you on the floor?" he asks with an angry glint in his eyes.

"I don't know. Not too long, I think."

Tanner grabs the bottle of medicine and a bottle of water from the nightstand. "Well, since we don't know if you've done any more damage, I think you should take another one. We can check everything out after you've had some sleep and some pain relief."

I take both bottles from him gladly, wanting nothing more than to not feel anything. After taking another dose, I close my eyes, feeling him slide in closer beside me. As much as I hate him, I don't want him to leave right now. I know damn well that nothing good will come of this when I wake up again, but right now I don't want to be alone. I feel so pathetic that I don't even care he's stroking my hair and telling me everything will be okay.

As I wake again to a pain that I'd swear is worse than what I felt waking up in the hospital, I hear hushed arguing coming from the direction of the living room.

"What the hell would have happened if I hadn't come by to check on her, Quinn?" Tanner asks angrily. "She would've laid there until you came home. She would've been on that floor for hours. I told you I didn't think this was a good idea."

"I didn't want to leave her alone, but she insisted. What the hell am I supposed to do?" Quinn says, sounding just as irritated as Tanner.

"I can hear you, you know," I yell from my bed. If they're going to bitch about me, they might as well do it to my face.

"Good," Tanner calls back before barging into my room and stalking toward the foot of my bed.

"Why are you still here?" I growl. Why does he always have to be the one to save me? Why does he always have to be the one to see me at my lowest? I'm so tired of him. I fucking hate him, but he doesn't seem to care, which only makes me hate him more.

"Because you need someone here. You can't do this by yourself, Ashley. You need to let people help you." He sounds frustrated. If he's so annoyed with my attitude, then maybe he should just leave me alone like I'd wanted him to in the first place.

"I didn't ask for your opinion, but I do let people help. I let Quinn help me all the time," I point out.

Quinn appears in the doorway, sighing. "I can't be here all the time, sweets. You need to let more people in." Her shoulders sag as she sits on the end of my bed.

"Sorry I'm such an inconvenience to you, Quinn." My bitchiness seems to be out in full force today. I blame it on the new bruises and Tanner's presence.

She frowns and shakes her head.

"That's not what she said and you know it," Tanner scolds. "Stop being such a brat. She's dropped her entire life to be here for you, and you're going to pull this crap? What happened to you was awful, but I'm not—*we're* not—going to sit here and watch your pride make things worse for you. You need someone with you all the time right now. Deal with it."

I get lost in the authoritative nature of his voice. It reminds me of why I fell in love with him in the first place. Suddenly, a painful twinge in my knee snaps me back to reality, and I remember he's the reason for this whole mess to begin with.

"Fuck you," I spit back.

The cocky bastard smirks. "I wish, sweetheart. I wish."

I want to slap him.

"So," Quinn says, clearing her throat, effectively ending my staring contest with Tanner. "What are we going to do?"

"Well, you have two choices," Tanner says. "You can come stay at my house during the week—"

"Absolutely not! Not a fucking chance in hell." I shake my head adamantly.

"Or," he continues, giving me a hard stare. "I can stay here with you while Quinn's at work."

"Nope. That's not happening either."

"Well, I didn't ask for your *opinion*. I gave you two choices. Pick one. How much longer do you think it's going to take you to heal if falls like today's keep happening?" he asks, raising an eyebrow as if daring me to argue. Fucking smug asshole! The fact that he makes a good point pisses me off even more.

"He's right. Tanner will come here while I'm at work. Sorry, sweets, but it's the best option," she says, not sounding the least bit sorry. "I don't think moving her in with you is good for anyone, Tanner. She might try to kill you… or after a few days of spending all day with her, you might want to kill her." She laughs. Fucking traitor of a best friend.

"Umm, do I get a say in this?" I ask in annoyance at these two making decisions for me as though I'm not even here.

"No!" they both say in unison.

"You aren't thinking with your head," Quinn says.

Tanner steps toward the door. "Okay, since that's settled, I'm going to head out. I'll see you in the morning. Quinn, can you call the doctor and see if she needs to be brought in to get checked out after that fall? I know she won't do it herself."

Quinn nods.

I watch him walk out as though he owns the fucking place. In this moment, I'm certain there's no better motivator for rehabilitation than getting that smug, super-hot asshole out of my life. God, I hate him.

Chapter Twenty One

ASHLEY

THERE'S ONLY SO much sitting on one's ass and watching TV a person can do, and I've been doing even more of it in the past two weeks than I had been before falling and hurting my leg worse. When Quinn called the doctor and told him what happened, he wanted me to come in as soon as possible so he could check my knee, so Tanner got to take me the next morning. Super fun! The caring boyfriend act was enough to make me vomit. It would've been nice if he'd cared when I'd needed him to instead of bailing and calling me a worthless whore.

After an MRI, the doctor had concluded there was more swelling but no additional damage. Since then, I've been on strict bed rest while my leg stays propped up on a pile of pillows and no getting up except to use the bathroom or wash up. The doctor ordered me to let people help me and said it was a bad idea to be alone until I have more strength and mobility. It seems like a bit of an oxymoron since I can't get either of those while stuck in a fucking bed… But hey, what do I know? I'm just a girl who can't do anything for herself, and he's a doctor.

With Tanner always here, my days have been stressful and anger-filled. He's here every fucking day… Sometimes I can ignore him, but others I can't—like when he bitched that I hadn't eaten my lunch yesterday. I don't want to eat anything that asshole makes me though, and I have no appetite most days anyway. Staring at these same four walls is already driving me insane without his constant attempts at small talk. I usually pretend he isn't here by distracting myself with meaningless thoughts like what the hell had I been thinking when I picked this storm cloud gray color for the walls?

I'm getting better at ignoring him, but I feel his annoyance each time his attempts to get me to engage fail. At least he's stopped trying to sit in here and hang out with me. The first few times I told him to leave, he'd just smirked at me and said it wasn't a good idea for me to be so isolated. Since he wouldn't leave and I couldn't, I just slept. It's easy to sleep these days. I feel as though all I have to do is close my eyes—probably because my dreams are way better than my reality.

You'd think he would've gotten the fucking hint by now to just leave me the hell alone. I'm doing everything in my power to avoid talking to him at all, and I'm just waiting to add a bladder infection and a UTI to my list of ailments because I refuse to let him help me to the bathroom. I don't know what he and Quinn were thinking when they decided having him here would help me.

My angry thoughts of Tanner are momentarily halted when I notice the forgotten TV. A commercial for diapers is on. On the screen, a sweet little baby is bundled up and laid down "for a better night's sleep" or so the commercial claims. Who gives a shit about getting a better night's sleep if they have a precious little miracle at the end? Ungrateful mothers! I'd never sleep another night for the rest of my life if it meant I got Daniel instead.

My torment doesn't stop when the commercial ends because the show that comes back on is *A Baby Story.* A very pregnant woman and her husband sit in front of the camera, talking about how they've gotten ready for the arrival of their baby. The smiles on their faces are luminous. Then the shot cuts to clips of their everyday lives, scenes of them with the son they already have, asking him if he's excited for the arrival of his baby sister. The little boy squeals as he talks hurriedly about all the things he's going to do with his new sister.

My heart cracks as I envision Daniel getting excited about being a big brother and jumping for joy at the thought of having someone to play with, having a new person in his loving family—a loving family which will never be because his father didn't want him. Who knows though? I might've moved on and found a man who loved my son and me unconditionally. I don't realize I'm crying until the big drops of tears hit the backs of my hands. I let them build and fall.

They come faster as I hear the woman on TV telling her husband it's time. I watch the two scurry around their house, grabbing this and that, huge smiles adorning their faces. The woman winces in pain as a contraction hits, and I wish I could trade my pain for hers. I would've savored every contraction because each one would have meant that I was closer to holding my sweet baby. I didn't get that chance, and I'll never get it back… not ever.

The dam holding my pain and sorrow at bay breaks as the doctor delivers a beautiful baby and places her on her mother's chest. The husband brushes his wife's hair out of her face and kisses her, telling her how amazing she is and what a wonderful job she did.

I can't take the pain searing through my heart. I would've given anything to experience the joy those two obviously felt in that moment. Why couldn't I have that? Why was my baby taken from me? I did everything right. I loved him from the beginning. I did what was necessary to ensure things would be good for us. I did everything a mother is supposed to do. Where did I go wrong?

When I think about it, I know where I went wrong… I got Daniel, the greatest gift in the world, from the most selfish asshole ever… Damn you, Tanner.

I don't realize I've been screaming until Tanner comes bursting through the door.

"What's wrong, Ashely?"

The sight of him only adds to my pain.

"Get the fuck away from me!"

"What's wrong?" he asks again, ignoring my request. "You're screaming bloody murder. Does something hurt?"

He walks toward the bed, and when he gets close enough, I can't help but take a swing at him with my good arm. The punch hits him in the chest, the only body part I can easily reach. I hit him once more before he grabs my wrist.

"Did that make you feel better? Tell me what's wrong." There's a mixture of emotions on his face, but I don't care enough to worry about which ones they are.

"You're what's wrong. Get the hell away from me. I hate you! *I hate you!*" I yell. "But you're always fucking here. Because of you, I lost the most important thing ever, and I didn't even get to see him. But you did. You, the one who did everything wrong, got what I should have."

He sighs. "Ashley." He releases my wrist but only to run his hand up my arm.

I yank my hand from his grasp and hit him again.

"GET THE HELL AWAY FROM ME! DON'T TOUCH ME!" I scream. My screams turn into sobs. I sit in my bed, hunched over, my head in my good hand as I continue to cry for everything I've lost.

"Ashley," Tanner whispers.

"Go. Just leave me alone. Just get out of my life. Please."

I hear his footsteps as he retreats toward the door, and when it clicks closed, another round of sobs leave my body.

Chapter Twenty Two

TANNER

***WHAT THE HELL** just happened?*

I stand outside her door, listening to her cry her heart out, and she won't let me do a thing about it. I have no clue what set her off, but I'm becoming more and more worried about her. She's just so goddamn angry all the time. I understand her pain, really I do, but how long is she going to keep this up?

I slide down the wall to sit on the floor outside her door, wanting to stay close, just in case she fully breaks. I feel it coming. Maybe today's her tipping point. It's hard to tell with her refusing to talk to me. Well, she talks to me sometimes, but only to tell me to go fuck off or leave her alone. Ashley telling me not to touch her cut me deeply, more deeply than I'd like to admit. Nothing has ever brought me as much joy as touching Ashley—the feel of her skin, the way her eyes used to shine brightly when she smiled at me, her laughter, the way she fit in my arms as though there was nowhere else she ever belonged. I would give anything to have her look at me with adoration again instead of hatred.

Her wailing grows louder and more high-pitched just as Quinn comes through the front door. She stands at the end of the hallway, a look of sympathy on her face.

"What happened?" she asks quietly.

"I don't know," I say. "She just started screaming, and when I went to check on her, she threw a huge fit. She punched me and kicked me out after telling me for the thousandth time how much she hates me."

Quinn slides down the wall to sit next to me. "I'm so sorry. I know how hard this must be for you."

"It's okay. She needs you, though. You should go check on her. I'm sure she'll talk to you." I don't want Quinn to comfort me. I don't deserve it.

"Okay, are you going to hang around until I find out what's wrong?" she asks, standing again.

"Yeah, then maybe I'll figure out how I pissed her off without being anywhere near her, so I can avoid doing it again tomorrow," I say, feeling resigned as I watch Quinn head into Ashley's room.

I push myself off the floor and head to the living room to give the girls some privacy. The idea of hanging around the door now that Ashley has someone in there to confide in makes me feel like a weird stalker. I take up my post on the couch again and wait for Quinn to come out.

It feels as though hours pass before Quinn comes out, but a glance at the clock tells me it's only been half an hour. She heads to the kitchen before coming into the living room with a glass of wine for her and a beer for me.

"It's worse than I thought," she says after a sip of wine.

"What's going on?"

"She was watching some dumb show about babies—pregnant woman and their roads to becoming mothers or some shit like that," she says, staring into her wine glass as if it holds all the answers to her problems.

"Jesus." Why would she do that to herself?

"I don't know what to do, Tanner," Quinn says, bringing her eyes up to meet mine. There's a pleading look in them, as though she's begging me to help her figure this situation out.

I rub the back of my neck, feeling a bad headache coming on. "Quinn, I'm more clueless than you. She won't talk to me unless it's to tell me what a piece of shit she thinks I am."

Tears well in Quinn's eyes. "I love her. I do. But how much of this am I supposed to take? I get that she's angry, but what the hell did I do? I've done nothing but support her. Her mood swings are giving me whiplash, and since I cut back on her meds so she can't use them as an escape, she's gotten even bitchier." She doesn't deserve Ashley's anger, and she's most likely its target because of me.

I sigh. "I can only go by what she tells me, which isn't much. I didn't realize things were so bad. Maybe she needs to speak to someone who can help her through this. You and I can't do this alone." A professional could help our girl start to heal.

"She won't go for that," Quinn says, seeming defeated as she wipes a stray tear from her cheek.

"Well, we won't give her a choice. I have no problem being the bad guy. I'll take her, make her go. I bet she'd rather do that for an hour than spend it with me," I point out.

Quinn chuckles. "Good point."

I know she doesn't mean anything by laughing, but it hurts to admit that Ashley would rather do almost anything other than be near me. I can't help the frown that spreads across my face.

"I'm sorry, Tanner. It must be rough. You're not an asshole or the bad guy, so don't let her convince you otherwise."

I smile sadly as I push myself off of the couch. "Doesn't matter if I am or not. I've already made my bed with one mistake." I hold out a hand to help Quinn up. "Come on. Let's go tell Ash we're making her see a therapist. I wonder how loud the explosion will be this time."

Quinn laughs. "She's going to blow a gasket."

Is this what dealing with Ashley has come to—us plotting behind her back, making decisions for her, and laughing at the fact that there's a good chance she'll go nuclear on us? Either way, no matter what I do, she's going to hate me, so I might as well force her to deal with her problems and get better.

Quinn knocks on Ash's door before we head in.

We find her sitting in the same spot she always is. It's not as though she can sprawl out or move around much. Tears are rolling down her face as she stares at the TV. The couple on screen talk about waiting for the arrival of their baby as the husband rubs his wife's very pregnant stomach.

A piece of my heart breaks looking at the longing and sadness in Ashley's eyes.

"Dammit, I told you to stop watching this shit," Quinn yells, walking over to grab the remote from her hand.

Ashley just continues to stare at the screen that is now thankfully devoid of soon-to-be parents.

"Ashley, you can't keep doing this to yourself," I say softly, almost apprehensively, not stepping through the door. I don't want to set her off more by getting too close.

"I didn't do this to me. You did this to me," she answers, her gaze snapping up to meet mine. The fire burning there is almost hot enough to melt me on the spot.

"That's enough," Quinn says, directing Ashley's attention toward herself and effectively ending the "blame the world's problems on Tanner" session before it gets started. "You're not doing this again. You need to speak to someone. It's time to start thinking about a therapist."

"I don't need a shrink," she growls. "I'm grieving. I'm allowed to grieve my losses." She snaps her head around to glare at me, a not-so-subtle reminder that I'm to blame for her losing everything.

"You do need a shrink… and maybe an exorcist at this point," Quinn quips. "I'm not too sure which right now. I love you, but you need something that I can't give you, and you sure as hell don't want to talk to Tanner."

I have to bite my tongue when she says *exorcist*. Leave it to Quinn to make a joke in the middle of a serious conversation.

Ashley grits her teeth. "Of course I don't want to talk to that…"

"Asshole? Yes, we know, Ashley. He's an asshole. You hate him. Same shit, different day. He's still here, and he'll be here to help you as long as you need it. Want to get rid of him? Start getting better."

Well, this is the first time I've been used as negative motivation. Thanks, Quinn.

"She's got a point. Don't want to see me anymore? Get better." I smirk even though it pains me to say the words.

"Fuck off, Tanner," Ash snaps. "I don't need you here. I keep telling you that, but you can't seem to get it through your damn head. If I was able to get around on my own, you wouldn't get the fucking time of day from me."

I grin. "I would love to be off fucking right now, but since you refuse to work on getting better, I'm here instead. And I'm not even getting the time of day from you now, so is that really a solid point?" Baiting her is easy. I just hope that it doesn't backfire in my face.

"Shut the fuck up. I. Don't. Want. You. Here." She glares at me, a steeliness in her eyes I can't quite place.

"When I'm ready to talk, I'll talk," she says, directing her anger back at Quinn.

"The time is now, sweets. You either talk to someone or I'm sending you to your mother's. You two can bitch back and forth at each other until you're blue in the face. Let her be your punching bag because we're not doing it anymore."

"Hell, Quinn can commit you if you don't shape up," I say with a smirk, earning me a look of pure venom from Ashley.

Quinn sets her jaw. "We love you, but we're not going to sit around and watch you waste away. Don't think I haven't noticed that you haven't been eating lately."

My head snaps in Quinn's direction. I know Ashley won't touch the food I bring her, but not eating for Quinn is news to me.

Quinn gives me a sharp nod, which confirms what she's saying is true.

"You're supposed to start physical therapy in three weeks, Ashley. How the hell do you plan on doing that with no strength? You need to eat," I bark at her.

"Don't tell me what to do," she says, sounding like a child who's been scolded.

"Well, since you want to act like a child, we'll treat you like one. Do I need to sit in here with you now that I know you can't even be trusted to eat by yourself?" I ask.

"Hell no! You aren't sitting in here with me all day. It's bad enough that you're even here at all."

"Well, get your shit together, and you'll be rid of me all the quicker."

A light of comprehension switches on in her eyes, as if she's just solved the most difficult problem in the world, and she smiles.

"If I agree to see the shrink, will the two of you get the hell out of here and leave me alone?" she asks.

"Yes," we answer together.

"And if you promise to start eating again," Quinn adds.

"Fine. I'll go and eat." Ash agrees.

I can't help but think that this is the beginning of the end for us. She seems way too happy at the prospect of getting rid of me, and I've just stupidly agreed to leave her alone.

"One more thing," Quinn says, grabbing the remote from the bed. "No more TLC for you." She scrolls through the channels before landing on the Game Show Network with a grin.

Chapter Twenty Three

ASHLEY

Q**UINN MOVED FASTER** than I'd anticipated after I'd agreed to see a therapist. She came bouncing through the door the day after my breakdown to tell me and Tanner, who of course had to be included in the conversation, about how she'd gotten me an appointment with a "fantastic" therapist her mother recommended.

"If anyone knows how to find a good therapist, it's my mother. Lord knows she's seen enough," Quinn had said. Apparently, the best part was that she had an opening at the end of the week and could squeeze me in, avoiding the month-long wait for a spot to open up in her schedule.

So here Quinn and I are, driving toward Dr. Michelle Paterson's office—certified psychologist and grief specialist according to her website. I'd rather be on my way to the gynecologist right now than heading in to have my head examined. I really don't want to spend the next hour with some woman who's going to ask a gazillion questions I don't want to answer.

"Her office is in this building," Quinn says as we pull around the corner, heading for the parking garage. The building's tall, with the cityscape reflecting in its mirror-like windows. It's shiny and pretentious-looking. The only thing that feels welcoming about the place are the flowers that are starting to bloom in the beds along the front.

As we pull into a parking space and get out of the car, I hope the building isn't a reflection of the good old doctor. For some reason, this building feels oddly familiar, as though I've been here before. But with a job that had me traipsing all over the tristate area, everything starts to seem familiar sooner or later. Once you've been to one city building, you've been to them all.

"We should've taken up the knee doctor on that handicapped parking pass. That way you wouldn't have to trek across this damn garage," Quinn says as we reach the elevator at the front of the parking garage.

I smirk at her. "Or next time, you just drop me off by the elevator and trek across the parking lot by yourself."

"Haven't you ever heard of the buddy system?" she asks earnestly.

"Yeah, because I'm doing you a lot of a good with fighting off possible muggers, carjackers, and rapists." I laugh shaking my head.

"Touché," she says with a grin.

We take the garage elevator up to the main lobby.

On our way toward the main elevators, I hear someone call my name.

"Ashley, is that you?" a familiar voice asks from behind me.

Quinn and I both turn toward the voice to see Jason approaching us.

"I thought that was you," he says as he gets closer. "What are you doing here?"

"Are you fucking kidding me?" Quinn sneers, not trying one bit to hide her disdain. "What do you want, dipshit?"

"Quinn, a pleasure as always," he says. "I just wanted to see how you were doing. The accident was all over the news."

"Yeah, I'm aware the whole country got to hear all about the worst day of my life. I was nearly killed by a drunk driver, and my son *was* killed by him. How the hell do you think I'm doing, Jason?"

His face pales at the mention of Daniel. We were careful to keep him out of the news, so of course he had no idea. Doesn't matter though… Every time someone asks me the same idiotic questions about the accident, I have to think about my sweet little boy who didn't make it through.

"I'm sorry. I didn't know. Nothing was ever said about that," he says, embarrassment evident in his voice.

"Yeah, I know."

"Come on, Ash. We're going to be late." Quinn puts her hand on my shoulder, attempting to guide me forward as the elevator in front of us opens. "I'd like to say it was great to see you, dickhead, but it wasn't," she says, leading me inside the elevator car, careful not to use much force.

Cautiously, I follow her lead. It's hard to balance with only one good leg and it's even harder using a crutch with only one good arm on a marble floor.

"I don't want to keep you. I'm sorry for your loss. It was good seeing you." He says before we walk into the elevator.

"Ugh, if I never see him again, it will be too soon," Quinn says as soon as the doors slide closed. "He's got balls though. I'll give him that. First, the flowers he sent to the hospital, and then actually approaching you?" She shakes her head. "I wonder what he's doing here. And what the hell was up with the 'It's good to see you'?"

"I forgot he works in this building. It didn't dawn on me until I saw him. And who gives a shit what he wants or says? Like you said, if I never see him again, it'll be too soon. Let's go get this shit started."

An hour later, I can't get out of that office fast enough. Sixty minutes of psychobabble bullshit should be considered a torture technique. I'd wanted to stab my own ear drums out the entire time I was listening to that uppity woman with her damn librarian bun and glasses on a string ask question after question.

"What do you hope to get out of therapy, Ashley?"

My best friend and stalker ex-boyfriend off my damn back.

"Are you familiar with the grieving process, Ashley?"

No, I've never lost a kid before, dumbass.

Sometimes smart people say the most stupid shit. I'd tuned her out after I asked her if she'd ever lost a child and she said no. She has no idea what I'm going through.

Chapter Twenty Four

TANNER

"I'VE SET EVERYTHING up, Quinn. Just get her to meet with him," I say.

"She's not going to like this, Tanner. The minute I tell her you set this all up for her, she's going to flip her shit again," she says, sounding tired and stressed.

"So don't tell her that I set it up for her. Tell her you did. I don't need credit for this shit. I just need to know she's going to be okay. Who knows how long she's going to keep shutting me out? She may never take me back, but at least I'll know that she's set."

"Okay, I'll try. I'll let you know how it goes," she says before hanging up, not sounding terribly optimistic.

Ashley's been even more hostile in the two weeks since she began going to therapy. She also started physical therapy at the beginning of the week, and both have made her more aggressive toward Quinn and me, which we hadn't thought possible. We've become the enemy, although me more so than Quinn. At least she isn't hostile to Quinn all the time. I'm starting to think it would've been a better idea to hire a private nurse for Ashley since my presence only makes her madder. I offered myself up to help her out of my own selfish need to be nearby, but at what cost?

With her pulling further and further away, I'm more and more afraid of what the future holds for Ashley. She's shown no signs of wanting to get back to her life. She doesn't want to see anyone. From what I can tell, she has no interest in writing at all anymore. What if she never finds a way to movè on with her life?

With her refusing to rely on me, I've wanted to do something to make sure that Ashley would have resources to fall back on no matter what. Recently, I contacted a lawyer to discuss the possibility of filing a civil suit against the driver of the car who hit her.

After all of the trauma and pain Ashley's gone through, she's entitled to a settlement, especially when the bastard who killed our son is only going to sit in jail for ten years—not nearly long enough. When I explained Ashley's fragile state to the lawyer, he agreed to do all the leg work he can before meeting with her. Even so, he has to sit down with Ashley at some point to get her medical record release form and have her sign off on everything. With all the initial prep work out of the way, the lawyer needs to meet her soon. If I have it my way, that drunk bastard won't have two pennies to rub together when he gets out of jail.

I hope Quinn can get her to meet with the lawyer. I don't know if she'll want to bother since she's already pretty set with the sum the insurance company gave her—not that it will fix a damn thing, but at least she can take her time healing and doesn't have to rush back into life—a life she had been planning completely around having Daniel.

Yesterday, I received a call from the cemetery. Daniel's headstone has finally been erected. I haven't been to visit since the funeral, and I think heading there will do me some good. As weird as it may sound, I want to see my son. Even though he never took a single breath, he's still my son… and every boy needs his dad. I want to see the headstone marking his eternal resting place, and Daniel deserves visits from his parents. I know Ashley isn't up to it, but I'll go gladly.

Pulling into the cemetery brings me back to the last time I was here. Sadness washes over me in waves, and I suddenly want to turn around and go back home, but I won't. I force myself out of the car and make the trek over to Daniel's plot.

The headstone stands at the head of his grave, and I can't tear my eyes from the name engraved on it. I couldn't be more proud to have this little boy bear my name. I would've fought Ashley until the end of time over it, so I'm glad she didn't get a say.

I place the teddy bear I've brought for him next to his headstone and lean over to place a kiss on the cool slab of rock.

"Hey, buddy," I say, looking down at his grave. It feels odd to stand here, talking to the memory of my son, but it also brings me a weird sense of calm. "I love you. I want you to know that. From the beginning, I loved you. It may not have seemed that way, but I promise I did. I messed up, but the moment I realized that you were mine, my whole life changed. All I could do was think about being a father—your father. I'm not proud of my behavior. I like to think I'm a good man, but I wasn't at that time. I'm really sad I missed you growing in Mommy's belly. I wish I could've sung to you and told you stories. I wish I'd gotten to listen to your heartbeat and feel you kick. I missed all that and it's all my fault, but that doesn't mean that I don't love you. I hope you're at peace, sweet boy."

I place another kiss on his grave marker and head back to my car. It feels like a "hang at home and drown your sorrows in a few beers" kind of night. Putting up a strong front is becoming more and more difficult, and lately, I've been waking every morning to thoughts of Daniel and wishing for everything that could've been. I'd bought a pint-sized Garrison jersey for the baby almost as soon as I'd come to my senses over Ashley, and now it just lies on the dresser in the corner of my room, mocking me. I can't bear to part with it. I hadn't known for sure that Ashley was having a boy, but deep down, I'd felt she was. Now, that jersey just reminds me of all the ways I failed her, and each day feels like more of a battle than the last. I don't know how much longer I can keep it up.

Chapter Twenty Five

ASHLEY

THIS HAS BEEN the most grueling week I've had since coming home from the hospital and burying Daniel. I'd thought when I got my cast removed, it would make me feel better—the same with my huge leg brace—but I hadn't factored in physical therapy, and that shit is a bitch. Everything fucking hurts, but in a completely different way to being broken and injured, so I'm not even used to it. So even though I'm slightly more mobile now, I'm in more pain.

Quinn doesn't seem to understand that fact, and she keeps telling me I'm more of a bitch now than when I was stuck in bed. On top of that, we got into a huge argument over some stupid civil suit shit she set up a few days ago. All she would tell me was that a lawyer was coming by so I could sign a bunch of papers and that he would handle the rest.

I tried to explain to her that I didn't want any more money, but she wouldn't have it.

"The asshole's lucky that he only got ten years. He's lucky I'm not a judge. His ass would never see the outside world again. Think of this as part of his plea deal," she'd reasoned.

"That doesn't even make any sense."

"It does to me, and that's all that matters. I know you have plenty of coverage between both your car insurance and your health insurance, but who knows if that's going to be enough. Major surgeries, a seven-day hospital stay and a year's worth of physical therapy come with a hefty price tag," she said, raising her eyebrows as if daring me to argue with her.

She had me there. I'd never thought of that, so I'd conceded.

A huge smile had spread across her face then, as if she'd just won't the battle of her life. "That was easier than I thought."

Today's battle isn't so easy.

When Dr. Paterson tells me it's time to warm up to the idea of visiting Daniel, I'm immediately against it. I don't know if I can go through the agony of leaving him there again. It was hard enough the first time. I don't trust myself not to do something crazily morbid, like dig up his coffin and try to bring it home with me. The fact that I've even thought about that scenario at all should be a red flag that I'm royally fucked up, but I'm in denial, so it's okay.

I bitch about it to Quinn the whole way home.

She sits there listening quietly, yet intently, only to tell me she agrees with Dr. Paterson as soon as I finish my rant. "She's right. It's time."

Quinn's off today because she's pissed at her dad. At first, I'd been glad not to have to deal with Tanner, but right now, I'm thinking it would've been better if he were here instead.

"No, it's not," I say harshly.

"Yes, it is. Today's a perfect day. It must be fate that my daddy dearest is a douche-bucket and pissed me off. It's a sign!" She sounds far more excited than she should at the prospect of visiting my son's grave.

"No," I say, raising my voice. I won't budge on this, but apparently neither will she.

After another ten minutes of fighting, I tune her out. I take out my phone to distract myself, and distract me it does, so much so that I don't even notice we've pulled into the cemetery until Quinn puts the car in park.

I want to yell and scream at her for making this decision for me, but it's too late for that. Regardless of if I feel ready or not, Quinn has deemed me so, and that's that.

I sit in the car for a while, staring out the window in the direction of Daniel's grave, wishing that I could just tell Quinn to back the fuck off and take me home. As much as I'm not ready for this, I can't be this close to him and not see him.

When I finally get out of the car, the ground is wet and mushy, which seems appropriate for a cemetery. Most of the funeral is a huge blur in my memory, and I only really remember the hole in the ground and Daniel's casket. Today, an eerie fog mixes with the drizzle, making the ground look too somber to be the place my little boy will spend all of eternity.

It's colder than normal for late an April day, and the wind gives me goosebumps as I walk along, my crutch sinking slightly into the soggy ground. I'm almost worried I won't make it to him. Before we've made it a few yards, Quinn pulls the crutch out from under my arm and replaces it with her shoulder.

"I don't want to have to pick your ass up out of the mud. You know you don't really need it that much anymore anyway." She smiles and urges me forward.

Being here gives rise to a storm of emotions inside me. Knowing Daniel has been here all alone makes me mad at myself for not visiting sooner. At least the yellow sunflowers that Quinn's holding for me will bring some color to the gray of this awful place. I don't know how she managed to buy them without me noticing, but I'm grateful. I must have been more zoned-out during the ride than I'd realized.

We stop when we reach Daniel's plot, and I'm surprised to see it now has a headstone—a headstone I didn't pick out. It was one of the things I'd told Quinn to handle. It's beautiful, and I'm so glad Quinn went with a standing one as opposed to the kind that lay flat on the ground. It's a gorgeous dark marble with etchings of angels, a simple rectangle of stone that has Daniel's name, birthday, and a beautiful quote engraved on it.

This is not goodbye, just time to rest your head.
The moon will be your pillow, the stars above your bed.
Sweet dreams our little angel, until we hold you once again.

I wipe away the tears flowing from my eyes and look at Quinn. "It's perfect. You did a great job picking it out. Thank you."

"Don't thank me. Tanner handled this. He handled everything," she says squeezing me tightly.

I have no words. We stand there together for a while, Quinn wrapped around me in support. Looking the headstone over, something at the base catches my eye—a small teddy bear. I smile to myself, glad that someone, anyone has been visiting Daniel while I haven't been able to. I take the sunflowers from Quinn and reach forward to lay them on top of the headstone.

A flood of images runs through my mind—images of Daniel and me together, of the life we should have had. I had so many plans for us. Would he have looked like me? Would he be like me? Would he love to write? Would he be shy or popular? I picture his smiling face on our first trip to the zoo, to the aquarium, to Disney World… I'd looked forward to seeing him grow and thrive and find his place in the world.

I would never have been the type of mother my mother is. I'd have loved and supported him no matter what. I was ready for motherhood, even if I had to do it alone, because I'd have had him and he'd have been all I needed. But he's gone, and I don't know what to do. I feel the tears streaming down my face. I was so prepared to be a mother, and now I'm not. I'm trapped in a world of could haves and should haves. I can't go back to who I was before Daniel because that woman is gone. I can't move forward without him. I don't know who I am anymore or what I'm supposed to do. I just want my baby, and he's gone.

Chapter Twenty Six

ASHLEY

DR. PATERSON STARES at me. She sits in her pompous, high-back black leather chair, her legs crossed and her hands folded over the pad where she writes down all her notes and judgments. Her staring makes me want to punch her.

I hate these sessions. I've been sitting here week after week, listening to her prattle on about this and that and asking me about my feelings. *How does that make you feel? Why do you think you feel that way? What can we do to change that?* Hell if I know! Isn't that what she makes two hundred dollars an hour for?

Leaning forward, Dr. Paterson sets her precious pad on the glass table. Sitting back again, she levels me with a hard stare. "Tell me, Ashley, what do you hope to get out of therapy? We set goals when you first started, but based on your limited participation, I don't think you actually want to be here. It's been six weeks, and the only real progress you've made was visiting Daniel's grave, and that was by force. Two things have to happen in order for therapy to be effective: one, you have to want to get better, and two, you have to be willing to do the work. I don't think either of those things apply to you at this moment in time."

I shrug. "I never wanted to be here in the first place. I only agreed to it to get Quinn and Tanner off my back."

"I think we should revisit the topic of medication. Have you reconsidered seeing any of the psychiatrists I recommended? Medication used in conjunction with therapy can be very effective…"

"I don't need more drugs. I'm not crazy, and I'm just not going to sit here and pour my heart out to you," I say through gritted teeth.

She crosses her legs. "Then it seems we're at an impasse. I think it's best we cancel further visits until you're ready to be an active participant in your life."

"What the fuck is that supposed to mean?" I ask, glaring back at her.

She puts the cap back on her pen and places it on top of her pad. "You're angry. Rightfully so. What you've been through is horrible. While it's reasonable to go through a period of grief and depression, in order to keep functioning, you have to want to break free of the pain, you have to want to be happy again. It's clear you are not there. You've stopped living. You're only existing right now, festering in your rage. Lots of people follow this path after trauma. It's not uncommon. But I'll warn you that the longer you let the anger dominate your life, the harder it'll be to come out of the darkness. Perhaps when you're ready, you'll come back, and we'll try again."

"So what? You're quitting on me because I'm not ready to be Mary freaking Sunshine?"

She smiles. "Of course not. I'm here for you whenever you're ready, but you've made it clear that you're simply not ready. You want to hold on to the anger, and that's not how therapy works. Therapy isn't a punishment. It's a way out of the pain."

"You're just like everyone else. No one fucking cares!" I'm so tired of everyone pushing me off onto other people as though I'm someone else's problem. Quinn pushed me off onto Tanner, and Tanner pushed me off onto this bitch.

"I do care. I care very deeply. Seeing you sit there week after week carrying this heavy burden of guilt and anger, I worry that one day it's going to become too much and you're going to implode. But until you're willing to see the damage you're doing to yourself, no one can help you.

And honestly, I think that's what you want. You want to be isolated—just you and your pain."

"You want me to be like everyone else? Just move on with my life as though the accident never happened? As though Daniel never happened?" I will not act as though things are fine. They aren't. Not with Daniel gone.

"Is that really how you see things? Have Quinn and Tanner moved on? Look at their lives. What do their days consist of? From what you've told me, it sounds like the two of them have committed themselves to you," she says as though that's a gift I should be thankful for.

"I never asked them to," I snap. "In fact, I've told them over and over to leave me the hell alone."

She flashes that condescending smile again. I hate that smile. It makes me want to smash her teeth in. "And that's why you're not ready. You have people in your life who care about you, who are putting their lives on hold to focus solely on you, and you want your solitude."

"I lost my son," I scream. "I deserve to grieve!"

"Of course you do, but grief is a stage, not a permanent residence. Until you decide that you want to start living again, there's nothing I or anyone can do but watch you slowly self-destruct. This is your choice, Ashley."

"This is not my choice! Nothing has been my choice! Tanner abandoning me, the accident, losing Daniel… None of that was my choice. Don't you dare put this on me! It's all Tanner's fault, and the fact that I have to see him day in and day out… it feels like a God damn knife is being stabbed into my heart over and over. I despise him with every ounce of my being, and yet he's everywhere, reminding me of all the pain he's caused me. You want to know why I can't move on? Because he's still in my life."

"And why is that?"

"He won't leave me alone. It's like he has some sick need to pour salt in my wounds. He and Quinn have taken over everything and …"

She shrugs. "If that's how you feel, then why have you chosen to stay?"

"What are you talking about? I couldn't do a damn thing for myself for months. I haven't had a chance to leave! They make all the decisions."

She shakes her head. "They presented you with options, and you refused to make choices, so they chose for you. They haven't done this to you. You've allowed it to happen."

"Bullshit! I didn't allow this to happen. Tanner did this to me!" I shriek. It feels as though I'm talking to a brick fucking wall.

"Was Tanner driving the car that hit you?" she asks, cocking her head to the side.

"No, but it's his fault I was working that late. If he hadn't left me, I wouldn't have needed that job!" This is so exhausting. It's pretty simple. Why can't she understand?

"So Tanner never offered to support you? Never offered to help?" she questions with an unsettling smirk. Every single one of her facial expressions evokes more rage inside of me than the last.

"Only after it was too damn late!" I yell, gripping the arm of the sofa so hard my knuckles turn white.

"So you chose not to take his help. You chose to take that job."

Why does she keep trying to place all the blame back on me?

"Fuck you!" I shout. I'm done with this shit… Done! "This. Is. Not. My. Fault! It's his. Daniel would be alive if Tanner hadn't…" I'm seething, so angry I can barely see straight. My nails are digging into the upholstery so hard I'm sure they'll leave marks in the fabric. Oh well! It's either that, or I deck her.

She grabs a pitcher from the table beside her and pours me a glass of water before placing it on the table in front of me. "Ashely, this isn't about fault. You're so desperate to assign blame, but as you do that, it allows you to cling to your rage like a life raft. You got into an accident. The only person responsible for that accident is the man who drove drunk and hit you—not Tanner and not you. Continuing to blame Tanner will not bring Daniel back. It will not erase your pain. It will only trap you in this dark place you're in now."

I gulp down the water, trying to pull myself together.

"It's up to you to decide when you're ready to leave the darkness," she says calmly—almost too calmly. For some reason, the tone of her voice breaks my resolve.

"If I move forward, I'll lose him," I whisper so quietly I'm not sure she hears me.

"Lose who?" she asks.

"Daniel," I reply. "The hurt is all I have left of him. I didn't even get to hold him. If I let go of the pain, I'll lose everything I have of him." I feel a few tears trickle down my cheek but make no move to wipe them away.

"Daniel will always live in your heart. But you've shut down your heart and filled it with rage. You're not allowing yourself the chance to feel the good things he's brought to your life."

"I feel like all the good was inside him. Without him, there is no good. If I let Tanner get away with what he's done, does it make me an awful mother?" I ask, wiping my tears away at last.

"It makes you a great mother. A good mother knows how to forgive, to accept those we love in spite of their flaws and mistakes." She smiles a sweet smile this time, the first one that doesn't make me want to throttle her.

I snort. "I've never been good at forgiveness. I wouldn't know how to start."

"Perhaps it's time you tried. If you find a way to stop drowning in all the pain you carry around, maybe you'll be ready to move forward. Not moving on. Not forgetting Daniel. But moving forward. We can start with something simple."

"Like what?"

"How about something small that'll make you feel a bit better, something you enjoyed doing for yourself before the accident? You don't have to decide right now, but think about it. Think about things you used to do that made you smile or made you feel good about yourself. Sometimes it's the littlest thing, but it can really help," she explains.

"Okay, that seems easy enough."

She claps her hands together and says. "While we're thinking about things that are small, I want you to picture a spring cleaning for your emotions. Think of the anger that's been cluttering up your heart and find something small you can let go of, something you won't miss."

I think back over the last year of my life, searching for something that fits those criteria. "Jason, I guess. Maybe my parents, if I'm being honest. I used to feel so much animosity toward both of them, but now, after everything that's happened, they seem so insignificant."

She picks up her notebook and pen from the table and says, "That's a good start. Maybe after you've had a little practice, you'll find a way to forgive yourself... and maybe Tanner as well." Her hand moves furiously over the paper.

"I'm not forgiving Tanner. And what do I have to forgive myself for?" I ask, feeling defensive again. I haven't done anything wrong.

She raises an eyebrow. "That is the question of the hour, isn't it?" She looks at her watch. "Times up. Why don't you let me know if and when you're ready to resume your appointments again? I'm always here for you."

WHAT I HATE most about spring is how the sun comes up earlier and shines through the damn window, waking me up much earlier than I want to be. I could swear Quinn comes in here before she leaves for work and opens the curtain on purpose so I can't sleep the day away.

I sit up in bed and look around my room. While it's bathed in sunlight, nothing about it is bright or cheery. Dirty dishes litter the nightstand. Empty water bottles and soda cans spill out of the garbage can. The mountain of dirty sweat pants and t-shirts in the corner is almost as tall as I am, and I'm pretty sure there's a funky smell coming from my bed sheets.

I don't remember the last time the room was cleaned. Quinn cleaned it regularly in the beginning, but she hasn't been in here as much since my cast was removed and I was downgraded from the immobilizer to a smaller stabilizing brace. That was last week. I've let my room become a complete shithole in seven short days. I guess it's time to pull my head out of my ass if this is the first time it's crossed my mind to clean up after myself.

It takes close to two hours to get my room into a state of cleanliness, but I get it done. Changing the sheets is the hardest part. Even though I can move my arm now, it's still weak and kind of useless, so tucking the sheets under the mattress isn't a walk in the park, but they get changed, the nightstand is cleared, and the garbage is taken out to the kitchen. The mountain of laundry has even been reduced to one small load. Surprisingly, I feel lighter somehow—gross and sweaty as well, but definitely lighter.

When I head to the bathroom, I look in the mirror, taking stock of the person staring back at me. I don't recognize her anymore. Her face seems hollow. Large purple bags have formed under her eyes, eyes that used to shine brilliantly. Now they just look jaded. They match the frumpy bun sitting on top of her head. Everything about her screams angry hermit.

I leave my bathroom for Quinn's to grab her expensive shampoo and conditioner and her girly coconut lime body wash. Maybe using some high-end bath shit will help me feel a little bit better. I'd love a long soak in a bubble bath, and I'm sure that would help me pull myself out of this funk, but I still can't pull myself out of the tub alone, so a shower will have to do for now.

I turn on the shower and slip out of the nasty funk-infused sweats I'm wearing before stepping into the shower and letting the warm water run over me. I try to clear my mind and let all the dumb emotional shit wash away, just as Dr. Paterson suggested. None of the little stupid grudges, assumptions, and miscommunications matter anymore. I can forgive Jason. I can even let go of the resentment I hold toward my mother. I may never live up to her expectations, but I don't have to. I just have to live up to mine.

I smile to myself as I lather Quinn's shampoo into my hair, realizing it's okay to be done with everyone else and just live for me. I have a great best friend who has stood by me through the worst of the worst. She's the only person whose opinion I should ever let matter to me.

When I emerge from the shower, I feel like a new person. I even consider blow drying my hair before I remind myself to take baby steps. I catch the time out of the corner of my eye on the wall clock and realize I only have twenty minutes until Tanner gets here to take me to physical therapy. I seriously cannot wait until I can drive a car again. I'd be happier taking the bus than riding with him, but with Quinn and Tanner plotting against me together, I don't stand a chance of getting out the door alone. But hey, at least I look halfway human now.

TYPICALLY, I'D RATHER do anything other than go see Dr. Paterson, but as I head into today's appointment, I realize this is the first time I'm not dreading it, which surprises me considering how she laid into me during our last session. There must be a bit of truth to the things Dr. Paterson has been trying to drill into me, and I'm finally seeing some sense in them. I've been hanging on to so much anger, and it's exhausting being angry all the time. I wouldn't say things are suddenly all rainbows and sunshine, but it feels as though some of the darkness and gloom hanging over me has lifted.

I'll never be over Daniel's death, but I've realized I've been stuck on pause, refusing to push past the moment I found out he'd died. I've been keeping myself trapped, clinging to the hurt and despair. It's all I have left of him, and I haven't been ready to let go. Yet despite my protests, the earth has kept spinning and the world has kept moving forward, and it's demanding me to move with it—or at least shower on a regular basis. It's excruciating to think of living my life without Daniel in it, but what Dr. Paterson has me considering is that maybe I don't have to let him go completely. Maybe I just have to find a way to carry him with me.

"I'm very happy to see you here today, Ashley," Dr. Paterson says as I enter her office.

I'm so busy taking in her office properly for the first time that I don't say anything back. I don't know how she spends all day here. It's like a sterile glass box. One wall is floor-to-ceiling windows. The other three walls are stark white, and all the furniture is black, the tables glass. It's hard to believe I've never noticed before, but I've always been so focused on the clock, waiting to make my escape, that I just haven't.

"I'm very proud of your breakthrough. Keeping today's appointment tells me that you're embracing moving forward," she says with a sincere smile.

"Thanks?" I say, my tone rising. It feels odd to receive praise for coming to a shrink

"If we can approach every session from here on out with an open mind and the same honesty you gave me last week, you'll start to see an improvement in yourself. I promise. You'll also see a big difference in the way you feel about life if you actively try to pull yourself out of your self-imposed reclusion."

I nod.

She clicks her pen closed and lays it down on her pad before bringing her eyes up to meet mine. "I like the new haircut. Want to tell me what prompted it?" Dr. Paterson asks.

I'd decided to go for a new look last week after cleaning my room and taking a shower had made me feel better. When I told Quinn, she'd suggested that it might be fun to play around with my appearance and reinvent myself, so we'd gone to the salon. Quinn suggested a color change but I love my hair color, so I decided on a more extreme cut, from straight and super long to a medium-length with angles and layers—even a side bang. After leaving the salon, I felt even better, fresher, than I had after my cleaning spree. All of the focus on my makeover had directed my attention away from the pain in my body and heart, making it slightly more bearable.

"Thanks. I decided to try out your advice about pulling myself out of hiding and getting back into the swing of things," I admit.

"I'm glad. How did you accomplish that?" She asks, peering over the top of her black box-style frame glasses.

"Well, first I cleaned my room," I say, laughing.

She nods. "That's a good place to start. Anything else?"

"I took a shower, decided to care a little more about my appearance. I also made some strides in physical therapy this week. I can balance on my bad leg for twenty seconds now. I did it ten times before my leg started hurting pretty badly." I smile, remembering how proud of myself I'd felt, but I'd regretted pushing myself so hard later when my leg was throbbing in uncontrollable pain.

"That's very good, Ashley. You should be proud of any accomplishments, no matter the size. Every step, even a small one is progress," Dr. Paterson says, writing more notes on her pad.

We spend the next God knows how long talking about how my progress in physical therapy makes me feel. I don't really know what the point is though. How am I supposed to feel about having to learn to walk again? How am I supposed to feel about the fact that I can't raise my arm up high enough to take off my shirt without difficulty? All the physical therapy does is cause me more pain. I nod when I'm supposed to and give the answers I think she wants to hear, but inside, I'm back to staring at the clock again.

Dr. Patterson must notice that I've checked out because she surprises me with a topic change, and I miss the question.

"Huh?" I ask, having no idea what she's just said.

"I asked if you've put any effort into letting go of some of the stress and tension you've been carrying around by holding on to all those meaningless little things." Her eyes meet mine.

I nod, and we delve into my progress on releasing some of my past grudges, particularly in regard to Jason and my parents.

Dr. Paterson spends the rest of our session offering different methods for finding closure for unimportant things from the past. She says that a good way to deal with my anger is to channel it into an activity. "Have you written anything lately, Ashley? Writing can be a great form of therapy."

"For the paper? No, they told me to take my time coming back. It's not like I could go check out any of the places lined up for features. To be honest, I haven't thought too much about work at all. Quinn's parents have been covering my half of the rent for our condo since the accident, so I haven't had to worry about that, and Quinn has been taking care of all of my bills. I also had a good chunk of change saved up before the accident, and I've been getting disability supplements as well. There's also the two huge checks from the accident."

"Well, maybe those are two steps you can take to reclaim some sense of independence in your life. You could start writing again, even if just for pleasure, or you could pick up a journal and just write your feelings down, work through them on paper. You could also take back the reins on your finances." The way she says those words, with such positivity in her voice, makes me feel as though she finally has faith in me.

I don't know why but her faith makes me want to follow through.

"Both of those are very easy things to do," I say.

She smiles. "The road to recovery isn't always grueling."

"That journal will probably be filled with nothing but my hatred for Tanner," I point out.

"That's not the point of the exercise, Ashley. It's not another way for you to hang on to your anger. We're trying to move forward, remember?" she says, shaking her head.

"I'll always hate him. No amount of moving forward will change that," I say, gritting my teeth. My suppressed rage pushes itself to the front of my mind, and I'm suddenly pissed at myself for letting thoughts of Tanner bring me back down, but it's so hard to ignore him when he consumes so much of my life even though I don't want him to.

"Let's save this topic for another time. Our hour is coming to a close."

I give her a slight nod before standing and making my way out of her office toward the elevator.

My anger is still swirling around in my head when the elevator arrives and the doors open.

"Hello, Ashley."

I look up to find Jason standing inside all by himself.

"Hi, Jason. How are you?" I ask, attempting politeness.

The shock on his face tells me that he hadn't been expecting a friendly tone.

No time like the present to start letting go in the real world, not just in my mind.

Chapter Twenty Seven

TANNER

THE FUCKING ROADWORK has made me ten minutes late, and I hope that Ashley isn't stupid enough to take a cab home instead of waiting for me. I know she'd never call to check in with me. If Quinn hadn't forced her to choose between her parents and me, she would've never allowed me anywhere near her.

I pull up to the building where Ashley's therapist is and turn into the parking garage. Luckily, there's a spot open right by the elevator.

At least she won't have to walk far to get to the car. She may not have to use the crutch anymore, but she still has a heavy limp.

After parking the car, I rush into the building and board the parking garage elevator. I hurry through the doors toward the lobby as soon as they open again and round the corner, heading toward the main elevators.

Just in front of them stands Ashley, having what appears to be a very intimate conversation with Jason, who's standing far too close to her for comfort. I don't want that fucking asshole anywhere near her. The whole situation makes my hackles rise. One of his hands rests on Ashley's forearm as she smiles at him. Fucking smiles! At him! I'd give anything to have her smile at me again, and there she is, smiling at that shithead.

I slowly step a little closer, trying to catch what they're saying. My stomach drops as soon as I'm in earshot.

"For what it's worth, I know how wrong I was with the way I treated you. Me being a cheating asshole had nothing to do with you. I don't even know why I did it. I do love you. I mean, I did love you."

He loves her? You've got to be fucking kidding me. I swear to God that if she falls for that bullshit, I'll kill someone—probably someone named Jason.

"It's okay, Jason. I forgive you."

Hearing those words makes my blood boil and breaks my heart simultaneously. She forgives him? After everything he did to her? After all the cheating, the lying, the spending, the destruction of her self-esteem?

I've been begging for forgiveness for months, since long before the accident. I've done everything I can to make things up to her. I've stood by her side through all the pain and the drama, and I'm still nothing but the asshole who ruined her life. I don't think she's ever going to let me back in. It's an earth-shattering revelation.

"I just wish I could've realized what I had before I went and destroyed it all."

I can't believe he's making a move to get her back. I'm sure that's what he's doing. Because I know what it feels like to lose Ashley, I can't say that I blame him, but if she takes him back, it will kill me. Right here. Right now.

I can't bear to hear any more, so I clear my throat to make my presence known. "You ready to go, Ashley?" I ask.

"Hey, Tanner," Jason says softly. He must suspect that I overheard their conversation because he looks as though he's afraid I'm going to deck him, which is a definite possibility.

I nod.

"You're late." Ashley points out, as if I didn't already know.

God, what I wouldn't give for her to say something to me that wasn't laced with contempt.

"I know. There was road construction."

"I'll let you go. It was good seeing you again," Jason says before turning away and heading off through the lobby. Smart move on his part.

"Bye," Ash calls after him before turning to me. "Let's go."

After I help her into the car, which is a battle in itself, I climb in on my side. Before I can stop myself, I ask, "What was Jason doing there?"

"He works in the building, not that it's any of your business." Animosity. It's always animosity—never civility.

Remembering the flowers that he sent to the hospital after her accident, I ask, "Do you see him often?"

"Here and there. Why? What's it to you?"

"Just curious…" I know I should just let it lie, but I can't, not after overhearing the two of them. "Curious as to how you can so easily forgive him after a few casual run-ins but still have nothing but hatred for me, even after I've been trying everything I can think of to get you to forgive me for months now." I struggle unsuccessfully to keep the anger and hurt out of my voice.

"I can forgive him because I wasn't head over heels in love with him when he hurt me. He didn't leave me pregnant and alone. He didn't accuse me of chasing after a meal ticket. He didn't kill my son," she says, holding nothing back.

"Goddammit, Ashley. I know I played my part in what happened to you, but I'm getting really fucking tired of you throwing it in my face every chance you get! Not for nothing, but the crash wouldn't have been nearly as bad if you weren't such a stubborn brat and had driven the perfectly safe car sitting in the parking garage of your building. I told you over and over again that something bad was going to happen in that death trap of yours. And look, it did. Maybe you should take some responsibility for your actions too."

I regret the words as soon as they leave my mouth, but I couldn't have held them in if I tried. I know they're harsh, but I'm sick and tired of being blamed for the accident time and time again. She never mentions anything I've done to help her heal over the last four months. I might as well have been driving the fucking car that hit her myself with the way she talks about it.

"Fuck you, you asshole! How dare you blame me? I'm the only one of the two of us that gave a shit about Daniel, yet you wonder why I'll never forgive you."

"I shouldn't have said that, but how can you say you're the only one who cared about Daniel? I did everything I could to try and be there for you both. You know I did." How can she still believe I didn't care?

The look on her face is on of pure disgust. "Oh, please! You bolted the minute I told you about him and didn't contact me for over a month. Then you waltzed back in thinking you could buy your way into his life, which I never would've allowed, but we don't have to worry about that now, do we? Thanks to you."

"I made a mistake, Ashley," I say. "One fucking mistake! I tried to be there for you in any way I could, and you shut me out, repeatedly. No one can say I didn't try."

"One mistake that cost me everything."

It's always back to her. She's the only one who lost anything.

"I lost everything too. If you pulled your head out of your ass, you might see that."

She sets her jaw, looking firmly out the window, and I stare out at the road ahead. It's obvious that there is no reasoning with her. Every word that leaves her mouth cuts me deeper, leaves more scars. The sad part is that she couldn't possibly blame me more than I already blame myself. I just wish she would realize she played a part in creating this reality as well. If she had only given me a second chance, everything would be completely different.

As much as I want to be back in Ashley's life, her behavior over the last few months has me worried about what would happen if that ever became a reality. How would she react the next time I made a mistake? What would I have to endure every time I make a bad call? Would every fight be this bad? I'm worried I'll find myself walking on eggshells all the time, always afraid of doing or saying the wrong thing. Is that a life I would want to live even if it were with Ashley? I want someone who can love me unconditionally, someone who can forgive me with ease, not hold things over my head. I want Ashley to love me the way I love her, but I don't think that's possible anymore.

"I don't trust you," she says out of the blue, as though our connection is still as strong as ever even though we're at odds. "You left me when I needed you the most. How am I supposed to get past that?" For once, there's no malice in her voice, and it's jarring.

"I don't know," I admit. "I was just wondering the same thing myself." It seems it's time to acknowledge the impasse we've reached and lay everything out on the table.

"Huh?" Her brow furrows in confusion.

"I was just thinking that same thing regarding you—"

"Me? What the hell—?"

"I don't want to fight with you. Can't we just have one conversation without killing each other? Don't you ever get tired of it?" I ask, feeling completely spent. I can't keep this up anymore.

She glares at me, which I'll take over the yelling and cursing any day.

"I was just trying to say that I was thinking the same thing. If by some chance we were ever to get past everything that's happened and you actually forgave me, how could I trust you not to treat me this way again? I'd be constantly worried about making another mistake and being raked over the coals again. I don't think that I could live my life like that. So while you don't trust me, I guess I can't trust you either. So what's the point? We can't trust each other, and you can't forgive me. I'm just trying to figure out why I've been fighting so hard. As much as I don't want to admit it, you're right. I guess it's time to move on."

I feel her gaze boring holes into the side of my head, but she doesn't say another word, even as I pull up in front of her building and park to help her out of the car. When we reach the front of the building, she turns to stare at me some more.

I decide to take her silence as a sign that she agrees. "Goodbye, Ashley," I say and head back to my car, trying to figure out what comes next.

Chapter Twenty Eight

TANNER

AFTER SAYING GOODBYE to Ashley, the last thing I'm in the mood for is Melissa.

I hear the excitement in her voice when she calls me, and I ask her to come over.

My blood has been boiling since I got a text message from her last night saying she's back in the States and wants to get together. I've been waiting to confront her for months, and I haven't spoken to her since finding out about her backstabbing ways after Ashley's accident. I've only agreed to meet her in person because I know I won't get the same satisfaction out of dealing with her over the phone.

At this point, I'm really questioning her intelligence. How can she not have gotten the hint that I've been avoiding her when I haven't answered her calls or returned her texts in months? Even my mother stopped taking her calls. She must have no idea I've been made the wiser about who she really is.

I haven't given her much thought lately, but finally confronting what she did head-on really has me enraged. What if Ashley had taken her seriously? Would Melissa really have been okay going through life keeping something like this from me? It makes me wonder what else she's lied about over the past seven years. The irony of the situation isn't lost on me. Six months ago, I'd though Ashley was the lying manipulative bitch, but it turns out that the real one had been right under my nose the whole time.

I should be the better person and quietly cut ties with Melissa, but I can't—not this time. I need to fuck with her just like she fucked with me, which is why I have a fake smile plastered across my face as the devil herself sashays her way across my kitchen as though she's Miss Fucking America.

"Oh my God! I missed you so much." She beams at me so brightly you'd think I just hung the fucking moon for her. She wraps her arms around my neck and kisses my cheek.

It takes everything I have not to recoil from her touch. Her closeness is enough to make me nauseated, but her actually touching me takes me to a whole new level of disgust.

"How was your trip?" I ask, pulling away from her as casually as I can. All I want to do is throw her across the fucking room, but that would probably arouse her suspicion that I'm not glad to see her, and I don't want that to happen just yet.

"It was amazing. The first two and half months were focused on Fashion Week—Paris, London, Milan. Being surrounded by all of those beautiful clothes and people was such a rush."

How have I never realized how truly shallow this woman is until just now? The bullshit coming out her mouth reminds me of the nonsense sounds the adults make in the old *Charlie Brown* cartoons. It's all so insignificant in the grand scheme of things that it makes my stomach turn.

"It was so nice to lounge on the French Riviera. You know how much I love the nude beaches. No tan lines."

The look Melissa is giving me is clearly meant to be seductive, but I'm only repulsed by her pouting lips, the hip cocked to the side, and the hand resting on it as if to draw attention to where a tan line should be. Now I see why Quinn and Ashley have never liked her. They must've seen through her façade from a mile away. I've been so fucking oblivious. All I want is to get as far away from her as possible.

I attempt to smile sweetly, but I'm not sure it comes across as sincere. "I'm glad you had such a nice time."

"I'm so sorry that I wasn't here for your big win," she says. "You deserved it after all your hard work and all the crap you've had to deal with, and I would've loved nothing more than to celebrate with you, but there was no way I could bail on all the prep." She rubs a hand up and down my arm, petting me as though I'm a purebred horse as she talks about the big win, not once mentioning the accident.

"I didn't celebrate it. There were other things going on. You didn't miss much except the funeral for my son." I feel my face fall as I consider the fact that she would've probably liked nothing more than to celebrate the death of Daniel. It's what she's wanted from the beginning.

"I feel terrible about not being here for that." She forces her mouth into a frown, at least attempting to pretend she cares.

"You know… I thought about you a lot while you were gone," I say, closing in on her the way a predator would his prey, setting the stage for her exit from my life forever.

A huge smile spreads across her face. "You did?" she asks.

"Yes, you said something the last time we were together that stuck with me. You told me you couldn't stand around, watching me be naïve and made a fool of." I smile again.

Melissa looks a bit confused but seems more pathetic than anything else as she hangs on my every word as if it were biblical scripture.

"Well, you seem to be doing much better. At least the pro of the whole situation was that you were finally able to separate yourself from that wretched woman. She was never right for you."

"Not like you, right?" I ask, still holding the smile on my face that I'm sure now looks more evil than happy.

Nevertheless, she appears oblivious to the change of emotion, too wrapped up in claiming the prize she thinks she won. "I always knew we were meant to end up together. I'm just glad you see it now too." Melissa steps closer and leans in as if to kiss me, but there's no way she's getting her venomous lips on mine.

"Is that why you went over to Ashley's place and told her that I wanted her to kill my son?" I ask, no longer able to keep the hatred out of my voice. With the trap sprung, I don't think I'll be able to control anything else I say now. My body vibrates with a fury, and I do everything in my power to contain it.

If Melissa were a man, I would've beaten the shit out of her already.

"I have no idea what you're talking about, Tag. What did that lying whore tell you now?" she asks, her voice steady, but the paleness of her face gives her away. She knows exactly what I'm talking about.

I unwrap her hand from around my arm and push her back a few steps, giving myself some room. I don't trust myself not to strangle her when she's that fucking close to me. "I think you know exactly what I'm talking about: your little visit to Ashley's to tell her she'd better abort the baby because you and I were getting married and planning our future. Where was I during this supposed planning, Melissa?"

"That's exactly where we were heading before that stupid bitch came into your life," she yells, stomping her foot like a spoiled child who's just been told no. "Things were perfect between us until she royally fucked up everything by getting herself knocked up. I can't believe you even put yourself in that position in the first place. Six years we'd been together, and you never once went bareback." She has a lot of fucking nerve to yell at me after everything she has fucked up for me.

"Pissed off because it was you who was really waiting to trap me but I never gave you the chance? Careful, Melissa, your true colors are showing."

That accusation must push some button of hers because her face turns a deep shade of red, and I think I even see some foam forming at the corner of her mouth.

"I've stood by you through every fucking thing! You're supposed to be with me—not some poor, mousey reporter! She doesn't belong in our world. I was doing you a favor," she shrieks. The veins in her neck bulge, and her face goes even redder—if that's possible

I've never seen this side of Melissa before, but I guess that means my character detector must be way off.

"A favor? Telling Ashley it was in the best interests of everyone to get rid of our baby—that's your idea of a favor? Guess it's a good thing I won't ever be needing another favor from you again."

She blanches suddenly, the various shades of reds that had taken over her face just a moment ago vanishing. She shakes her head in denial as she realizes I won't be forgiving her.

"Tell me something, Melissa. What would've happened if Ashley had gone through with your suggestion? Were you ever going to tell me about your little meeting with her? Or did you just want her to assume that was what I wanted so you could get to your ultimate goal—my last name?"

"Whether she went through with it or not was up to her. It wouldn't have been my fault if she was so easily swayed in making a decision like that. Is that what you want in your life Tanner—someone you can bend to your will? We both know how well I follow your demands," she says, sidling up to me and rubbing herself against my side like a cat in heat. Her mood swing speed is impeccable. She's gone from rage to fear to horny in three minutes flat. It must've been exhausting for her to keep up all these pretenses over the years.

"Well, how about you follow this one: get the fuck out of my house. Get the fuck out of my life. We. Are. Done! I want nothing to do with you from here on out. I don't know when you changed or if you've always been this way, but you are ugly, Melissa. An ugly, bitter bitch. You are the epitome of everything I hate in a person."

Melissa's face becomes more contorted with anger with each insult I hurl at her and each step closer to the door I push her. I loom over her, giving her no choice but to retreat. I've never hit a woman in my life, but I'm coming really close to knocking her out.

"You'll regret this, Tanner," she threatens. "I'm the one who stood by you all these years, keeping you in line and out of trouble. Who the hell do you think you are, treating me like some slut you picked up at a bar? You can't possibly think that gold-digging bitch is better than me. What happened to the real Tanner? I don't like this pussy you've turned into," she snarls as though her threats mean a damn thing to me.

"I'm the same person I've always been. It's you who's changed. Either that or it just got to be too much trouble for you to live two lives. Get the fuck out of my house, Melissa. Don't let the door hit your lying ass on the way out." I nod toward the garage entrance, just in case she's forgotten the way.

Melissa lets out an evil laugh and shakes her head, "You stupid motherfucker. No one treats me like this. You think you're better than me? That your precious Ashley is better than me? Let's see who comes out on top. We could've been great together. Too bad you're going to be nothing now. I always win, Tag," she says menacingly on her way out.

Thank God! I was sick of talking in circles with her.

I head directly for the liquor cabinet. Between dealing with the constant disdain from Ashley and confronting the shit Melissa pulled, I'm exhausted. I'm tired of being the bad guy, but I guess that's the role I'm destined to play in life. No matter what I do, I always seem to be the one who comes out of everything smelling like shit.

I grab my phone from the kitchen counter and text Alex. I'm not in the mood for company, but I'm not in the mood to be alone either. The only person who might understand what's going on in my head right now is Alex.

Me: *Just had it out with Melissa. Feel like drinking with me?*
Alex: *I was wondering when that would happen. Yeah, I'll be by in a bit.*

Knowing I won't be the pathetic asshole who drinks alone tonight, I hit the bottle hard. By the time Alex arrives an hour later, I'm pretty drunk.

"So, what happened?" Alex asks, swiping the bottle of Jack from my hand and taking a swig as he sits next to me on the couch.

"The bitch has gone fucking bananas. That's what happened," I tell him before grabbing the bottle back.

"You know you're a Super Bowl MVP, right? I'd think you'd be classy enough to use fucking glasses," he says, stealing the bottle again.

"You're drinking from the bottle too, dickhead," I point out.

Alex chuckles. "I'm not a superstar."

"Yeah, some superstar I am. My life has basically imploded. It's over with the love of my life, one of my best friends has gone completely mental, and now I've only got you. What's going to happen to you? They say everything comes in threes, you know?" I reach for the bottle again but decide it's too much effort, so I sit back on the couch and let Alex hold on to it for the moment.

"I'm just going to continue being awesome. Don't you worry about that," he smirks at me.

"Your smugness is pretty fucking annoying," I growl.

"Oh, please. It's payback for all those years of watching you be on top of the fucking world." One best friend is certifiable, and now this one is an arrogant bastard.

"Fuck you! Give me back my whiskey," I say, snatching the bottle from his hands.

"Seriously though, what went down with Melissa?" he asks.

"Dude, she basically confirmed what the girls have been saying. She's been holding a candle for me and thought we were going to wind up married."

"Holy shit, man! I wasn't really sure what to believe. She never seemed like that to me over the years, but then again, I never really paid attention to signs for shit like that from her."

"I know. I can't believe I missed it, but she did do a damn good job of hiding it. She threatened me too. I can't deal with her crazy! I have enough on my crazy plate with Ashley. I don't know what to do anymore. Maybe I should just give up on Ashley. I mean, I've been at her side for months now, and she's only gotten more hostile. How much more am I supposed to take, man?" I ask, wanting an honest answer.

"I don't know. I'd like to tell you to stick it out, but I know what you've been through. At the end of the day, you're only human," he answers shaking his head. "I love Ashley, but the way she's acting isn't fair to you anymore. She can't seem to get it through her head that you lost just as much as she did. Maybe you're right. Maybe you should step back and focus on you. You haven't had the chance to deal with the loss of Daniel, and I think you need to. Hanging around being Ashley's punching bag isn't doing either of you any good. She may be getting better physically, but mentally, she's still hanging on by a thread. I know she's been seeing a therapist, but it hasn't helped much. Even Quinn has had just about enough of her."

I sigh. "She's cut me out of her life as much as possible, and even I know she's not making any progress. I honestly think she's getting worse. I have her back up on a fucking pedestal, but she still finds new things to blame me for day in and day out." I hate throwing these sorts of pity parties, but I just can't help myself right now.

"You don't need to figure everything out tonight, buddy. Just cozy up with the bottle you have there and turn your mind off for a while. I think you've more than earned it."

For the remainder of the night, Alex and I drink, joke, and watch that stupid practical joker show on TV, laughing as though we don't have a care in the world. It's a nice change of pace, and I find myself relaxing for the first time in a very long time. Maybe letting go of Ashley really is the best thing for everyone.

Chapter Twenty Nine

ASHLEY

BETWEEN WORKING WITH Dr. Paterson and worrying about Tanner, my mind has been swirling with thoughts of everything that's happened in the past few months. My therapy session this week isn't as intense as the last, but she says that I'm continuing to make progress and that's all I need to focus on. We discuss my encounter with Jason and how I've forgiven him.

I believe it was a sign that Jason was in the elevator after I'd left that previous session, even more so that Tanner's late arrival gave us a few minutes to talk. I'd been surprised when Jason had been the first to apologize. I hadn't seen that one coming. His confession of his infidelity not having anything to do with me was reassuring as well. I'd racked my brain for months trying to figure out what I'd done to push him into the arms of another woman.

Dr. Paterson has pointed out that I gave Jason too much influence over my self-image. She'd quoted Eleanor Roosevelt, saying, "No one can make you feel inferior without your consent". Even though I've heard that quote many times, I'd never given it much thought until now. Eleanor was right, as was Dr. Paterson. I had given Jason too much power. Not anymore. We spoke and apologies were given. Time to let it go.

Letting go and beginning to heal has also consisted of lots of physical therapy. I've been going three times a week for two-hour sessions, and it's fucking brutal—especially for my leg. I go home after each session and end up in bed, icing my knee and eating pain killers like candy. I'm surprised I haven't become an addict yet. This is the position Alex finds me in when he shows up to take Quinn out to dinner, except I've settled on the couch instead of in my room.

"Hey, Ash. What's with the ice pack? You didn't eat floor again did you?" He chuckles.

"No, I had physical therapy earlier, and this is how I spend my nights afterward—ice and mind numbing pills," I say, shaking my prescription bottle at him.

Alex approaches the couch. "You shouldn't need those after a therapy session. Let me see your leg." He sits beside me.

I move the bag of ice and roll up the leg of my sweatpants for him.

Alex pokes and squeezes, rotating my injured leg first to one side then the other. "You shouldn't be this swollen either. What the hell do they have you doing?"

"A bunch of things—pointing and flexing with those colored rubber band thingies, leg lifts with weights on my ankles, squats," I tell him as I roll my sweats back down and replace the ice on top of my knee.

"Weights and squats? Jesus Christ. You're nowhere near ready for that shit. Where the hell have you been going?" he asks, sounding angry. The look on his face isn't pleasant either, and he seems genuinely mad.

"The Heal Better Therapy Group."

"Never heard of them, but you aren't going there anymore. They're going to do more damage than good. You should be a little sore after your sessions, but you shouldn't be swollen or need ice and pain killers. I'm taking over your physical therapy. I should have offered from the beginning." He shakes his head.

"How are you going to do that? You have an office you haven't told us about?" I ask, wondering how the hell he plans to take over my therapy without a place to actually do said therapy.

Alex grins. "Technically, my office is part of the team's facilities, but we'll use Tanner's home gym. He has almost everything that we'll need, and I can pick up the few missing aids from the medical supply store. No biggie. You can keep some of the smaller items here too, so you can do lighter sessions on your own whenever you feel up to it. We can also start going for walks now that the weather is getting warmer. The vitamin D might help with that pasty thing you have going on. I'm surprised Quinn hasn't tried to make you go to a tanning salon yet."

"Don't give her any ideas," I say. "But I don't think Tanner's place is a good idea, Alex. I haven't heard from him in almost two weeks, and I think it's better this way. I doubt he'll want me hanging around his house." I don't want to mention that I don't think it's good for me to be there either. I'm in a weird place emotionally when it comes to Tanner, and I haven't sorted through my feelings about everything that's happened since our last encounter.

"It'll be fine. Tanner's not here anyway. He won't be back for a while either, and when he does, he'll be in full pre-season swing. You guys won't run into each other, and I'm sure he'd rather you get proper treatment."

He won't be back for a while? Where is he? An unexpected feeling fills my chest, but I can't explain it any better than my other emotions.

"Hey, babe. You ready?" Quinn asks, emerging from her room.

"Yeah," Alex says, standing up. "I'll set everything up tomorrow, Ashley. Don't go back to that hack place again." He winks.

"Okay," I say absentmindedly, still distracted by the unsettling feeling overtaking me.

"You going to be okay?" Quinn asks while putting on her coat.

"Yeah, I'm just going to head to bed. Have fun, you guys," I say before waving them off.

As soon as they've left, I make my way to my room and force myself to sleep. I don't want to decipher whatever the hell is going on in my head right now.

"HAVE YOU GIVEN any more thought to talking things through with Tanner?" Dr. Paterson asks. "Have you thought about forgiving him? You felt much better after getting proper closure with Jason."

"I don't think I'll be getting the chance to talk about forgiveness with him for a while," I say, the words flying out of my mouth before I realize it. My subconscious must be eager to talk about Tanner.

"Why do you say that?" she asks as she writes down something in that godforsaken notebook.

"He left."

"What do you mean?" Her attention shifts from her notebook to me.

"I haven't heard from him since he picked me up from my session here two weeks ago. I found out that he left town, and he isn't due back for a while." That same stupid feeling from the other night rises up in my chest again.

"What happened after your session?" Dr. Paterson asks.

"He overheard my conversation with Jason and was upset that I forgave Jason but not him. He asked how I could do that so easily."

"What did you tell him?" She returns to making notes.

The scribbling of the pen on the paper is driving me crazier than usual today.

"I told him the truth."

Dr. Paterson looks up from her pad, giving me a reprieve from the nerve-wracking sound. "Which is?" she asks.

"I didn't love Jason the way I love Tanner, and Jason didn't leave me high and dry while pregnant. I left him." I try to ignore her stare because I know I've just made a crucial step by saying that out loud, and I suspect she's about to broach a topic I'm not going to enjoy.

"But Tanner came back. He didn't leave you high and dry," she says, proving my hunch correct.

"It didn't matter at that point," I insist, repeating the same words I've been saying for weeks but without screaming like a crazy person.

"Why not?" she asks, probing further.

"Because the damage was already done," I huff out, trying to focus on anything but her face so I don't have to see that damn expression she gets whenever we talk about Tanner. It looks like sympathy, and I don't think it's sympathy for me.

Dr. Paterson uncrosses her legs and rests her forearms on her knees, leaning in as though she's going to tell me a secret. "It seems as though you're feeling more than you'd care to admit. I can't help you if you don't talk about it," she says.

"I can't trust him." I sigh, unsure as to why I hadn't wanted to tell her when I've already told Tanner as much.

"Why can't you trust him?"

"I can't trust him to be there for me. Last time I needed him, he bailed."

"Did he?" she questions, cocking her head to the side like a quizzical child. The pose is almost condescending.

"Yes. He ran the minute I told him I was pregnant," I remind her.

"Was that the last time you needed him?"

I grit my teeth. "Yes," I say, trying to keep my anger at the level of mild irritation.

"You didn't need him after the accident?"

"No, I could've managed without him." As long as I had Quinn, I would've been just fine.

"Could you have?" she asks, leveling me with a gaze.

We're back to her being a brick wall, I see.

"Yes," I say again.

Dr. Paterson sits up straight in her chair, clearly not willing to back down until I acknowledge her point. "Ashley, do you honestly think that you would be where you are right now without Tanner's help?" she asks.

A series of images flashes through my mind: Tanner scolding the doctor for shining the light in my eyes when I woke in the hospital, Tanner scooping me off the floor after I fell on my first day without Quinn, Tanner bursting through my bedroom door after my breakdown.

"I don't know. Probably. There wouldn't have been an accident if he'd been there in the beginning."

"Ashley, you can't keep holding on to that theory. It's just that: a theory. I want you to think about the facts instead— the fact that today you've been more affected talking about Tanner leaving than you have been about any other topic, the fact that you referred to your love for Tanner in the present tense." She gives me a sad smile, as though she's waiting for a light to click on in my head.

So I said "love" instead of "loved." Big deal.

"I want to talk about one more point before we end: how did you feel when he said goodbye?" Dr. Paterson asks.

"I don't know," I say. "I couldn't really form any coherent thoughts after everything he'd said, but I hadn't thought he meant goodbye forever."

"But that's what you wanted, isn't it?"

"Yes."

"So what do you think it means that you aren't happy about him finally honoring your wishes?" She asks.

"I don't know." I honestly have no idea why I'm not happy, and I have no idea what not knowing means.

"I want you to think about what has happened instead of what may have happened. You don't know for sure what the outcome would've been if Tanner had been by your side from the beginning. Fate is fate, Ashley."

Fate is a bitch, a bitch who isn't my friend.

Chapter Thirty

TANNER

"**YOU LOOK SO** much better, man," Alex says, returning to the table with a new round of beers.

I take a long swig of my beer, glancing around the club. "It was nice to get away for a little while. I haven't focused on just myself for months. It was nice to be free."

"How'd you do with the training schedule Max laid out for you?" Max is one of the new trainers the team has brought on for the new season. He's different from most of the trainers I've worked with. His philosophy on getting back into the training mindset after a long break—such as for athletes like myself who haven't focused on anything other than helping rehabilitate an ex-girlfriend who hates his guts for months on end—is to isolate oneself from outside influences as much as possible. When I'd decided it was time to break away from Ashley, I began working with him in the hopes of getting back into shape and building a better mindset.

Before I could really get down to training though, there were a few kids' camps I'd agreed to participate in for Mathis, but as soon as I'd finished those up, Max had set me up at a resort in Oahu. The complex had sort of reminded me of one of those monasteries monks live in. It was quiet, serene, and had everything you would need to rebuild yourself physically and mentally. The scenery alone was a sight to behold—just what you'd picture a Hawaiian getaway to look like. It was off the beaten path in a town on the North shore that had a name I couldn't pronounce properly, not yet a huge tourist attraction, and there was a beautiful lookout spot not too far from the resort. Everything was green and lush on one side with a great coastal view on the other.

The facilities lacked for nothing. They had this amazing state-of-the-art gym with floor-to-ceiling windows along one wall, providing a beautiful view of the beach. There were several different pools scattered throughout the complex as well—one for swimming laps, a really cold one that was better than an ice bath for soaking sore muscles, a hot tub for relaxation… Another pool even had exercise equipment set up in the water for training. There were mediation rooms, yoga classes, and even running trails down on the beach. Anything you could think of related to shutting off and relaxing, they had it.

"Max is definitely onto something with the way he does things," I say. "It's almost like strength and conditioning rehab. I plan on going back again. It was definitely beneficial."

"I'm glad, Tag. You definitely needed some serious downtime," he says before bringing his bottle to his lips. It hits me that Alex has been such a great support system to me over the last few months, and I realize now how important it is to have good people around you.

"It was an experience I needed. Being there put me in a mindset to really look at my life and see a clear picture. Honestly, I can feel a difference. I feel lighter and ready to have my life revolve around me again. I'm ready to find something to be happy about." I smile at him, feeling like a new man.

He clinks his beer bottle against mine in a toast. "Well, like I said before, you look great. I can see the difference. I'm happy for you, man."

"I'm glad to be home though," I say. "Listen, I don't know if I've told you this, and if I have, I haven't said it enough. Thank you for being here for me through all of this. I know it wasn't easy for you, always being in the middle. I appreciate you staying by my side even when you were pissed at me."

"I never would've been anywhere else. We're family. Family sticks together. Now let's get drunk and enjoy the night like old times.

I look around the club again. Nothing appeals to me about it, but I'm working toward reclaiming my independence, and some guys from the team had wanted to meet up this weekend to hang out, so here I am.

An hour later, I'm still not feeling the club scene, but I am enjoying the company of my friends. I find myself laughing heartily, which I haven't done in a long while. It feels a bit foreign to me.

"Hey, handsome," a sugary voice says from beside me.

I look left to see a beautiful blonde looking up at me with a bright smile.

"Hello," I reply, giving her a smile of my own.

"Feel like dancing?" she asks, placing her hand on my shoulder and slowly running it down my arm.

My first instinct is to say no, but I should be trying to get back out there. What can one dance hurt?

"Sure. Why not?" I finish the remainder of my beer and leave the empty bottle on the table as I grab her hand to lead her out to the dance floor.

She presses against me as we maneuver through the sea of bodies writhing to the music. When we find an opening, I swing her around in front of me and pull her toward me. Pushing my reservations out of my mind, I concentrate on enjoying the warm, willing body molded to mine. I close my eyes and try to get lost in the music. There's no fighting, no blaming, no nasty comments. When I open my eyes, my subconscious fights back. The blonde hair is all wrong. The barely there clothing isn't right either. The nice but very large, fake tits pressed into my chest feel hard and unnatural.

"You know, I've seen your picture all over. I told myself that if I ever ran into you, I would do whatever I could to spend the night with you," the scantily clad girl purrs into my ear. As if the physical differences between her and Ashley hadn't been enough, those words just sealed the deal. Why do I need to keep reminding myself that sluts are a dime a dozen? I guess the only things I can count on to go right are my career and reputation.

"I'm not sleeping with you, sweetheart," I say, pushing her back. "I'm used to your kind, and I don't fall for shit lines like yours. You're a beautiful woman. Do yourself a favor and learn some self-respect. Groupies and gold-diggers are everywhere. Be better than that."

I walk away, leaving her wide-eyed and open-mouthed in the middle of the dance floor. What woman in her right mind tells a man that she'll do whatever it takes to spend the night in his bed? That might be appealing to some guys but not to me. For a minute, I had almost tricked myself into thinking maybe things had changed. Not in my world. Everyone wants something from me—except for the one person I want to share everything with.

I'm not just pissed at myself for thinking things had changed. I'm also pissed that Ashley's still invading my mind. What does a guy have to do to move on with his life? Fuck if I know, but I'm done with this place. I'd rather go home and throw a few back with Alex in peace.

"What happened to the blonde?" Alex asks when I've finally made my way back to the table.

"I left her slutty ass on the dance floor," I say.

He shakes his head and chuckles. "What'd she do?"

"Told me she'd do whatever it took to wake up in my bed tomorrow. Wanna head back to my place and hit the good scotch I've got saved?" I ask, nodding toward the door.

"Sounds good to me."

I WAKE FEELING dazed and annoyed at the blaring of my cell phone, which is ringing loudly from somewhere in the vicinity of my sofa. My head is pounding, and I don't remember passing out in the den last night.

"Dude, find that phone and shut it the fuck up before I break it into a million pieces," Alex grumbles from under a throw pillow on the other couch.

"I'm trying. I don't even know where the hell I am right now. Give me a fucking minute."

Whoever is on the end of that incessant ringing had better be fucking dying. I shouldn't joke about that though.

I manage to detangle myself from the mess of throw pillows and blankets and get up to follow the shrill ringing of my phone. I find it on the kitchen counter. Naturally, it stops ringing as soon as I get my hands on it. I pick it up to see notifications for twenty missed calls and thirteen text messages. Is the world fucking ending? The majority of the calls are from Davis, but training camp doesn't start until next week, so I don't know what the hell could be so fucking important.

I don't get to check a single message before the phone starts ringing again.

"DUDE! Shut it the fuck up," Alex yells.

"Hello?" I say as I answer.

"Tanner, where the hell have you been? Please tell me it isn't true." He rushes through his words all in one breath, sounding as if the world is about to end.

"What the hell are you talking about?" I ask confused. It's too early for this shit, and I'm way to hungover for guessing games.

"Are you under a fucking a rock? Turn on SportsCenter, NFL Network… hell, check your fucking Twitter, man. You're trending. You're pretty much the number one googled person right now! Please tell me it isn't true. I'm a damn good agent, but I'm not a fucking magician."

"What the fuck? I only got back from Hawaii two days ago. I haven't done shit, Davis. Not here or there," I tell him as I head back to the couch to search for the remote.

Davis babbles on and on, but I don't hear a word he says once I see the headline being run on ESPN.

"According to a source close to Garrison, he broke off relations with his girlfriend after finding out she was pregnant," the anchorman says. "It was after a shift at her second job as a waitress at a local sports bar, she was hit by a drunk driver, which resulted in the death of the couple's unborn son. As we already know, this happened the night Garrison and the Jets won the Super Bowl. The same source has stated that Garrison's ex had picked up that second job because Garrison had refused to have any involvement with or provide any financial support to the baby, claiming he didn't know whether or not the child was his. It was later confirmed that the child was, in fact, Garrison's. Does anyone else see the irony in this situation? Garrison is the face of The Tony Mathis Foundation, a charitable non-profit that supports underprivileged children."

I gasp. "What the fuck?" Where the hell did this story come from? There are only a few people who know any of the information being reported, and I don't think any of them would've done this.

"TANNER!" Davis yells from the other end of the line.

I'd forgotten I was still holding the phone to my ear.

"Yeah?" I ask as I stand in front of the TV, staring.

"How legit is this story?" he asks, the worry evident in his voice.

I sigh. "It's pretty accurate," I admit dejectedly. "There's no point in refuting it. I doubt Ashley put this out there, but if she decides to back this up when she's undoubtedly tracked down, I won't lie."

"I don't know if I'll be able to do anything about this without trying to spin it as a lie," he says.

"It is what it is at this point, Davis." I hang up.

There's no point in arguing with him, and he knows me well enough to leave me be for now, but he does text me another important piece of information that hasn't been flashed across the TV screen yet.

> **Davis:** *Mathis is meeting later today to discuss cutting you from the foundation.*

One mistake has now officially cost me everything I care about. One mistake has cost me my son, my girl, and now my reputation. What else is left?

"Tag, where the hell did this come from?"

I look up from my phone to find Alex staring at the TV in utter disbelief just as I had been.

"I have no idea," I say, shaking my head. I scroll through my texts to see who else has been trying to get ahold of me since this news hit. Most of the messages are from Davis, but a few aren't—one from mom, one from my dad, and a couple from my sisters. The one that stands out the most though is from Melissa.

Melissa: *I told you I always win. Have a nice life, Tanner.*

"That crazy fucking bitch," I say through gritted teeth as I turn to Alex and hold up my phone for him to see. I'd taken her threat as a bluff, and weeks have passed since I kicked her ass to the curb. That's what I get for not giving the bitch enough credit, but I hadn't thought there was a thing she could do to me. I never saw this coming.

"You've got to be kidding me. I can't believe her. She knows how much your reputation means to you. She couldn't get her way with Ashley, so she went to the fucking press. What are you going to do?" he asks, seeming just as stunned by this turn of events as I am.

"There's nothing I can do, Alex. It's true. Who knows if Ashley's going to jump on this bandwagon or not? If she does, she can more than prove it's all true and that I did unintentionally kill my own son."

"You know that's not true," he says angrily.

"But it is. Just ask Ashley. She'll tell you all about it."

Chapter Thirty One

ASHLEY

TODAY HAS BEEN an emotional roller coaster, to say the least. Only now do I fully understand how Tanner must have felt when he realized he'd made the mistake of leaving me. I would sell my soul to fix all of this for him, and I'm angry at myself for being so stubborn for all these months. Unfortunately, after the news had broken, it still took Quinn slapping the shit out of me for me to realize what I had to do. Quinn's words still haunt me even hours later as I drive to Melissa's.

"How can you just sit back and let this happen to him, Ashley? What the fuck is wrong with you?" Quinn had yelled while we watched Tanner's life implode on the morning news.

"He did this himself. It isn't my fault," I said. That was when she got in my face and slapped me—literally bitch-slapped me.

My hand shot up to cover my cheek, and tears welled in my eyes.

"What the fuck, Quinn?"

"'What the fuck' is right. That man made one mistake that he's tried to make up for tenfold, and you still insist on nailing him to the fucking wall," she screamed.

"He killed my baby!" I shrieked back, unable to keep my tears at bay.

"*He didn't kill your baby.* Fate did. The drunk driver that hit you did. Tanner did no such thing, but he's let you blame him time and time again while silently keeping all his grief inside because you've been too damn selfish to let him mourn the death of his son!"

I'd never seen her so livid—ever.

"Why are you taking his side?" I cried, falling to my knees in the middle of our living room. The pain that shot through my bad leg made me cry harder.

"Because. You. Are. Wrong." She stomped her foot after each word.

My tears couldn't be stopped, and neither could Quinn's words.

"Alex and I watched him break down over your unconscious body, holding your stillborn son. He stood there telling that sweet little baby how amazing his mother was and that he couldn't have been luckier to have you. He apologized to him, said it was his fault that Daniel didn't make it. He took full responsibility then and has continued to without so much as a peep because he thinks it's his penance for losing his mind for a short period of time. He tried to make it up to you over and over, proving repeatedly that he was worthy of redemption, and you only proved that you weren't. He loves, or loved, you unconditionally, and you're going to let his life fall apart because you're a selfish stubborn bitch!" Tears streamed down Quinn's face.

I'd known that she and Tanner had developed a close friendship over the last few months, but I'd never thought she would take his side over mine.

"Did you know that he told Alex he would've gladly switched spots with you in that car or that he would have stepped away forever if it meant you and Daniel would have made it out okay? Did you know how badly you broke his heart when you forgave Jason for all the horrible things he did but wouldn't even give Tanner the time of fucking day? He practically gave up his life for you by being there every day, even when you treated him like total shit. Who do you think set that settlement in motion for you? I sure as hell didn't. That was Tanner. He wanted to make sure you had a cushion so you could heal without worrying about money." She shook her head at me in disappointment. "I talked to Alex this morning. He said Tanner won't even let his agent try to get him out of this. He won't do anything about it because he said it's the truth. That's what you've been telling him for months."

Each word she spoke weighed down on me more than the last. I knew she was right. I needed someone to blame, and that role had been filled by Tanner. I hadn't known half of the things Tanner had done and said until she'd told me. Now that I did, everything Dr. Paterson had been shoving down my throat all clicked into place. I've made a grave mistake, and I don't know if I'm going to be able to fix it.

I'd called Alex immediately after Quinn's scolding to get all the information I could. Apparently, the foundation is meeting today to make their decision about Tanner's position as spokesman, and it isn't looking good. The board finds it extremely unethical to keep him on with allegations like these. Donors will start to pull their funding if a man whose abandonment of his own child led to the child's death is the face of their organization.

According to Alex, the story came from Melissa—that fucking bitch. Alex told me that she and Tanner had had it out after she got back from France a few weeks ago, when he'd confronted her about her surprise visit to me. She must not have liked being thrown out of his life and had decided to destroy the one thing that means the most to him: his reputation.

Now that I know all the facts, I have work to do. I have to make it to that board meeting before they make a decision, but first, I'm making a detour to that backstabbing twat's house to tell her just what's going to happen. Thanks to Alex, I have the address in my GPS, and I'm working on getting my ass over there as fast as my neglected BMW can get me there.

She opens the door to her apartment with a snarky smile on her face… until I slap her the same way Quinn slapped me. It would have been nice to knock her the hell out though.

"You think you've won, don't you? Guess again, bitch. You can't break him. I won't let you. Thanks for making us stronger. We'll see how great your life is after tomorrow," I say, a smile now on my face. I leave her standing there in the doorway, holding her cheek staring at me in confusion. The easy part is over.

Getting into that board meeting is the hard part. Once I get to the foundation headquarters, the stupid bimbo secretary won't let me in to see the board.

"I'm sorry. It's a private meeting. Board members only," she says.

"We'll see about that," I reply, setting my jaw. Refusing to give up, I stomp and yell and make a huge scene.

It doesn't take long for one of the higher-ups comes to find out what the hell's going on in the lobby. "What is all the commotion about?"

"Sir, it is imperative that I speak with the board before they make their decision," I say firmly.

The dipshit in the suit gives me a dirty look. "They aren't taking character witnesses."

I fold my arms across my chest. "I have a press conference scheduled in an hour. I suggest you let me speak to them before I speak to the press."

After a few moments of deliberation, he shows me the way to the boardroom, and I'm finally granted access to the people deciding Tanner's fate.

I nervously look around at all the unfamiliar faces seated before me. "I'm sorry to have made such a big scene today, but it was very important that I speak with you before you made any rash decisions regarding Mr. Garrison," I say earnestly.

"And who might you be, miss?" an older gentleman sitting at the large conference table asks.

"I am Ashley Mitchell, Mr. Garrison's girlfriend," I say proudly. It might not be the truth at that moment, but it will be by the end of the day if I have anything to say about it.

"We weren't aware that Mr. Garrison had a girlfriend," some snooty redheaded woman comments.

"Well he does," I say. "I need to set the record straight before you make a huge mistake based on outlandish gossip and uncorroborated lies. These allegations against Mr. Garrison are false. He did not abandon me or our child. It was unfortunate that on the night of the Super Bowl I happened to be hit by a drunk driver. The crash, not Mr. Garrison, resulted in the loss of our baby. He was by my side for as much of the pregnancy as he was able to be with his crazy football schedule. He did not cause the death of our child, although he will claim responsibility because he wasn't with us that night. This rumor was started by a vicious ex-girlfriend of his who couldn't handle the fact that their relationship is over." I tell the story with such conviction that I think I might choke on it.

"What's your point, Ms. Mitchell?" another gentleman asks.

"My point, sir, is that I don't find it fair that Mr. Garrison's facing losing something he loves because of one disgruntled ex-girlfriend," I say. Over my dead body will that bitch succeed in taking Tanner's reputation and the foundation away from him.

"It's more than that, Ms. Mitchell. It's now a matter of the public opinion," yet another older gentleman says—or maybe he's the same man who spoke first. All of them look the same now—old, fat, balding, and judgmental.

"Well, sir, I can clear that matter up with something as simple as a press release. I'll be giving an interview in just a short while to clear up this misunderstanding. By this evening's newscast, this ordeal will be just another story of some scorned woman trying to get her fifteen minutes." I know I need to take care of this situation by myself and quickly. I don't want people thinking Tanner made me recite some stupid scripted speech to cover his ass.

"Just how do you plan on pulling something like together so fast?" a third condescending asshole asks.

"I'm a journalist, sir. I work for *The City Press.* I have many contacts and many friends in high places."

Okay so that last part is a lie. I don't know anyone in high places other than Tanner, but thankfully James, the sports reporter I covered Tanner's first interview for, does. When this whole crazy scheme came to life in my head, I'd called him right away to see if he could hook me up with someone who could get my side of the story out fast. Lucky for me, he has a friend at ESPN who owes him a favor. Even luckier is that said friend is the anchor for the evening edition of SportsCenter.

"May I ask with whom you are doing this interview?" one of them asks.

"The evening anchor for SportsCenter. It will be a special segment. They've assured me it will be viral by the time it's finished airing," I say proudly.

"I'm assuming it will be done via video chat," the same gentleman says.

"Yes," I reply.

"Would you mind conducting the interview here so we can see the footage before it airs? It will give us a jump on the story, and we may be able to come to some conclusions before it airs. Of course, no decision can be concrete until we see how the public reacts."

Before I know it, I find myself in an empty conference room at the headquarters for The Tony Mathis Foundation doing a video interview with ESPN. I make sure to recount everything exactly as I did in the conference room and do my best to drag Melissa's name through the mud. Afterward, the board assures me they'll hold off on making any permanent decisions for the next few days to see what trickles back to them after the press release airs—just an hour from now.

Chapter Thirty Two

ASHLEY

I'M IN THE driveway of Tanner's house, sitting in my beautiful BMW he bought for me months ago, before the hour is up. I have no game plan for this part. I've been flying by the seat of my pants since I set up the interview, and I'm still trying to wrap my head around the fact I just told the entire nation about losing Daniel with my head held high. That was the first time I've been able to talk about him honestly and openly, and I didn't even break down into a sobbing mess.

Dr. Patterson's voice echoes in my head. *Progress*... I wish her voice would tell me how to fix this mess with Tanner. I don't know how to make things right between the two of us, but I guess this is exactly how he felt trying to wade through the mess we created for ourselves. I find myself wanting to follow the same path he did: start with a simple apology. I don't expect him to be very receptive. I sure as hell wasn't.

I sit in the driveway for a good twenty minutes more before forcing myself to put on my big girl panties and face the music. Climbing from my car, I walk to the front door, each step more unsteady than the last. I raise my hand to knock on the door but pull it back. After a moment, I raise my fist again, this time managing to knock.

A few minutes pass before Tanner answers the door. I can tell from his appearance how much this whole media shit-storm is affecting him. It looks as though he hasn't showered or slept since the story broke. I haven't seen him look this broken since I first woke up after the accident—not while I was blaming him for everything wrong in my life, not while I was blaming him repeatedly for the death of our son, not when I told him I could never forgive him. It thaws another layer of the ice around my heart.

"What are you doing here?" he asks, visibly shocked and confused by my presence.

"I needed to see you," I say hesitantly, suddenly nervous. What if he gets mad with my meddling in his life? What if he's finally realized I'm more trouble than I'm worth? Lord knows I wind up disappointing everyone in my life, and I've already given him enough reasons to be disappointed in me for the next two lifetimes.

"You aren't supposed to be driving, Ashley," he says, sounding angry. "Your knee hasn't healed enough for a quick reaction time, and you know it."

"This is more important," I say, finding my backbone. If he can still find a way to care about my safety in the face of everything he stands to lose, I've definitely made the right choice in him.

"Is everything okay?" he asks, his face scrunching into a look of worry.

"It will be." I step toward him, closing the gap between us. I reach up with my good arm and wrap it around his neck.

There's confusion in his eyes as I lean in closer to kiss him, which gives me the time I need to make my move before he can step away. I mold my mouth to his as quickly as I can, and that familiar spark of electricity hits me as soon as our lips touch.

Thank God!

At least I now know our connection hasn't dissipated. With everything that has happened between us, I'll admit I'd been worried. Tanner's body stays stiff as a board, as if he's waiting for an anvil to be dropped on his head. I deepen the kiss, hoping to coax him into it, but he holds back.

I'm not sure what I'd expected him to do. I've made it very clear over the last few months that I want nothing to do with him, and now here I am, throwing myself at him—kind of like our night in the back of his town car.

Tanner wraps his fingers around my upper arms, careful not to squeeze my left arm, and pushes me away. "What are you doing?" His face is tired and lined in sadness.

I see now how awful I've been to this man. I've taken this incredible, confident, vibrant man and reduced him to a depressed, disenchanted mess.

"I need to talk to you, please," I say. It's probably not the best way to start this whole conversation, but I suddenly feel lost and so confused.

He could tell me he's finally had it with me, and I don't think I'd blame him.

"What the hell is going on? What are you playing at, coming here and pulling this shit? Hasn't my life fallen apart enough? You need to pour salt on the wound by playing games? You hate me that much? I've got a lot of shit going on, and I don't have time for whatever it is you're up to. If you want to talk, then talk, but I'm not hanging around for you to yell and bitch at me some more," he grumbles, the irritation apparent in his voice.

"I'm not here to yell or scream at you. I thought the kiss might've made that clear."

"Nothing is clear when it comes to you except that you want nothing to do with me. You haven't been able to stand the sight of me for months, so please excuse me if you kissing me doesn't make much of anything more *clear*."

Damn, he's definitely not playing.

"I'm sorry." I'm sorry? After everything I've put this man through, that's the best I can come up with? How pathetic… I wish I would've thought up a speech or something on the way here because I'm sinking fast. This is my only shot, and I'm fucking it up—first by kissing the man as though I still have a right to his body and then a lame *I'm sorry.* I wouldn't blame him for slamming the door in my face.

"It's fine," he says dejectedly as he runs his hands through his hair in frustration. "Just, please, no games. Tell me whatever it is you need to tell me and let me get back to what I was doing." The look in his eyes doesn't hold any of the reverence I used to see when he looked at me.

"I'm sorry," I repeat again.

"I said it's fine, Ash." His voice is hard, and I know he's trying to tell me I'm not welcome without saying the words.

"No, 'I'm sorry' is what I need to tell you." My voice wavers as I feel the emotion welling in my throat. I think I've lost my chance to fix this, and I just want to run—well, gimp—away as quickly as possible, get back in my car, and go home. That's not an option though. He deserves a proper apology, even if it won't fix things between us.

"Sorry for what?" he asks, still seeming confused.

"Everything! I've completely ruined your life. Look at what I've done to you, done to us," I cry. I'm tired of being such an emotional mess. I feel as though all I do nowadays is cry and feel sorry for myself.

"Ashley," he says. His phone rings in his pocket, momentarily distracting him.

The fact that he even looks toward his phone right now proves just how far we have fallen. A wave of sorrow washes over me as he pulls it out and answers with a brisk hello.

My body can't hold itself up under the weight crushing down on it, the weight of the knowledge that what we had is gone. I crumple to the ground, and pain radiates through my knee, but I relish it. I deserve it. Two days ago, I wouldn't have given a shit about being an afterthought to Tanner, but now that I realize what I've so rashly thrown away, it kills me.

I hold my head in my hands and let go of all the emotion inside me. I can't bring myself to be embarrassed right now. The only thing I hear clearly in my mind are the thoughts of regret screaming at me. I don't hear my sobs. I don't hear Tanner whispering in my ear. I don't even feel it when he scoops me up into his arms and carries me into the house. I don't feel the warmth from his hand smoothing over my hair or hear his comforting words. All I'm aware of are the thoughts of what I could've done to fix all of this sooner, to be grateful for everything I'd had while it was staring me in the face.

I don't know how long I've been huddled in Tanner's lap, but I do know that if this is the last time I'll be welcome here, I'm not leaving until he makes me.

"You did this," he says, no anger lingering in his voice even though he has every right to be angry.

I did do this. I did destroy us.

"I know, and I can't tell you how sorry I am," I say truthfully as I attempt to rise from his lap. "I know that you didn't deserve anything I put you through, and I'm sorry, even if it's too late for your forgiveness."

His arms squeeze me tighter. "Sweetheart, it's been a long couple of days, so my brain is pretty fried. What exactly are you apologizing for?"

Sweetheart? Did he just call me sweetheart?

"Everything! I just tried to tell you." We're going in circles again, and I'm fucking lost. "I've been nothing but awful to you for months, months where you've done nothing but stand by me and help me get better, all while suffering in silence as I blamed you for something that wasn't your fault."

He rubs circles on my back, trying to comfort me even though I don't deserve it. "You have every right to blame me, Ashley. It's my fault that this happened. You don't need to try to make me feel as though it's okay. I know it's not, and I'll have to live with the fact my choices led to the death of our son," he says, shame marring his beautiful face.

I feel my heart breaking. I've truly convinced him it's his fault Daniel died.

"STOP!" I demand, rising from his lap. "This isn't your fault. I'm so angry you've let me convince you otherwise. It's not anyone's fault but that asshole who's now sitting in jail where he belongs."

"How can you say that? You wouldn't have even been there that night if I hadn't been an asshole. You would've been in Miami with me, and there would've been no accident," he says, crying.

This is the first time I've seen Tanner break down over the baby. I suppose I've never given him the chance to show any emotion in front of me when it comes to Daniel. I've always told him he didn't have the right to grieve.

"Maybe not that night, but you don't know for sure that everything would have turned out fine. There's a reason that Daniel was taken from us. We might never understand what the reason is, but now I'd like to believe that part of it was to bring us back together," I say sincerely.

"You can't even stand to be in the same room as me, Ashley. You hate me, and I don't blame you. I don't deserve you, and I never did. You don't know how many times I wished it had been me in that car." He lifts his head, leveling me with a hard stare from his red, tear-filled eyes. "I'd gladly have traded places if it meant you both were okay."

"Stop it." I can't take hearing him say these sorts of things knowing how he's been going through all this pain on his own while he blamed himself, while I blamed him.

"I would've walked out of your lives forever, no matter how much it hurt, if it meant that he had survived with you." He sobs, hanging his head.

His sobs ignite mine, but I know it's time for me to hold him together just as he's tried to do for me over these last few months.

"I need you to know that isn't something I would've ever wanted. I know I've been nothing but a bitch to you since you apologized and tried to make things right, but I would never have traded one of you for the other. I love you both. Some things are just out of our control." I wrap my arms around Tanner's body, being the one to hold him for a change. All those hours of therapy are finally sinking in, and I see that what everyone has been telling me about Tanner's sincerity since the accident was correct, and I hate that Tanner's been keeping this bottled inside for Lord knows how long thinking it's his penance, thinking he needed to be strong for me.

"You love me?" he asks, pushing away to look up at me.

"Yes," I nod.

He lets out a sardonic laugh. "How can you love me after everything I've done? You hate me."

"I don't hate you, Tanner. I hate what's happened to us but not you. Even when I wanted to hate you, I couldn't bring myself to actually do it." I sigh. I never would've imagined it was possible for me to hurt this man the way I have.

"And people tell me that I have a funny way of showing my love," he says, chuckling cynically.

We sit there, my arms still wrapped around his frame, neither of us caring how much time passes until the tears finally start drying up.

"I honestly don't know if I can believe you," Tanner says, breaking the silence at last.

I lift my head from its resting place on his shoulder to look at him, a bit confused but mostly scared.

"We've been through so much. You've been through so much. How can we ever come back from all of this Ashley?"

"We can. I know we can. I believe with every fiber of my being that we can get past this," I say, grabbing his chin, forcing him to make eye contact.

"How? You don't trust me, and I don't trust you. We've had this discussion before," he says as though I could've forgotten that conversation.

I won't give up just because he has doubts and he's scared. I'm scared too. Hell, I'm petrified, but I can be the strong one right now. I can wade us through this mess. It takes a minute for me to figure out how to prove to him that I love him, but there's only one way Tanner and I have ever fully expressed our feelings in the past. Every monumental moment in our relationship has come after sex.

I know how I can show him…

Pushing from the couch, I stand in front of him. His eyes follow my every move as I take a few steps back and work myself out of my shirt. I wish I could make it more of a show, make it sexier, but the limited movement in one arm and the inability to fully support myself on one leg make for a boring strip tease. Even so, I'm really not too concerned with seduction. I have something else to focus on. I already know I can bring Tanner to his knees. I need him to see that I'm already on my knees, begging.

"What are you doing?" he asks, his voice wary.

"Shhh," I say as I continue undressing. I unhook my bra and slide off before letting it fall to the floor.

Glancing at Tanner, I'm relieved to find him watching me, his eyes hooded with lust. It's not only lust I see there though. A mixture of longing, disbelief, and a few other emotions swirl in his endless pools of emerald. Even though I'm not one hundred percent sure which emotions are there, the lust and longing are enough to fuel me, enough to fan this fire burning inside me.

I balance carefully as I guide my pants down my legs, thankful I'm only wearing leggings. Tanner must understand how hard the process of undressing is for me because despite his obvious apprehension, he rises from the couch and kneels in front of me to help me pull away the leggings pooled around my ankles.

Sliding my hands into his hair that's much longer than he usually wears it, I tip his head up toward me and lean down to kiss his lips. "Thank you," I whisper.

He gives me a simple nod as he rises back up to full height. I've always loved how he towers over my five feet three inches. It's always made me feel safe, even when I didn't want it to.

"What are you doing?" he asks again, his voice much huskier now.

"I do trust you, Tanner. I'm standing here completely stripped of everything. I'm standing here, scarred and bared, to prove to you that you don't have to be scared. I love you. I trust you. You were right—we do belong together. I have no doubt about that. I will never doubt you, or us, again," I stare him in the eye, spine straight, with the utmost confidence.

It doesn't escape me that this is the first time Tanner is seeing just how much of a physical mark the accident has left on me—the scar just under my left breast from my chest tube, the long scar across my abdomen from my splenectomy, the scars on my arm and leg from my surgeries. I try to ignore the little voice in my head telling me I'm damaged now and he couldn't possibly look at me the same way he did before. Any thoughts of self-doubt fade when I see the tears well in Tanner's eyes once more.

I step closer to him and reach out to wipe away the lone tear that stains his cheek. I grab his hand and kiss his palm before saying, "Please don't cry. It's okay. I'm okay. I'm still here." I bring his hand to the worse of the two scars, placing it there.

He runs his thumb along the jagged edge of it while tears stream down his handsome face.

"I never thought it was possible for you to become even more beautiful, but you are now. These scars are a reminder of what you've been through and just how much of a fighter—no, survivor—you are." He slides both hands up to my neck, pulls my face toward him, and kisses me.

My lips mold to his with no hesitation whatsoever, trying to convey the torrent of feelings inside me through our kiss until I realize one kiss couldn't possibly convey even a fraction of my emotions.

Reluctantly, I pull my lips from his and hold out my hand, not wanting this reunion to take place on his living room couch. He only hesitates for a second before sliding his hand into mine, still seeming slightly apprehensive. It's funny how the tables have turned. I did this to him though. I made him so unsure of himself that he can't even accept the fact I love him. Granted, I'd never said those words to him until today…

Interlocking my fingers with his, I feel possessive and sure. Every single asinine thing I've said since he broke my heart all those months ago fades away. Nothing other than reconnecting in the way Tanner needs—we need—is important right now. Full of self-assurance, I guide him through the house to his bedroom.

I pull him toward the bed in the center of the room and then stand back, taking in the sight of him. The doubt on his face, the slump of his strong shoulders, and the defeat in his eyes—all are still present but have taken a backseat to the lust I've evoked in him. I reach up on my tiptoes as I did earlier on his front porch and press my lips against his, resuming what I started downstairs. He doesn't take the lead like he used to. He just stands, his arms wrapping loosely around me, his pliant lips waiting for my next move.

Breaking away for the warmth of his mouth, I slide my hands up his abdominals and back down, rediscovering his wonderful body. I grasp the bottom of his navy blue t-shirt and pull it up his torso as far as I can before

I need a little help. Tanner obliges by leaning down, making it easier for me to pull the garment off over his head.

Even though it should have been impossible, it's as though I'd forgotten how beautiful the man in front of me is. From the square of his jaw to his thick thighs, everything is absolutely beautiful, a masterpiece to be cherished. I slowly drop to my knees, which with a not-fully-healed formerly-dislocated knee takes some time. I hear the anguish in Tanner's voice as he says my name and tries to prevent my descent to the floor. I shake my head to let him know I'm okay.

Once settled on my knees, I lean forward kissing the muscled work of art in front of me. Raining kisses over every hard plane within reach, I slide my hand under the waistband of his black track pants and push them down with excruciating slowness. Once he's completely naked, I fully take him in with my eyes before taking him in my mouth.

My eyes roll into the back of my head as if I were on the receiving end. My moan matches Tanner's as we both relish the union of his cock and my mouth as though they're long lost friends. I don't hesitate to look up at him, and I'm not surprised to find him staring back at me. The storm of passion in his eyes does surprise me a little, but it's the best kind of surprise I could ask for. Every past sexual encounter between us has been about the desire, passion, and the adventure we could find in it, but right now, it's about nothing but love, showing him the love that I have for him.

I pull him to the back of my throat and then back out, using the hand guiding his thick shaft to cover what I can't fit in my mouth. As much as I want to swallow him whole, that's not what this is about. This is about giving all that I have because I love this man, not because I have to prove anything to him. It's unrestricted, no holds barred, everything left on the table, an encounter meant to leave Tanner with nothing to doubt.

Running my fingers along his thighs, I reach up to find his hands, gaining the support I need to pull myself up. Once settled on my feet, I walk him back the few steps to the bed and nudge him down. He sits on the end of the bed and pushes himself backward until he's lying in the center, staring back at me in all my scared, naked glory.

Climbing onto the bed I straddle him, then lean forward to kiss his lips, his jaw, and his neck before getting to his ear, where I whisper, "I love you."

He groans, and his cock twitches at my admission. His hands, which had been gripping my hips, are suddenly gliding their way up my sides until he hits my scar. He runs a finger back and forth over it in reverence as his eyes tell me exactly what he's thinking and feeling.

I rock back and forth against his hardness, coating him with the wetness his emotional reactions have drawn from me. I don't know what it says about me that I'm getting turned on by watching this man get emotional over my scars, but it stirs something in me. I rise up onto my knees, putting most of my body weight on my good leg as I align myself with Tanner's rigid erection and sink down, taking him fully inside my body.

"Ahhh!" I moan, having forgotten how amazing it feels to be stretched to my limits by him. I give myself a minute to acclimate to his size again. I already have a difficult time walking, and I don't need to add to my struggles.

"Christ," Tanner hisses out after nearly a full minute held in that position. "Are you okay? I need you to move before I explode."

Nodding, I roll my hips, letting out little moans every time his cock hits that sweet spot deep inside me. I can't help but throw my head back and let the sensations take over. I continue to ride Tanner for a few minutes before dropping my head back to his chest and burying my face in his neck to kiss every spot I can get my lips on.

"You feel so amazing," I say. "Stretching me to the point of burning, filling me so completely that there is no spot left untouched." I know Tanner's number one weakness is dirty talk, not that I would consider those words dirty talk, but I'm sure they will have the same effect on him and accomplish what I need them to.

My suspicions are confirmed when Tanner digs his fingers into my hips and thrusts up a little harder, a little deeper.

"Mmm… Yes, right there!" I cry out when Tanner finds the spot he's been searching for. "Feels so good. I'm close." I'm thankful I'm almost there because my knee can't handle this position much longer.

"Ahh, me too." He moans, picking up the pace even more as his hips ram upward over and over with enough force to bring me to the edge.

"Come, baby," I order, turning the tables on him.

He's always been the one to demand my orgasm, but hearing my words, his eyes light up with something I can't decipher. I feel him grow impossibly hard before he pulls me down roughly as he comes. I feel the pulse of his cock as his orgasm rolls over him wave after wave. Watching him let go pushes me over the edge, and my body is racked with pure pleasure, a pleasure I haven't had since the night I hate-fucked Tanner in the bathroom at the New Year's party.

My body's completely spent, and my knee is screaming at me to move, but I just can't find the motivation to remove myself from Tanner's embrace. I don't want to experience the feeling of loss that will come when he pulls himself out of my body. I have no idea if I was able to convey any of my feelings to him, and I have no idea if he's going to kick me out of here as soon as we get up. I feel him stir under me, and panic starts to take over. My hands cling to him of their own volition, desperate to hold on to anything that they can.

"It's okay, baby." He chuckles, kissing my head. "I know you can't be comfortable like this. I just want to move you to give you room to stretch your leg." He shifts under me, his cock falling from my body, which elicits a whine of protest from me. Tanner rolls us onto our side and pulls me flush against his chest.

I instinctually bury my face in the crook of his neck and inhale deeply. He smells like home. There has never been a scent more comforting. Ever. His hands run up and down my back in a loving way, giving me hope.

"I do love you," I tell him. I need him to understand that I truly do.

"I'm starting to see that." He sighs into my hair.

"I don't think I ever stopped. I needed to turn that love into hate because I was angry—angry at you at first and then just angry at the world. A hundred hours of therapy kicked in this morning, making me see everything I've been trying to avoid —you included. I can't begin to apologize for all the terrible things I've done and said to you over the last six months. Nothing will ever make that okay." I feel the tears coming back again, and I promise myself this will be the last time I cry over the time we've lost together.

"Shhh," he whispers. "It's not as though I didn't play my part in this, Ashley. I'm just as culpable as you are."

"I really want to kill that stupid bitch friend of yours," I say, my voice full of anger. "Most of this is her fault. Things probably would've never gotten so bad if she hadn't planted those awful thoughts in my head."

"I know. Trust me, I know. Why do you think I kicked her ass to the curb? I would've never asked you to do something like that. Although, as I've already told you, it hurts to know you could actually think that low of me. I know I was an ass, but I'd liked to think you'd see through that crock of shit." I hear the hurt in his voice, and I know that misjudgment is just another thing I have to try to make right.

"I know. I don't know how I didn't see it before… but no one likes a Monday morning quarterback, Tanner," I say hoping to lighten the mood. It's not as though we can fix everything all in one day. It's going to take time.

My comment gets a laugh out of him before he says, "I think you misunderstood me earlier."

My stomach drops. I push back from my warm spot against his chest to look at him, frightened that even after all we've just shared, he's actually done with me.

"No, no, no," he says, shaking his head. "I mean, when I said, 'You did this.'"

I give him a perplexed look, having no idea what he's talking about.

"I was referring to the press conference you gave earlier today. Davis called me and told me to turn on the TV because there was something on I might want to see."

"Oh," I say. "I'm sorry if that was going too far, but there was no way I was going to let that fucking twat ruin the foundation for you. I can't believe they would actually think something like that was true. For a bunch of educated people, they're really a bunch of idiots."

"I can't believe you did that for me. You were honestly the last person I'd ever have expected to speak up for me."

No matter how true that statement is, it still hurts. This man who has done everything within his power to help me piece my life back together couldn't allow himself to believe he could count on me.

"I know, Tanner, but that's on me, not you. I know I have a lot to make up for." I sigh, nestling in closer to him, still afraid that, at any moment, this will all disappear.

Epilogue

TANNER

2 YEARS LATER

"**I LOVE IT** when you get all demanding," I tell Ashley, nuzzling her neck and kissing that spot she loves so much under her ear.

"I know. You've only got yourself to blame. You've created a monster," she says, the smile evident in her voice.

"I love my monster." I smile at my wife. "Don't you have some business to take care of?"

"I knew there was an ulterior motive to you waking me up with your head between my legs," she says, sitting up to stretch.

The sheet falls from her shoulders in the process, revealing her torso and giving me a view of the most beautiful sight in the world. I could stare at her for hours, and I find myself completely entranced by her more often than not.

Memories of her in her wedding gown flash through my mind. She's beautiful every day, but on that day, her beauty shone through in ways I'd never seen before. Her hair had been clipped to the side and curled, framing her flawless face. Her eyes had practically glowed, the color of the ocean. She'd worn a smile so big her happiness was undeniable. I cried like a baby as soon as I saw her standing there at the end of the aisle. That day has been years in the making.

I wish I could say that everything had been rainbows and sunshine for us after we'd gotten back together, but it wasn't. We'd had a lot of things to overcome before we could move forward. After the press conference, things had started to look up for us, but neither one of us was naïve enough to believe everything would just fall back into place.

After careful consideration, the foundation had found it was in their best interests to keep me on as their main spokesman. My fans had been outraged that they were even considering removing me based solely on a terrible rumor. Ashley had been a damn good actress. We both know that Melissa was right, even though Ash still denies it was my fault. Countless hours of therapy together still haven't convinced me otherwise.

Ashley had insisted I join in her therapy sessions, so we could start healing together. It was hard at first, admitting to a total stranger that I was the reason for all of Ashley's struggles. They both attempted repeatedly to help me understand that fate has its own plans despite our best intentions. I'd eventually agreed with them just to get them to lay off, but deep down, I know this is my cross to bear. Ashley was right about one thing though: Daniel was a gift. Even though his life ended tragically before it had even begun, he brought Ashley back to me—well, him and that fucking bitch Melissa.

Ashley and I ran into her once after the fallout from all the turmoil she'd caused, and she'd been shocked to see us together. I could tell Quinn has really rubbed off on her because Ashley had smiled the sweetest fake smile, thanked Melissa for bringing us back together, and then proceeded to show off the huge, princess-cut solitaire I'd given her when I'd asked her to marry me. The satisfaction we'd gotten from the look on Melissa's face was indescribable.

"Are you coming?" Ashley calls from the bathroom.

"Of course. I wouldn't miss it for the world." I most definitely will not miss this experience ever again. "How long do we have to wait?"

"Three minutes." She smiles. "Are you nervous?"

"Not at all," I say, coming to stand behind her at the bathroom counter, watching the plastic test that could change our lives resting right in the middle of it.

"Why does three minutes have to be so long?" she asks.

We decided about three months ago that it was time to try to add to our family again. Ashley had been disappointed when it didn't happen during the first two months, but I told her it would happen when it was meant to and not to worry. The hope had been obvious in her eyes when she told me last night that her period was two days late. I'd immediately grabbed her hand and dragged her to the car. We grabbed just about every test in stock from the shelf at the pharmacy, but the instructions on the boxes all seemed to be written in a foreign language. I'd wanted her to take one as soon as we got home, but she said that it was best to wait until morning.

I woke up this morning earlier than usual, too excited to sleep, so I'd decided to wake Ash up with a few orgasms. What better way could there be to start off the day than with some bliss and hopefully a baby?

I chuckle and take her hand. "It's only three minutes, baby, and two of them have gone by already."

"I can't look. Can you look and then let me know?" she asks, turning away from the counter and wrapping herself around me.

I glance over her shoulder, looking at the window on the test, where the results are waiting.

I drop to my knees and kiss Ashley's bare stomach, a stomach that's now holding the most precious thing in the world.

"Hello, baby. I'm your daddy."

Want more Tanner and Ashley?

Freed

An Uninhibited Series Novella

Now Available

Acknowledgements

Where do I even begin?

There's been so much love and support behind this book. Never in a million years did I think people would embrace Tanner and Ashley in the way they have and I thank each and every reader from the bottom of my heart.

My biggest thank you goes to amazing Isabelle Richards!! You have been the biggest help anyone could ever ask for!! I couldn't have gotten any luckier the day Facebook brought us together!! You're the best support system anyone could ever ask for and you happen to be one the most amazing people I've ever met! Thank you for being such a rock star!!

Thanks to my hubby for being a huge support! I've changed careers as often as I change my underwear and he's always been supportive no matter how crazy the new career I set my sights on can be. Love you!

Yolanda Ann, Deanna Hill, Terri Peterson, and my street team, THANK YOU for taking your time to pimp out my book simply because you liked it!! It's so amazing to have so many people in my corner!!

Thank you to Ena and Enticing Journey Promotions for working your asses off putting together my blog tour, cover reveal, release blitz and thunderclap!! You absolutely rock and I'm so glad I chose you to promote my books!!

Xoxo

About The Author

Kimberly is a stay at home mom to four beautiful, crazy children by day and a steaming hot novelist by night. She's a Jersey girl at heart and that's where she currently calls home with her amazing husband and children.

Her debut release Inhibitions and the subsequent Uninhibited Series as well as the spin-off Apprehensive Duet both show her love of all things football. But not to worry, she'll still bring you plenty of steam!

When not writing she can be found curled up with a good book or watching her beloved New York Jets. Lover all things romance, including a little M/M action as well as the dark and twisted. She enjoys video chats with her best friends and always loves to hear from her fans on social media.

Connect with Kimberly

Website: www.KimberlyBracco.com

Facebook: www.facebook.com/authorkimberlybracco

Facebook Fan Group: Kimberly's Knockout Fangirls

Twitter: @AuthorKBracco

Instagram: @AuthorKimberlyBracco

45192108R00135

Made in the USA
Middletown, DE
27 June 2017